NOT MY DIAMONDS

Ruth Zanger Barron

Novels by Ruth Zanger Barron

The Commission Trap
Hell-Bent on Fraud

Contents

Family Trees

The Berger Family Tree

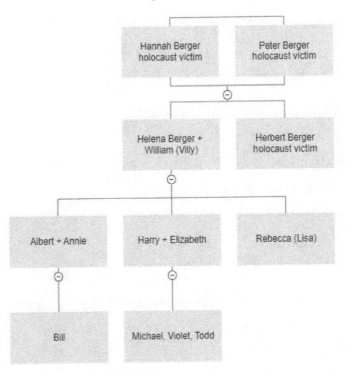

The Ellis Family Tree

Devora Kazan
(Russia)

Leon Kazan
(Russia)

Mikhail Kazan + spouse

Deborah Ellis (Kazan) + Jack Ellis

Titus Ellis + Sally Ellis

David Ellis, Maddie Ellis (Celeste)

The Casualty

He was one of the casualties in the aftermath, but he had seen the faces. He could see all of them, lying in a hospital bed, while waiting for somebody to pronounce him dead. He saw them not through his own eyes, but by way of some invisible instrument or ability. His three children surrounded him, daughter Violet, and sons Michael and Todd. All the grandchildren came and a few cried. His brother, with whom he had been close, stood there silently, a little apart from everyone, seemingly frozen in his grief. Elizabeth, the love of his life, looked stone faced and pale. His next-door neighbor was there, too.

He knew they would be sad that he was gone from their lives. He had never ceased to be essential to them: Violet and her occasional depression, Todd and his large family and meager income, and Michael, who shared his inventive thoughts and ideas. He was not sad for them; he was serene, assured that his children were able to thrive even without him, and that they would always help each other. They knew since early childhood that they were to stay close.

Elizabeth stayed, sitting by his bed and holding on to his hand. He did feel unease about her, his wife of forty years, not old enough, perhaps too attached to him, to become widowed all at once. That was one thing that he had not spoken about with anyone: were the unexpected to happen, how to help Elizabeth overcome and move on with her life. Not financially; that would be covered by his insurance and retirement fund. The missing parts would be the untouchable, irreplaceable ones-- the missed smiles, the intimate moments, the wisecracks. Who would have ever thought to bring this up?

Had Harry been able to foresee his violent demise, he might have had a chance to ponder those things. It's one thing for a person to die from a long illness, when there is time to prepare. It is more daunting to lose a loved one unexpectedly, and worse when the loss was caused by a violent act. Making sense of it is difficult, he would have known. Elizabeth plausibly pondered why he had chosen that particular day to go out for lunch, when he usually packed a sandwich. She might even be angry with him, but it would be a fleeting anger.

The monotonous electronic beeping abruptly stopped. He barely heard the frantic voices that came from everywhere around his bed, but could not make out any of the words. Elizabeth left his bedside... His life on earth had now ended.

Following Harry's Jewish tradition, his funeral took place the day after he passed away. They put his body in a coffin and many of the mourners, one after the other, used a shovel to cover him with earth.

The police and FBI began hunting for Harry's attacker—perhaps the driver that swerved off the road and barely avoided the lunchtime crowd.

"Careful, everybody down!" He had heard a single scream that drowned in the deafening noise of the blast, and his instincts shouted "run!" But it was too late; Harry felt a huge darkness, right there and then. He never heard the aftermath--the falling, the chaos of police and ambulances, or the paramedics who tried furiously to revive him and wheeled him away.

It had been a rare event; Harry offered Esmeralda to go to lunch with him and another colleague, and when it was over it appeared they all had enjoyed the outing. He had become somewhat of a father figure to young Esmeralda, the bright intern at the desk across from him.

"We should do this again," Harry had said when they finished lunch, and slumped as the killing machine roared around them. In the last seconds of light, he saw a face hovering over him.

During his life, Harry had been a senior FBI investigator who worked in a Financial Crimes unit. Quiet and unassuming, he had become very skilled in spotting suspicious transactions, and had his own confidential contacts in several investment brokerages. The victorious outcomes were those which resulted in saving the consumer from financial doom and apprehending the wily culprits. Harry had been satisfied and successful in his job.

The Intern

Esmeralda Santoro, a second-year student at Glendale Community College, had recently started a volunteer internship at the FBI office in Los Angeles. She was a slim young woman of medium height, with flowing dark hair and green eyes that often gave people pause. Although she had crossed the U.S. border illegally, she had participated in an operation that helped nab a band of human traffickers. The Bureau, recognizing the young woman's bravery, and helped initiate the fast-tracking of her green card application. She cherished the realization of her life-long dream to become "a real American."

She didn't miss her native El Salvador; there were only bitter memories of her mother's death, her alcoholic father, and two siblings who had run off to become criminals. Her most important treasure was a small framed photo of her deceased mother, who had died when Esmeralda was in her early teens, and she deeply missed her.

Relentless about mastering English, she had worked in a hotel and earned a high school diploma through a GED program. Her internship opportunity came about thanks to the intervention of Ms. Fields, the FBI agent she had met. That meeting happened while she had played a major role in apprehending her own brother, a major culprit in a human trafficking case. Internships were officially offered only to college juniors and seniors, but Ms. Fields had known about an opening and miraculously slipped her in. She easily passed a personal security interview, a comprehensive background check, and drug and polygraph tests.

Esmeralda had been granted only the minimum-security clearance for her stint with the FBI. Her main job consisted of routine paperwork, and, in addition, she attended training sessions and briefings on past cases. Unfortunately, the latter, more fascinating to her, usually took place only once a week, sometimes twice. Still, she was so thrilled about being a part of the Bureau, that she stayed late whenever possible. She often sat at her desk after hours and re-read the briefings to assimilate the details. Definitely, Esmeralda thought, crime fighting was going to be in her future.

She planned to have a career in law enforcement and enrolled in classes that prepared her for a degree in criminal justice. Her internship was in the Financial Crimes investigations unit, but her hope was to have a career in the human trafficking area.

"Mamá," she whispered in her native Spanish to the small picture early one morning, "I am an American woman now. I know you will be happy to know that I am getting an education, like you wanted me to. I always think about you, Mamá, and I am sure you are still watching over me."

Esmeralda longed to have some friends. Since her relationship with her boyfriend had recently ended, she started feeling lonely. On a Tuesday evening at the end of a late class, she noticed another student, a short, somewhat stocky girl with a friendly smile. They had exchanged a few words occasionally, and she decided to reach out to her.

"Hi," she started. "I don't think we met before; I am Esmeralda, but my friends call me Esme." To her displeasure, her Hispanic accent was still distinct.

"Hi," the girl responded with her bright smile. "My real name is Alexandra, but I go by Lexi. Our parents sort of went overboard with those long names, huh?"

They both laughed and walked outside together.

"Do you want to grab a burger or a salad?" Lexi asked her.

"Sure, why not? Do you have a place in mind?"

They walked to a small eatery close to the campus that advertised their home-made split pea soup. It was a popular pub with checkered tablecloths and an eclectic collection of hanging light fixtures of all styles and colors. They ordered at the counter and sat down.

"Does your family live here?" Esmeralda asked. "I mean, in this area?"

"No, my mom lives in San Diego and my dad moved to San Jose. They divorced a long time ago. What about your family?"

"I don't have any; I came from El Salvador, and my parents are both dead."

"Wow," her new friend said, her smile gone. "That's so sad; I'm sorry."

"It's okay," Esmeralda said without emotion, "I have been on my own for a long time, so I'm used to it."

"Me too," Lexi said. "So, what do you do for fun?"

"Not too much... I have a job, so between school and work I don't have a lot of extra time."

"What kind of job?"

"Oh, I have a government internship." She was careful not to divulge any details. "How about you? I can tell you're bright, because you ask smart questions in class. So, what do you do for fun?"

"Thanks," Lexi said and smiled. "I love getting to understand how government works. I want to get into law school and work in constitutional law. But for a distraction, I took a dance class last year, and since then I've been going to a ballroom dance club. I like it a lot."

Esmeralda was pleased to meet an intelligent person, and decided to pursue the friendship. "That sounds nice," she said, her green eyes brightening. "I think ballroom dancing is very glamorous."

Their conversation was interrupted when their food orders were called and Lexi brought them to the table.

"This soup is delicious," Esmeralda said over her steaming bowl.

"It's their specialty," Lexi replied confidently, took a thick slice from the bread basket, and they ate in silence for a few minutes.

"If you want, you can come to the dance club with me sometime. I go every Thursday."

Esmeralda eyed her silently, considering the idea.

"But I don't know how to dance. I never learned."

"They have lessons at eight o'clock, and then at nine the music starts and everybody dances. It's a lot of fun, and you get to meet different people."

"But I don't know anybody there, so who is going to dance with me?"

"Oh, everybody dances with everybody. Don't worry; with your looks, you'll have lots of guys waiting to dance with you."

They agreed to meet on Thursday. As soon as Esmeralda entered her studio apartment she smiled at the mirror and twirled around the bedroom, her long hair fanning about, and then crashed on the bed. Sleep eluded her for hours while she pictured herself in a shimmering yellow ball gown, waltzing with tall, handsome men.

Dancing

On Thursday evening Esmeralda waited for her new friend at the college library. The weather was warm with a slight breeze. Lexi arrived a minute later, looking elegant and slimmer in a blue dress and dance shoes. She drove them to Stardust Dance Studio.

"You look so pretty," Esmeralda told her, worried that everyone would be looking at her outfit of a skirt and a blouse, definitely not ballroom dance attire.

"Thanks," Lexi replied and pulled into the parking lot.

"I don't have the right clothes for this," Esmeralda said awkwardly, "but if I decide that dancing is my thing, I'll buy some."

"Don't worry, nobody will pay attention; you look great."

The dance club was a large room with a polished wooden floor and a few tall stools scattered along the walls. Music was playing, and she saw a few couples practicing their steps.

There was a beginner's lesson of cha-cha, and Esmeralda joined the group. Lexi stood off to the side; she was past the beginners' level. The instructor, a bubbly woman with a British accent, taught the steps and moves, then two moving circles were formed. Each woman got to dance with the man facing her in the inner circle—a different person each time; so she practiced with some older men and a few younger ones, good dancers, others not. She hardly paid attention to her various partners, and focused on remembering the cha-cha steps. Later, the floor opened for everyone, and after being asked to dance all evening, she was disappointed when it ended.

"So, how did you like it?" Lexi asked when they walked out.

"It was amazing!" Esmeralda said breathlessly. "Too bad it was over so soon. Can I come with you again next week?"

"Definitely," her friend said. "I knew you'd like it. By the way, you did a great job dancing the cha-cha. I was watching you."

While changing into her pajamas, her thoughts went back to the thrill of dancing, so new and exhilarating. She knew she had to find a way to cram it into her busy life. She then sat down and turned her attention to an assignment for a finance class, a course in which she enrolled to improve her skills at her work.

Intersected Roads

After a few weeks, Esmeralda felt confident enough to go to Stardust without Lexi, who was away visiting her ill mother. During a dance break one evening at the studio, Esmeralda was standing at a corner, laughing with one of the instructors. As soon as the announcement came that dancing was about to start, a young man approached.

"Hi," he extended his hand. "My name is Brent. Will you dance the next number with me?" he smiled at her.

She scrutinized him briefly—a young man with unruly curly blond hair and blue eyes, not bad looking, she thought.

"Yes, of course," she replied and moved forward. "I am Esmeralda, Esme for short," she shook his hand briefly.

Soon after the music began, she noticed he did not know the steps. Definitely not a dancer, she thought, but said nothing.

"I'm new here, so I guess I still have a lot to learn," he said with a bashful smile.

"Don't worry," Esmeralda replied, "just take a few lessons and then you'll be all set."

"My girlfriend is a great dancer, so I want to learn just enough to pick up some moves. I want to go dancing with her without making a fool of myself."

During the evening they danced together two other times, and the rest with others. The crowd at Stardust was mostly made up of older people, so there were not many young ones to choose.

"I've got a feeling this fellow has a bit of a crush on you," a fellow dancer, a woman she had gotten to know, told her quietly. "But there is something different about him; too smooth, maybe."

"He says that he has a girlfriend and he wants to impress her with some dance moves. It's pretty believable."

"If you ask me, he didn't take his eyes off you the whole night."

"Then he should figure out," Esmeralda said defiantly, "that I'm not interested".

Brent was at the studio each of the following three weeks.

It was nearly a month before Lexi came to the club, but to Esmeralda's surprise, she excused herself and hurried toward a side exit when she noticed him.

"What's the matter?" Esmeralda rushed over and asked her.

"I'll tell you another time. It's someone from my past, and I'd rather disappear."

"Hi, Esme!" he called out when he saw her. "There's my favorite dance partner!"

She froze, desperate to think of how to distance herself. Be honest, but polite, she told herself.

"Look," she replied with a half-smile. "They want us to mix with everybody here. Do you mind if we dance with other people?"

"Of course," he replied. Still, he managed to pull her hand to join him.

Over the few weeks that Esmeralda had danced with her new acquaintance, she learned that he was an investment adviser. She wondered why Lexi was so adamant about avoiding him.

"I handle transactions in stocks, bonds, annuities, even life insurance," he boasted.

"It sounds very complicated," she replied, trying to show interest.

"Maybe sometime we can talk about it so I can teach you some tips," he said.

"Yeah, maybe."

That was her last time at Stardust Dance Studio. She decided to take a break from dancing, and eventually find another club.

The Unthinkable

It was an ordinary morning, and Esmeralda was at her desk at the FBI office, scanning a computer monitor over a cup of coffee. Harry, her supervisor, an older Senior Special Agent who had been teaching her how to interpret codes and messages, raised his head from his papers with a smile.

"Hey, Esme, how about you, Judy and I go out to grab some lunch today? I think we can all use a change of pace."

"Oh, of course," she replied with a questioning glance to Judy, a woman in her thirties.

"Sounds good," Judy said, and they all went back to work. What a nice day this will be, Esmeralda thought.

It felt unusual for her to be walking outdoors on a work day. She looked around her, as if seeing for the first time the cedars that flanked the sidewalk. In spite of the heat there were many people out, entering and leaving office buildings and shops.

They ate sandwiches at a coffee shop two blocks away, and Harry shared a few funny anecdotes about his children. He obviously enjoyed the break, but then it was time to return to work. They got up to leave and Judy excused herself to go to the bathroom.

"I'll catch up with you outside," she said. On their way out, Harry started to tell a joke, and then, while he followed Esmeralda out, the unthinkable happened. Her world was forever changed.

He held the door for her to exit first, so she was a few feet ahead of him. At the second that he took his first step outside, the door exploded, and she saw him fall. The people who had been sitting at the outdoor tables disappeared from view in the smoke, and Esmeralda froze, uncertain if she was injured, dead, or alive. Her ears were ringing and her eyes teared so she could barely see.

She noticed a car that had swerved to the right onto the sidewalk, but was too numb to try to think of a connection to the bombing. It was a black sedan, and as it screeched away, she could see a large dent in the rear left corner. When her eyes cleared some, through the thick smoke, she ran toward Harry who lay on the sidewalk. His blue shirt was soaked in blood and his face was dark gray with ash. A paramedic rushed over to him and placed an oxygen mask on his face, while Esmeralda knelt down and tried to talk to him.

It was then that she noticed that her white top was nearly completely black, and that her legs were bleeding. A female paramedic rushed toward her, but she motioned her away.

"I am fine, go help the others," she yelled and kept talking to him.

"Harry, you'll be okay. They are taking you to the hospital, so they will take care of you." While she held his hand for a moment, she felt something rush through her. Maybe it was the shock of witnessing the horror that affected her, she thought. She shivered when they wheeled him to an ambulance, then realized she was sobbing. Judy came over and put her arm around her.

Judy called the office to give them the news. "I don't think Esme and I are coming back to work today," she said, and Esmeralda watched her co-worker swallow hard, visibly controlling her emotions. A New Agent Trainee, Judy immediately began to scan the scene, cellphone camera in hand, and checked on the victims on the ground. Esmeralda rushed over to a middle-aged woman who was gasping for air. The woman whispered something inaudible, and then she was lifeless. It was the second time she had seen a dead person, and she could hardly calm her own trembling. The scene brought back memories from a day long-ago, the day she had discovered the bodies of the two people who had saved her life at the California-Mexico border. She had been helpless then, but she thought that perhaps this time she had resources, and a purpose. Instinctively she straightened the deceased woman's rumpled skirt and whispered tearfully "I am so sorry."

Judy and Esmeralda, the two FBI women, slowly walked away, but a policeman stopped them.

"Nobody goes anywhere. We need to take statements from you."

Neither of the two could offer much information to the officer. Esmeralda thought the black sedan was relevant, and described every detail she could recall about it. Judy explained that they had eaten lunch in the restaurant with Harry, and that the bomb exploded exactly at the time they exited.

"You were apparently not injured. Where were you when the bomb went off?" he questioned Judy.

"Harry and Esme went outside first, because I told them I was going to use the bathroom, but then I changed my mind."

"How about you?" he asked Esmeralda.

"Harry and I went toward the exit together. He held the door open for me to go first, so I stepped outside a few seconds before him. I can't believe I'm alive."

"Did either of you notice anything suspicious?"

They both shook their heads. It was difficult for the women to talk even after they were allowed to leave.

"Poor Harry," Esmeralda finally spoke. "He's always been so good to me; he taught me so much. I hope with all my heart that he'll be all right and come back." Then she started crying again.

"I hear you," Judy replied. "But I'm not so sure he will." She closed her eyes and shook her head in grief.

Sleepless

Esmeralda was waking up every hour or two at night, and was barely able to get up in the morning. Things in the office were not the same with Harry gone, and nightmares about the bombing haunted her.

"How was it that Harry died, and I didn't?" It was a question she kept asking herself, a riddle that plagued her constantly.

The nightmares did not stop, and a few times she woke up screaming in terror. In her dreams, a flaming car was racing towards her and she was running from it, breathlessly watching as it kept rushing closer to her until she awoke. Then the visions changed, and she was climbing up a ladder, hiding from a giant brown cricket with big, bulging eyes, that was hopping toward her. The chirping was so loud that she had to cover her ears, and then woke up. She finally decided to confide in Judy.

"It just doesn't stop," she told her when they sat in the cafeteria at lunch. "I am so tired all the time, and I am scared to go to sleep."

"You know," Judy said quietly, "there is a task force investigating the attack. When they solve it, you'll be able to have some peace."

"But what should I do in the meantime?" Esmeralda pleaded.

"I am not a psychologist, but it may be good for you to talk to somebody about it. This case may take a while."

"Do you think they will let me get involved with this task force?"

"I don't have that much clout, so I can't say. But maybe you should take a sleep aid before going to bed. Could be it will help you sleep."

The nightmares did not reappear that night, but Esmeralda's sleep was light. In her brief dream she saw a column of small crickets hopping towards her, but she didn't fear them. She tried to peer at the spectacle closely before it disappeared. The vision came back the following night. At least, she thought, sleep finally came.

Celeste

Maddie Ellis was five years old, a thin, light brown-haired girl with bright unruliness in her eyes. Her father, Titus Ellis, was a tall, handsome man, who always seemed irritated to her. He looked at her the way he always had, with those unsmiling, angry eyes. The girl had just come home from kindergarten, her orange shirt splattered with dried mud, and her hair tangled.

"Hi, Daddy!" she yelled and ran into the house. The screen door remained open behind her as she bounded into the kitchen.

"How did you get so dirty?" her father asked, glaring at her with his deep frown marks and hard glare. "You left the door open again!" She couldn't help noticing that every time he screamed at her, one of his eyebrows rose and remained higher than the other. She thought he looked funny, but always had to hold herself back not to laugh.

"I'm sorry, Daddy," she mumbled and ran to close the door. "Randy and I got into a fight and I fell in a puddle," she said weakly and looked down, spirits deflated.

"You have such a crappy nature," he always told her that. "Did you start the fight?"

"No, he did."

"You know, Maddie," her father, frowning, spoke sternly, bent down and brought his face very close to hers. "I don't believe you. You're such a liar."

"Daddy," she pleaded. "It's true; I'm not lying. He grabbed my paper from my hand and smooshed it, so I tried to get it back."

"What paper?"

"We drew pictures of animals today, and I wanted to show you how I drew a camel. Ms. Sharp told me it was very good. She told all the kids to show their pictures to their mommy and daddy."

Maddie didn't have a mommy; her parents divorced when she was just one, and her father had full custody of her and her brother David. He was two years older, a second grader, and always called her a baby. The children had never known their mother—poor, weak and dejected, she had moved away to find more affordable housing.

Her father grabbed her by the waist, pulled down her pants, and spanked her bottom. The pain felt like fire searing her skin. She clenched her teeth until it was over, then marched to her room, lay down on her bed and broke into tears. She wondered if all her friends were getting spanked a lot. Her father never believed she was telling the truth, and she tried to remember how many times she actually lied. She recalled just once, when she had made up a story to cover for another girl who had stolen a five-dollar bill.

When David came home later, she told him about the fight at school.

"Randy is a boy! He shouldn't be fighting with girls! What a wimp…"

"I'll tell him tomorrow that you said he's a wimp," his sister said, more animated.

"Yeah, and you stop being such a baby. Tell him your big brother can teach him a lesson or two."

With that, the boy walked over to the kitchen, and she continued to stand in the hallway, her teeth clenched again. I wish there was a lady or a girl in our family, she thought. Men and boys are so mean…

When Maddie was ten, her father remarried and it appeared that his demeanor had relaxed. He told her and David that they had a new mommy who would take care of them, but she wasn't convinced. She had become quite self-reliant, making her own breakfast and lunch and handling her own laundry. She stayed out of trouble, having limited conversations with her father. No wonder his name is Titus, she thought. Is he as evil as the crazy Roman emperor we learned about in school?

She enjoyed studying and doing homework and earned top grades. There was a sweet joy in keeping this success to herself, since her father and brother never showed any interest. It doesn't matter if Daddy thinks I'm stupid, she told herself. As soon as I'm old enough I'll move out and do what I want.

Maddie's favorite subject was math. She was placed in a gifted program that allowed her to advance her math skills beyond her grade level. There was something about the interworking of numbers that fascinated her, and she knew this passion was going to be in her future.

When her class went to visit a food bank to serve food to poor people, she found that she enjoyed the activity. Helping people who were less fortunate than herself gave her a sense of power and convinced her to stop pitying herself.

Her father's temper gradually surfaced again, and he began beating her over any minute matter that aroused his rage.

"Your room is a mess again," he screamed at her and slapped her face. One eyebrow went up again. "You're making our house a pigsty! What a crappy nature you have! You'd better go and clean it up this minute!"

Maddie's eyes teared in spite of herself, and she shot a pleading glance at her stepmother, who stood by silently. She's not really my mom, she thought to herself as she ambled to tidy up her room. I am on my own.

Her father either ignored or forgot her fifteenth birthday, and beat her with a belt over not taking out the garbage the night before. He had stopped pulling down her pants now that she was older. She had trained herself not to cry, and had made a decision. She calmly carried out the trash can and scattered all its contents on the brick walkway. She then went into her room, gathered some clothes, her wallet, and a few toiletries in a duffel bag, then tiptoed out through the back door. It was getting dark.

She walked to her friend Lily's house and rang the doorbell. Lily's mother opened the door.

"Hi Maddie," the woman asked, clearly surprised to see the girl with a duffel bag in the early evening.

"Hi, is Lily home?" she asked, trying her best not to look helpless.

"Yes, Honey, she is," the mother said and pointed towards her daughter's room.

She didn't have to say much. They understood, and welcomed her to stay for as long as she needed.

Maddie didn't stay long. Since she had always been required her to have a part time job, she had earned some money by helping an elderly neighbor with yard chores. She kept the money to herself, because she was never given any by her parents, and had to buy her own clothes. Weeding and watering were activities she didn't completely enjoy, but it gave her time to think and analyze things for herself. She surmised that her father's habitual cheating on his tax returns must have been helpful to him. Since she had never been taught values of any sort, good or bad, Maddie formed her own beliefs. Cheating a real person was a no-no, but deceiving the system seemed an appealing victimless crime.

Her frugality enabled her to save enough to buy a dilapidated Chevy Malibu on an installment plan. She held her breath during the transaction, hoping the used car salesman would not ask her for an ID or a driver's license, and somehow it worked. At last she had wheels of her own, and she was delighted with the new taste of power and freedom. On Tuesday afternoons she went to a battered women's shelter to help cook and serve meals.

Maddie had to quit school and get a job in a fast food restaurant, where she told everyone she was eighteen. She rented a small room in a private home, and realized that she was in control of her own life. She resisted an impulse to call her father, knowing that he would report her as a missing child, only to have her dragged back home. Instead, she decided to find a daytime job, so she could go about getting her GED.

She was hired by a furniture store to become an office assistant to the manager, and enrolled in a GED program the following week. She found herself very busy but content about the prospects for a brighter future. Perhaps, she hoped, she would meet someone who would actually love her. She bought some clothes and makeup in a second hand store, and a few weeks later dyed her hair to a golden blond. Maddie was pleased with her new look.

Then, something happened that turned her world upside down. "Hey, Maddie," her manager came to her desk one late afternoon, pulled over a chair and sat down next to her, so close that his body pressed against hers. "You've been doing a good job here. I'd like to take you to dinner tonight, and then maybe we can have dessert in my house. We can go directly from here, or I can pick you up from your place. What do you think?"

That was Maddie's first experience with a sexual advance, and her face reddened in surprise and embarrassment.

She looked away from him and absentmindedly grabbed a pencil and started scratching lines on a piece of paper.

"Umm..." she mumbled. "I don't think so, sir. I'm sorry, but I can't come to your house. Thank you for offering..."

He rose from the chair, furiously glaring down at her.

"You're fired! Some people can't appreciate something good even when it's staring them in the face! Get out!"

With practically no money left, and after a few days of job hunting, she found herself homeless and hungry. Eventually, a friend let her stay with her for a few weeks, until she found her next

employment in a real estate broker's office. That's when Maddie, nearly seventeen, obtained a driver's license and assumed the name of Celeste Butler.

Bright and ambitious, she soon enrolled in a community college. She chose accounting and math as her main fields of study. Her organized mind and financial curiosity helped her grasp the structured nature of the subject, and she easily excelled in those classes. She was bored with the other required courses like English and history, but grudgingly managed to pass them. It was then that Maddie started suspecting that her father was much more affluent than he had pretended to be. She vaguely remembered overhearing him during phone conversations about "a couple of million dollars." She once heard him say "the money in the trunk." Why didn't Titus live a more comfortable life, and why was he so secretive about his wealth, Maddie pondered. She had always assumed that she had been cut out of his will and would never benefit from any of it, so she hadn't given it much thought. Titus and David had ceased to exist for her, and she was happy to depend on nobody but herself.

Thomas was Celeste's on again, off again boyfriend. They met in an accounting class, and discovered a strong connection. Their shrewd minds recognized the opportunity to earn much greater fortunes than what was offered by ordinary jobs, by the creative use of their knowledge and talents.

After graduation, Thomas had become an astute software expert, and started working at a brokerage firm as an assistant to a senior account executive. While there, he developed ways to breach clients' documents. The two began collaborating, with the idea of obtaining access to his firm's customers' asset records. He devised schemes to access money, and she found ways to funnel the funds into various assets. The romance was gone, but their working relationship thrived. Celeste's single priority had become her own self. Her wealth was now in the millions.

It was two years later that she met Steve, a handsome, athletic assistant manager in a mall where she often shopped. She was attracted to him shortly after they met, and they soon began dating.

"Why do you need this small job, being a mall employee?" she asked him. "You don't set your own schedule, and the salary is not great."

Steve adulated her, always telling her she was meant to do great things.

"Like I always say, you have the best of both worlds. You are smart and beautiful," he replied. "But I'm not as lucky, so what else do you propose I do? I enjoy my job."

"You can learn what I do," she said, raised her eyebrows and smiled.

"If you marry me," he said and took her hand, "I may consider doing that."

"Are you proposing to me?"

"You bet! It's the most important question I've ever asked, or will ever ask. Will you marry me?"

"Of course I will, silly!"

They kissed passionately and hugged in silence for a long time. Celeste's mind raced. He loves me... This is sweet, she thought, he truly loves me... but I may have to let him in on the business with Thomas. Then she stopped herself and took a long breath. Enjoy the moment... Hit the pause button on the brain.

Of everything about Steve, Celeste enjoyed their sex life the most, and the lovemaking later that evening did not disappoint. He undressed and caressed her slowly, arousing her beyond anything she had ever experienced. Steve appeared to have a talent, a natural ability in this area. His body was firm and muscular, and he skillfully traversed hers with his fingers and lips, until her moans signaled to him it was time to move on from foreplay to consummating the act.

"You are an amazing lover, you know..." she whispered to him. "I think this time was our best. You must have had lots of practice, but I'm not asking any questions."

"No, darling... I haven't really had much experience. It comes to me naturally when I'm with you. Besides, you're not so bad yourself in this area. You are so preoccupied with analyzing numbers and finances, that you don't realize what a sexy woman you are..."

They lay entwined together for a long time before going to sleep. Being married to a man like him, she thought, could never be all bad.

Thomas

After Celeste and Steve married, she had not heard from Thomas for several months, mainly because there was nothing they had been working on together for some time. She knew that he had changed jobs, and that he landed a senior position. Still, she thought he might be useful to her in the future.

He had recently become a professional "white hat" hacker. His title at his new place of employment was "senior computer specialist," and was charged with overseeing the company's cyber security. He was hired by a large stock brokerage that was trying to recover from a serious system breach. A nefarious hacker managed to access thousands of customers' records and alter financial transactions. This prompted the management to hire an expert who designed a program that detects and stops breaches as soon as they emerge. He had become a legitimate security systems specialist.

Thomas Snow proved himself immensely valuable to the brokerage when, on two separate occasions, his department intercepted irregularities they noticed. Those steps enabled them to block the theft of clients' data and avoid a public relations fiasco.

"Most hackers are not looking to cause any harm," he told the CEO shortly afterwards. "They're geeks who have a fixation with operating systems, and they hack into companies' computers to figure them out. The bad guys, the so-called 'black hats,' actually want to inflict damage and steal information."

"Well," his boss said with a satisfied smile, "It's good that we're set up to catch those black hats' intrusions and stop them before they happen."

With a comfortable nest egg and respectable earnings, he had decided to "go straight" and end his shady ties and dealings with Celeste. He hadn't heard from her for some time, and hoped that their association had dissolved.

His phone rang at eleven PM while he was preparing to go to bed. Fearing an emergency, he answered immediately.

"Hi," a familiar woman's voice greeted him. "It's Celeste. How's life in L.A. these days?"

"Hi, life's good. How are you doing? Actually, where are you and Steve now?"

"On vacation."

"Are you still working?" he asked, not expecting a truthful answer.

"No, not exactly; but I heard that you're in charge of computer security at a major brokerage firm. Congratulations!"

She sounded smug and condescending, and he was anxious to go to sleep.

"Listen, I was just getting ready to crash for the night, so can we talk another time? Actually, to be honest, I want out. I suggest that you don't call me again!" he blurted without thinking.

"Oh, I see," the cool reply came after a brief pause. "Have a good night."

She hung up, but then Thomas couldn't fall asleep. What is she up to this time, he asked himself, knowing she didn't just call to say hello. Celeste wanted something, and he was relieved he didn't give her the chance to tell him. He didn't care.

Harry's World

Crickets had always annoyed Harry and Elizabeth for entering their house in his years on earth. The chirping sometimes kept them up at night, and he would get out of bed to find the creature and shoo it outside. When Elizabeth was helping their daughter with her science project, she learned that certain spiders are natural predators of the despised crickets. They had shared a few jokes about the critters. During his living days, Harry had often contemplated the adversarial relationship between the insect populations.

Philosophical by nature, he often compared conflicts among people to those among insects. Unless it was about survival, he had always said, people should never try to destroy each other.

A loud argument erupted between two field agents about the best way to question a suspect in a fraudulent lending scheme. Harry stepped in.

"Disagree peacefully" he told the sparring duo. "Many good ideas come from arguments and disputes. I want each of you to write down your thoughts and email them to me. We'll take a look at them later."

The tension disappeared; when Harry spoke, everyone listened.

He, the experienced special investigator, had been working on several confidential files concerning bank fraud and money laundering. Although he worked in close quarters with others in the department, many of his communications were secret, to be shared only with those with the highest security clearance. Those were people who worked in a separate office, which he had often entered and closed the door behind him. The young staffers in the immediate work area nicknamed that separate office the "hush-hush cave", and had never asked questions about his projects. Much of his time was devoted to training and mentoring the New Agent Trainees and interns.

Esmeralda Santoro had attracted Harry's attention since her first days as the youngest intern in their unit. She was bright and eager to learn, which motivated him to help her understand some of the more complex concepts. As her mentor, he bonded with the young woman, and, since he knew she had no family, became her older role model. The Financial Crimes office was on the main floor of the FBI building. It was divided into sections where teams of three to four people worked together. Despite the austere design, Esmeralda enjoyed working there. She appreciated the opportunity to learn about law enforcement from the inside.

"I hope to have a real career with the FBI someday" she told him once during a lunch break. They were in the cafeteria, each eating their homemade meal.

"Esme, I know you have the brains and the desire to learn," he replied. "You are a strong and hard-working young woman. I am quite confident you'll attain that career. But tell me, do you get any time to enjoy yourself between your classes and this job?"

"I'm not looking for a lot of fun these days. I am focused on building a future for myself."

"No boyfriend?" he asked with a smile.

"I had a boyfriend some time ago, but we broke up," she replied, gazing down at the table.

Life in her unit continued, and she noticed Harry going into the "hush-hush cave" more often, and staying longer.

Schemes and Strategies

Of all the names and identities she had occasionally used over the past fifteen years, she liked her current one the most. Celeste Butler had a serious ring to it, suggesting a strong, possibly mysterious woman, and she decided to keep it permanently. Not that her past aliases were no longer useful; each owned a modest life insurance policy, never over $150,000, that provided easy returns. The best part was that nobody had to die in order for the policies to pay; each had a phantom name insured and beneficiary, designed so that when the policy paid out, the proceeds made their way into one of her bank accounts.

The false papers came from an expert, named Monroe, a crafty source in California. It was a forgery mill that produced a variety of counterfeit documents—passports, birth certificates, Social Security cards, death certificates, and more. Celeste had taken care to ensure that the forger did not know her name, and had everything mailed to a post office box under a bogus name. Payment was always made using money orders or bank transfers.

Her various accounts were spread over six different banks, under different identities and Social Security numbers. Celeste had the details printed on an index card that she always carried in her wallet, backed up by a file on her computer. The list had partial names and numbers that had the beginnings of each password, a hint of the rest. She had arranged the various user ID's and passwords in sequential order. The security questions and answers were duplicated for each of the fictional investors.

They lived in an ordinary house in Los Angeles. There was a small yard with drought-tolerant plants, and although there were neighbors living on both sides, they had never gotten acquainted.

Early one morning she was at the small desk they had set up in one of the bedrooms. She had logged on to each of her holdings to verify the security, when she heard Steve at the door. She stood up in shock when she saw that he was carrying a puppy with long floppy ears. Then, she instantly went over to admire the pup with joy, caressing and cooing.

"Oh, what an adorable doggie! It's a little Basset Hound!"

"It's a she, which I got as a present for you. I remembered how much you wanted a dog."

"She looks so dignified," Celeste chirped excitedly. "I always imagined having a dog named Lady Windsor, so that's what I want to call her. Oh, we'd better make a little place for her to sleep, and buy some dog food." She took the trembling dog and cradled it.

"I thought of everything, dear," Steve said. He went outside and came back with a bag of items from the pet store. There were a collar, a leash, food, a dish, and toys.

"Thank you, you're a sweetheart," she kissed his cheek. "Oh, look at her, she's so scared." The minute the frightened pup was down on the floor, she urinated. Not so dignified, she thought, but then reminded herself it was still a baby. Steve ran to grab a rag and wiped the wood floor, and she watched nervously while Lady Windsor stood, surveying her new surroundings.

"As soon as she gets used to the house, she'll be fine," he told her and sat down to play with the puppy. She went back to her laptop and searched the Internet to learn how to train and care for Lady Windsor. She didn't have the patience for babies, dogs, or any needy creatures. The reason she wanted to have a canine was that she recognized an opportunity, one that fit with her intricate plan.

Her income from various underhanded sources was being directly deposited into several bank accounts. While she made it a point to bond with Lady Windsor, walking her every morning, she spent hours formulating and planning her windfalls. Yeah, she smiled to herself, I had a rich daddy and he treated me like trash. But, guess what, I've got more millions than he ever had.

She bought a new laptop, since Steve had been using the older one more. She then prepared a document with the various details and locations of her investments, along with the details she had listed on her old-fashioned index card. Then she saved it on two tiny memory sticks.

"Even if our computers are hacked, nobody will find a shred of our details; I have everything on two duplicate flash drives," she told him one evening. That was not all; Celeste had also encrypted the document with the details on her own laptop.

"What if they find one of the drives?" he asked. "If we're ever investigated, they'll go through everything we have."

"Don't worry," she said triumphantly, "Nobody will find them." She had taped one flash drive, encased in plastic, to the inside bottom of a purple handbag, and the other in a tiny pouch that she sewed into the dog's collar. But her husband didn't need to know all the pieces, she thought. It was enough to tell him about the stick in the dog collar.

As part of her new sophisticated self-image, Celeste decided to create a minor fashion identity. She had always liked red clothing, which she had never had as a child. She now bought a bright red scarf, and wore it whenever she was outdoors. Regardless of who would notice, she would always be the woman with the red scarf.

The Next Move

Celeste feared that living in Los Angeles might make it easy for both the authorities and victims of her fraudulent activities to discover her whereabouts. Therefore, she, Steve, and Lady Windsor moved to Bakersfield, California, where they bought a small house in an upscale district. It was a single-story home with a well-tended flower garden in front. Away from the huge city, and a fresh start in a new place, they agreed. Steve began to look for work, and in the meanwhile took upon himself the task of landscaping, which allowed her time to work on their finances.

It took Celeste a few months to gather her thoughts and decide on her next steps, with Thomas out of the picture. She had supplemented her sizeable net worth by filing false death claims on the life insurance plans she had purchased for fictitious individuals. That activity had abruptly come to an end after Monroe, her reliable forger, had recently died of a massive heart attack.

She needed help with moving the funds to legitimate assets without leaving a money trail. In the past, Thomas had mentioned a young intern named Brent whom he was training. She had considered recruiting some new blood, and pondered if this particular intern could fit into her agenda. Without a last name, she was at a loss about tracking him down at Thomas' firm. Conceivably, he might no longer be working there; but it was worth a try.

After debating the matter for a few days, Celeste took on the task of tracking down Brent. She eventually managed to access the company directory, discovered there were three men with similar first names. One of them was Brent Bushnell, the young man who had worked with Thomas.

She initiated her approach by posting an "opportunity" through a private app on social media, then waited for a response. When nothing came after a week, she repeated the post, and immediately sent an apology for accidentally posting it twice.

Several weeks later, when she was certain that Brent was not interested, he reached out. He took the bait, she told herself, celebrating her triumph. She decided to move cautiously and give him the impression that he was one of several candidates competing for this "opportunity."

She identified herself as "Agent M" and instructed him to communicate with her by encrypted email to ensure confidentiality. She then dangled before him a generous offer of 25% commission on every successful sale or project that he would clinch.

"Please provide me your full resume, copies of your last two years' income tax returns, a list of your goals, in addition to examples of projects you worked on at your firm," she wrote him in the encrypted message. "We will review your application and inform you of our decision after we evaluate all our applicants."

Brent resigned from the company upon receiving his employment offer from "Agent M," and wrote her that he was eager to start. He recommended that they invest in commercial real estate in two cities that bustled with the high-tech boom. She agreed to let him arrange the initial investment in a new, small office complex in San Francisco. With the exorbitant rental income, it did not take a long time to show high returns, and the new recruit, whom she code named "Agent B", received his first commission check. He wrote her that he needed a few days off for a personal emergency, and drove home to Los Angeles.

Steve and Celeste settled into what turned out to be a comfortable routine. She liked to go to bed early, rise at sunrise, go for a run with the dog, then delve into her paperwork. He preferred to stay up long past midnight, watch old gangster movies on the internet, and rise late in the morning. They ate breakfast together after he finished getting ready for the day. Steve enjoyed gardening and spending time outdoors, so he had added more shrubs and flowers to the front yard. As a member of a hiking club, he spent hours getting acquainted with the canyons and trails in the area.

Brent's Gift

The great advantage that Brent brought Celeste was his small treasury of contacts with offshore companies, which offered safe havens for questionable cash. Unbeknownst to Thomas, his former boss, he had assembled this trove of confidential material while working under him. For her, this was a great solution to her challenge of where to stash the large amount of cash she had accumulated.

Celeste had her share of money that had been syphoned from clients' accounts when she and Thomas started working together. He had gained access to large fortunes by hacking their bank records, and wired money to her in exchange for handsome fees. These proceeds, along with the phony life insurance settlements, amounted to millions. Although they were safely hidden in various banks, she had always hoped to work with a foreign company that knew how to handle ill-gotten funds.

Thus began Brent's practice of traveling under various cover names, to Greece, Thailand, and Panama, posing as a wealthy tourist. He knew which individuals to contact at the firms, and thereby succeeded in moving his new employer's fortunes to more clandestine locations. He received a new smart phone with strict instructions it was only to be used for communicating with Agent M. Since using his own telephone was completely banned, Brent carried several burner phones with him.

Celeste believed that she was ensuring total anonymity and secrecy. She did not reveal her name to him or to anyone with whom she had dealt. He, grateful and loyal to his new benefactor/employer, did his utmost to mask his own identity. With his new earnings he purchased a seaside mansion in Malibu in southern California, and treated himself to a new red Ferrari. He ignored her warning against displaying his riches, so as to avoid undue attention by the IRS. He assumed that since there was no record of his affiliation with her, the relationship between them would remain in the dark. He knew nothing about his or her identity—gender, name, or location.

On a Saturday morning he noticed a secure message from Agent M. It was brief: "FBI is on our tail, urgently need to stop their investigation." He began scrolling through his contacts to find a phone number. He came across Lexi, his girlfriend from a prior life, and pressed the call button.

"Hey, Lexi, it's Brent."

"Hey yourself," came the surprised response. "I haven't heard from you in ages."

"I know… It's been a long time. My life has been a little crazy. I just changed jobs, but the best part is… Are you ready?"

"Yes," she replied, clearly not very intrigued.

"Look, I came into some money, so I bought this great place in Malibu. It's right on the beach. I want you to come over and see it. We should reconnect."

"Sounds impressive. Well, I admit I'm curious, so give me the address and I'll see you around three."

It was a warm afternoon. They walked on the beach, sat down on towels on the sand, relaxing and talking mainly about old times and people they had known.

"I have to ask you," she finally said. "Where did you get the money to buy this place? Only millionaires live here. I can't believe it."

"I made a couple of investments when I worked at this brokerage, and they paid off very well."

"That's incredible. Is it all legit?" she raised an eyebrow, trying to read his face.

"Come on, Lexi! Do you think I want the IRS after me? This is rightfully my own property."

"What kind of job to you have?" she asked. "I mean, who do you work for, or do you have your own business?"

"I work for a very high-rolling brokerage firm, and I am actually one of the account executives. We buy properties all over the country, and some overseas."

Brent paid for a pricey dinner in a small upscale restaurant in Malibu.

"How about spending the night in my beautiful digs?" he asked with a smirk.

"Thank you for treating me to a beautiful day and a very nice dinner. But I really can't stay—I have an early morning appointment tomorrow."

She called Esmeralda as soon as she came home.

"Hi Esme, it's Lexi."

"Hi, I haven't seen you for a while. Is everything all right?"

"I'm fine, but can we meet sometime tomorrow? I need to talk to you about something."

They scheduled to have dinner at the small café near the campus where they had gone the first time they met.

The women hugged when they saw each other. Esmeralda did not realize how much she missed her friend.

"So, you haven't been coming to Stardust," she began. "Actually, I stopped going too."

"Let me guess," Lexi smiled. "It's because of this guy Brent, right?"

"Yes, how did you know? He wasn't leaving me alone, and honestly, I don't like him so much anyway. I am also very busy with my work. But you wanted to talk, and I promise to keep it between us. So, tell me please."

Lexi kept looking down at her salad before she started talking. She opened her mouth, was about to speak, and then stopped again.

"I may not be doing the right thing talking to you about this, Esme. I'm sorry…"

"When you called me last night, I knew there was something on your mind that was bothering you. Go ahead, I will listen."

"OK, here it goes. Again, I don't know if you are the right person to tell this to. I met Brent years ago, and we dated for a few months. I broke it off because he always seemed to be involved in something shady. Here are a couple of examples: He wanted to get a position at a certain marketing firm, so he wrote his own recommendation letter and forged his professor's signature. He stole a computer and printer from his place of work, then reported them missing, and later insisted that they question everybody in the department about it. He always had his ways of cheating and double-crossing people. I am pretty sure he has gotten everything in his life by being corrupt."

Esmeralda watched her friend's tension ease when she finally ate some of her food.

"So," Lexi continued. "Let me tell you what's troubling me. Brent called me yesterday, out of the blue, and invited me over to his house. Good God, he has a mansion in Malibu, right by the ocean. He told me that he made his money from some great investments, hat he's working for a brokerage firm, and that he came to some money. According to him he works as a junior account executive for a successful company.

"The thing is, I don't believe that this guy is smart enough to be so financially successful. He also mentioned that they were investing in other countries, which makes me even more suspicious."

Esmeralda held her breath as she listened.

"Wow, Lexi. Your instinct may be good about this guy, and all I can say is that I'm relieved that I got away from him."

"This information should not necessarily stay just between us. See, the reason I wanted to mention Brent was not only to warn you about him, but also for something else. I wonder if, through your government job, you can get somebody to check into him. If I'm way out of line, I'm sorry. What do you think?"

If only she knew that the office where I work has exactly the right people for looking into the likes of this guy, Esmeralda thought. Lexi was right on. Without revealing the details of her internship, she replied.

"First of all, you are not out of line here. We are friends, and we can share things that bother us. Second, your former boyfriend Brent sounds suspicious. I have a friend who interns at the FBI, and I can pass this on to her. I can't promise it will go anywhere, but it is worth a try."

"You are so amazing! It's a good thing my first thought was to ask you about it. You are so smart, and always know what to do."

"Okay, give me Brent's full name, his address, phone number, email, anything you have." She took out a small notepad from her handbag and slid it to Lexi. "Write it down here, and don't email me anything about it, so we don't create an electronic trail. It was smart of you to decide to check into this guy."

Wildfire

Steve was still awake when he began to hear the howling sound outside. It was two in the morning, and he was preparing to go bed, but stopped. Looking out through their bedroom window, he saw the trees bending and twisting in the strong wind. Bakersfield is so flat, he always thought, nothing can obstruct your line of sight, maybe all the way to the Pacific. The horizon was orange red, and he could see flames in the distance. He rushed over to the bed and tapped Celeste on her shoulder.

"Hey, you'd better get up," he said aloud, watching her open her sleepy eyes. "There's a big fire. We need to pack a couple of things and get out of here." She rose from the bed, her hair disheveled, and looked out the window at the eerie glow.

"Let's call the fire department to see what they say," she told him and picked up the phone.

All she heard was "all emergency lines are busy." Steve made her coffee, which she began to sip, listening to the blustery winds, while he stepped from the kitchen.

"Let's grab some things us and drive somewhere away from here," he said. "Forget the coffee. Those fires spread fast; it may be too late for us if we wait."

She turned on the TV where the news was on.

"The Tehachapi wildfire is spreading toward nearby towns, and there is no containment at this time. Residents should be ready to evacuate at any time, so everyone is urged to be alert, and to wake up neighbors who may be asleep."

The only neighbor that she vaguely knew was an elderly couple who lived two houses away. She put on jeans and a t-shirt and opened the front door. Lady Windsor ran outside and disappeared through the open door, and Celeste ran to find her. She jogged over to the neighbors' house and rang the doorbell. When nobody answered the door she rang again, and turned around to try to search for the dog. Hopefully the second ring will wake them up and they'll hear the howling outside, she thought.

After fifteen minutes, she and Steve gave up on locating Lady Windsor. The wind was blowing and she could smell the fire. As soon as she entered the house there was a text message on her phone announcing the evacuation order. While he backed out the car from the garage, she threw their toothbrushes, sunglasses, underwear, sweatshirts and cell phone chargers in a duffel bag and ran outside.

A loud, foreboding voice came from a bullhorn. "You are ordered to evacuate immediately! Take your necessary belongings and drive away now! Follow the routes to the main highways!" The dreary announcement was repeated a second time, and then it was just the wind and the faraway rumblings of the approaching fire.

"I forgot my laptop!" Celeste screamed.

"Don't worry, I grabbed it," Steve said and started to drive away.

It was unclear which direction the fire was coming from, so Steve decided to go toward the main highway, which led out of town. To her surprise and relief, he took charge.

"We'll be okay, dear," he told her. "Just calm down."

The eerie darkness and the heavy smoke in the air made it nearly impossible to see through the windshield, and Steve was forced to slow down. They were in a long line of cars that were evacuating, and the low visibility slowed all of them down to a crawl. It looked like an inferno was approaching, but they couldn't see which direction it was coming from.

"I am really scared," he heard her say for the first time since he had known her. "Maybe we should pull over, park the car on the side of the road and run."

"All right, let's go for it," he said, drove onto to the unpaved shoulder, grabbed the duffel bag, and they started jogging down a small hillside. Steve pulled a flashlight from the bag.

They could see the flames moving toward them, and immediately changed direction, running to their left.

"This is getting from bad to worse," she screamed. "There is a small pond somewhere here, and I think I can find it. I don't mind getting drenched if it will save our lives."

The flashlight proved to be a life saver, because it illuminated the small trail that she knew would lead them to the pond. About fifteen minutes later, hot and thirsty with eyes burning, she saw the glint of the small body of water. She looked in all directions; there was no light.

"Steve, where is the flashlight?" she screamed a minute later, but there was no answer. She sat down on the grassy edge of the pond, but the fire now seemed to come at her from every direction, and the intense heat terrorized her. She couldn't see him in the thick blackness, and the dread of being alone overwhelmed her.

"Let's get into the water, okay?" she hollered and stepped in. "I'm going in! Where's the damn flashlight?"

Her husband had disappeared.

"Hey, Steve," she screamed louder. "Where are you? Come to the pond!"

She was alone with the flames surrounding the area, shivering in spite of the heat. Where is he, she puzzled, disbelieving. Sparks were flying and landing around her, but were extinguished the second they touched the water.

Calm down, she told herself, get yourself together. You're safe in the water, and Steve is most likely somewhere close, possibly on the other side. Still, she strained to look around, hoping the fire would offer some visibility, but nothing happened. She remembered that he had their bag while her hands were empty, and she was shaking in panic. Then she remembered her cell phone and pulled it out of her submerged jeans pocket. To her relief, it glowed as soon as she pressed the power button. She then tapped the flashlight app, and held the phone up towards the sky. She had read that emergency responders in rescue helicopters had night vision goggles that enabled them to see even a small light and locate stranded people. It was her only hope. She turned the device off every few minutes to conserve the battery. It seemed that nobody was coming to rescue her; on the phone, she saw that she had been in the water for over half an hour.

The sound of the wind, the fire, and her own sobs blocked out the whirring above her, until she saw a beam of light coming down. She then saw the outline of a helicopter, waded to the center of the searchlight, and waved her arms wildly. In the midst of the chaos, Celeste continued to aim her tiny device at the aircraft above her, and tried to hold still. She thought she heard a male voice saying something on a loudspeaker, but the words didn't matter. She saw a figure rappelling down a rope towards her, and waited for him to reach her. A huge sense of relief overcame her, and she silently congratulated herself for remembering to use a light to attract attention. But where was Steve?

"My husband Steve is still here somewhere, but I can't find him!" she screamed.

"Okay, ma'am, we have night vision goggles, so we'll look for him. Does he have any source of light, like a lighter or a flashlight?"

"I think he has a flashlight and a cell phone," she replied frantically, while the man secured her into a harness and she was soon airborne.

"We'll search for him, but for now I'm getting you up to the helo."

She shivered when she and the rescuer were hoisted up, and promptly started bawling when they pulled her inside.

"Thank you, guys," was all she could say. When did I become such a coward? Why am I sobbing? I am strong, she tried to reassure herself, but it didn't ease her anxiety.

"Look, ma'am, we will search for your husband Steve for a few minutes, but we can't take too long. The fire is spreading, and we've got some other places to search for stranded victims."

They didn't find him and Celeste sat down, strangely calmer, wondering where they were taking her. She was given a thin mylar blanket, which helped with the trembling. Her clothes were soaked, but she didn't have the strength to ask any questions. She survived, and recognized that she would have to deal with the aftermath.

The helicopter picked up a stranded couple who were huddled together on a large rock. How fortunate for them, she thought: both of them made it out safely. She began to lose hope that Steve was alive somewhere, and that he, too, was able to escape the inferno. Beyond that, she was unable to concentrate on anything, except landing somewhere dry and safe.

New Clues

A sudden, strong urge overcame Esmeralda to go to Harry's house, mainly to comfort his widow, but also to see where and how he lived. She hesitated, because she had never gotten to meet Harry's wife, and was uncertain about what to expect. Close to a month had gone by since the bombing attack, and the FBI group in charge of the investigation was developing leads. Clues came from several directions, but it was difficult to weave them together.

One Saturday morning, Esmeralda finally steeled herself and went to visit Elizabeth, Harry's widow. The house was in a quiet neighborhood on a tree-lined avenue in Glendale. In spite of the weather forecast, which predicted temperatures in the 90's, the sky was overcast. She easily got over her skittishness after Elizabeth invited her to sit at the kitchen table where she served tea and muffins. Esmeralda told the woman about her life of school, work, and how much she had admired her late husband.

She looked around and noticed a photo of Harry, approached it and gazed at the face, trying to connect with her old mentor. Perhaps the real clue would come from the man himself, she thought, focusing on his eyes. Another framed picture in black and white caught her attention. It was of a family of five: father, mother, two boys and a young girl. Her hostess came over.

"I can't bring myself to go through all his stuff in the garage," the woman told her. "He kept so many papers in his file cabinet."

Esmeralda perked up.

"Do you mind if I try to help you?" she asked. Elizabeth was quiet for a moment.

"Look, there's a lot of clutter there, so I hope you don't mind the mess."

They entered the garage, which was full of dusty cardboard boxes, a few old appliances, and a wooden file cabinet.

"May I?" she asked.

"Go ahead. I hope you can make some sense out of it," Elizabeth replied, hands on her hips. "I wonder if any of it has anything to do with his work."

Esmeralda had to struggle to pull the heavy drawer open, and then stared at the massive collection of folders, so tightly packed that it was difficult to pull one out. Then she saw something that astounded her. She stared at it for a long moment, trying to understand what it was.

Inside the file cabinets there were large labels in the front of each drawer. The top drawer was labeled "Crickets," and the second one "Spiders." Esmeralda stared at the two tabs and became light headed, so that she had to steady herself on the open drawer. She clearly remembered the disturbing dream about the giant cricket. She understood that Harry had somehow sent her a message, which was eerie, but also fortunate.

"Are you all right?" Elizabeth asked her with visible concern. Esmeralda ignored the question.

She pointed to the open cabinet and asked, "do you have any idea if crickets and spiders had any special meaning to your late husband?"

"Harry had a fascination with insects, and always tried to learn which predators each of them had. It all started with our daughter Violet's science project in the sixth grade. But I can't imagine he was keeping this much material on bugs. It just doesn't make sense."

"You know," Esmeralda looked at her, "these may be code words, and can possibly give the investigators some clues. It wouldn't surprise me to know that Harry is helping us solve his own murder."

Elizabeth stared and said, "this looks daunting. Who's going to go through all these papers?"

"With your permission, I'd like to tell my boss about this, so he can pass it along to the task force in charge of the case," Esmeralda said, waited anxiously and got a nod. "I'm going to snap pictures of the cabinet," she continued and snapped a few photos. "We have a special team investigating the bombing. You know that Harry was not the only victim; there were other casualties."

On Monday morning Esmeralda sent a message to Judy, who then forwarded it to another department. That afternoon she was asked to report to an office on the third floor. She had never set foot in the third-floor office; access to it was much above her security clearance. Her heart pounded when she entered the elevator and pressed the button to go upstairs. Just before the doors closed, a young man with reddish blond hair and freckles rushed in.

"Sorry," he said and looked down. She thought she had seen him somewhere, but couldn't place it at that moment. It slipped out of her mind as soon as she stepped out of the elevator.

The third floor was a large open space office with many cubicles that lined the long, gray walls. She noticed a few cameras overhead. Nobody was there to greet her, so she stood at the entrance, taking in the chilly mood, and waited. After about two minutes, a tall, stern looking man opened a side door and approached her.

"Are you Esmeralda Santoro?" he asked in an even tone.

"Yes, I am." Her heart beat so fast, she thought her chest might burst.

He pointed the way to a side office. "I am special agent John Pope; this way, please."

She followed Pope and showed him the photos she had snapped of the open cabinet drawers in Harry's garage. She waited while the images were forwarded and uploaded to a digital file.

"This is good work, Ms. Santoro," the tall man told her. "Thank you for bringing it to our attention. We will take it from here."

The heavy file cabinet was removed from Harry and Elizabeth's garage and transported to a warehouse in the basement of the FBI building. Esmeralda could barely control her eagerness to get involved in going through Harry's papers.

"I know I am only an intern," she pleaded with Judy again and again, "but I can help."

Two days later she received an office email asking her to go to the warehouse to join the team that worked on that part of the case. She was jubilant—she wanted more than anything to get her hands into the files.

The Face of the Aftermath

Celeste lay on a cot in a Red Cross shelter that was housed in a high school auditorium. She had slept fitfully, and in a daze walked over to a table where volunteers were serving breakfast. A cup of coffee sounded good now, she thought. It was difficult for her to accept the notion that it was not a dream. Did she still have a home? Was her husband alive? Where was her dog? That last thought jolted her into reality. What happened to Lady Windsor?

It slowly came back to her—the dog collar with the flash drive inside. With her laptop most likely destroyed, the only other record of her intricate transactions was on another tiny memory stick hidden in her purple purse in a closet. What if her house had burned down? When her head finally cleared, she questioned if anyone knew what happened to missing pets. Many other people were asking about their missing dogs and cats, but there were still no answers. Containment of the wildfire was only a meager 15%, with the main effort directed at saving people and homes.

The next day some news gradually came. About three hundred homes had been destroyed or damaged, and a number of bodies were discovered. It would take time to learn the identities of the deceased. She feared Steve was among them, and with him her computer. She briefly contemplated getting on a plane to escape somewhere to hide from the reality, but remembered she left her passport at home. In the public bathroom, she was shocked when she saw herself in the mirror. There were streaks of soot on her face, her hair was messy and her t-shirt dirty. I haven't washed my face since I got here, she thought, turned on the faucet and scrubbed off the grime.

It was then that her cell phone rang with Steve's caller ID.

"Steve!" She yelled into the phone. "Are you all right?"

"Sorry, Ma'am... This is fire captain Josh Miner. This phone was found near Pitts Pond near Bakersfield. It was hard to find anything on it, but one of our tech people discovered that your number was among the last outgoing calls."

"This is my husband, Steve Butler's phone. Where is it? Can I come to get it? Does anybody know where my husband is?" she asked frantically.

"Unfortunately, I don't have information on your husband. You can pick up the phone at the Bakersfield fire station number 88 as soon as the area is declared safe."

It took another day for the distraught who were missing relatives to go to a makeshift morgue. Celeste steeled herself for the grim prospect of seeing Steve's charred body. A kind woman who sat with her on the bus tried to chat with her, but she couldn't speak. The scene they came to was surreal, about a dozen cots with blankets that covered corpses. She froze when she saw orange sneakers that protruded from under a blanket, the ones she had always teased her husband about. The orange color was blackened, but still recognizable.

"We know this is very difficult. Please try to identify your loved one if you see them here," an older official said warmly. "We need the names of the departed."

She resisted lifting the blanket to see Steve's face, and looked at the kindly man helplessly. He walked over, and slowly pulled back the top of the blanket. The face was black, burned beyond recognition. The scalp was a charred mass which might have once been his hair. She nodded and moved away. "Steve Butler. His name is Steve Butler," she muttered and ran outside to vomit. A few minutes later, she went back inside to provide her details.

Two days later Celeste, along with the others, were allowed to check on their homes. With the certainty of her husband's demise, she mustered the strength to face what would come next. She had finally showered and changed into donated clothing, and prepared herself for the likely prospect of having lost her home. Her street was barely recognizable, but the house was standing, dirty with soot, but seemingly intact. The grass in front was covered with ash, and patches had been burned by flying embers. Two houses to the right looked like they had escaped the fire, but the roof of house on the left was partially caved in, its red tile turned black.

It was heartbreaking to see her beautiful neighborhood looking so bleak, and she waited a while before approaching her house. In their haste to escape, she and Steve had forgotten to lock the front door, so she opened it and entered the eerie emptiness. She smelled the heavy smoke that permeated the whole interior, opened the windows, but her mind was elsewhere. In her home office she opened the closet door to look for her purple handbag. She didn't see it in its usual spot on the top shelf or on any other shelves, and then searched every dresser drawer. The purse was gone. She sank into the sofa and covered her face in despair, anxious about surviving the nightmare.

It was three days later that she learned that the car they had driven to escape was destroyed. Their Audi that was still parked in the garage was covered with ash but otherwise unharmed. She used the garden hose to wash the car and drove to fire station 88 to retrieve her husband's phone. She regarded it as a personal reminder of his presence, and placed it in a drawer. At least it was something positive, she thought, a small thing to brighten her mood.

As the first week passed, Celeste grew more puzzled over why Steve hadn't made it into the pond with her. What caused him to die? Could he have tripped and broken a leg, or fallen somewhere? It was assumed that all the victims who perished in the wildfire had the same cause of death—by fire, mostly smoke inhalation. She had opted to forego an autopsy on her husband, so there was no way to discover any recent injuries.

Her emotions were mixed about his disappearance from her life. Yes, she would miss the romance and the passion they had shared. But she had always believed he was too fearful, certainly not sharp enough to participate in her financial dealings. He had ignored her repeated suggestions to learn more about investments. Concerned about his ability to be her true partner, she was glad that she had kept him in the dark regarding her various schemes. Still, in spite of his unsophistication and angst, she loved him. She had always believed she was protecting him.

Fearing the Unknown

Esmeralda was dividing her time between the basement and her desk, doing her usual research and summarizing reports. It was harder to concentrate on her tasks while thinking about the trove of information from Harry's garage. She understood that her low security clearance blocked her access to more than she had already seen.

The FBI unit in which Esmeralda interned handled financial fraud and money laundering. She had therefore given Brent's details to Judy, assuming they would make their way to the right channels. Nobody followed up or asked her about it, and since she had recently stumbled upon the new files, he slipped from her memory.

A text from Lexi reminded her of the disturbing young man.

"Hey," the message read, "can you meet me for happy hour at Effie's after work?"

"Yes, I'll see you there," she replied, went to the bathroom, and on her way back quietly stopped at Judy's desk.

"Judy," she whispered, "did anything come out of our discussion about Mr. Bushnell?"

"Actually, funny you should bring it up. The boys next door are very interested in this fellow, but it's complicated."

"What do you mean?" Esmeralda asked

"I'm hearing that he is not exactly who he says he is," Judy said quietly. "I don't know much, so I can't say anything."

"Come on, Judy… At least give me a hint!"

"I'm guessing that the name Brent Bushnell is an alias. But please go back to your desk. You know that we're not supposed to discuss open investigations, especially with interns."

She turned around and buried her head in papers on her desk, hoping nobody noticed that she had been distracted. She anxiously watched the clock, counting the minutes until happy hour. Maybe Lexi had more details.

She arrived at Effie's before Lexi and sat at the only available table. It was noisy and crowded. Why was the bar so full this afternoon, she wondered, then found a small table in a corner where they would have some privacy. Lexi came a few minutes later, sat down and ordered a beer. Esmeralda had never learned to like beer so she ordered a coke.

Lexi didn't bother with small talk. She leaned over and spoke quietly to Esmeralda, who had to cup her ear to hear.

"Listen, I have to tell you something. Brent has been asking me about you. He wants to know exactly what you do for work, where you live, even asked for your phone number. Of course, I didn't give him anything."

"What?" Esmeralda's mouth flew open. "What does he want with me? Is he a stalker or something? I just danced with him a few times at the club!"

"I told you he's a creep, didn't I?" Lexi continued. "He thinks you are a high roller at the FBI, and for some reason he's obsessed with finding you. It must have something to do with something sinister or illegal; I know it."

"Do you think he is dangerous?" Esmeralda asked, her forehead wrinkling.

"He said he likes you, and wants to get to know you better, but it's bullshit. It's about your imaginary high espionage job. I'm worried that he may try to follow you, so be careful."

Esmeralda was quiet for a moment, trying to absorb the disturbing news. She decided to tell Lexi the truth about her internship. After all, she was not required to keep it secret, and believed that her friend was trustworthy and smart. She had to confide in someone.

"If I tell you where I have my government internship, can I count on you to keep it to yourself?"

"Definitely. We've been friends for a while. At this point, we should be able to trust each other. I won't tell anybody, I swear."

"OK, it's actually not such a big deal. I am a lowly intern in the FBI, it's just a small part-time job, but I am very happy there. My dream is to work in law enforcement after I graduate. But I have no idea how he knows about it, and I think you are right that there's something fishy about him. I already passed on his name to somebody in my office. When I asked her if anybody had looked at it, all she just said was that they are interested in him. I have the lowest security clearance, so they don't tell me much."

They changed the subject and talked about hair styles and a new line of sandals that came out for the summer season.

"You know, Lexi, I am very blessed to have you as my friend," Esmeralda said and they hugged.

She couldn't stop trying to determine where Brent could have seen her that might have connected her to the Bureau. Did he know someone who knew her? Other than her previous boyfriend, nobody outside the FBI had known about her place of work.

The next morning, she asked Judy to meet her in the cafeteria during lunch. She told her the details of her brief interactions with Brent, and what Lexi had shared with her.

"Do you have a picture of this guy somewhere? Perhaps from the dance club? It would help to have it, so we can run facial recognition on him."

"No, I don't, and I don't think Stardust takes photos of the people who come there. Maybe there are cameras in the street outside."

"Don't worry. I'll mention what you said to the guys who are looking at him, and I'm sure they'll figure out what's going on. I'm sorry he's trying to follow you. Maybe you should change your routine a little; alter your route to school and to the office. Don't always eat in the same places."

Esmeralda stared at her, wordless.

"I am sure we'll know something soon. When our guys see that this is getting personal for someone inside the Bureau, such as yourself, they'll crank it up. By the way, I don't see him as being violent. He must be fishing for information."

The Third Floor

Harry had been amassing facts regarding suspected money launderers, identity thieves, and embezzlers, whom he code-named "spiders." Their victims were named "crickets." The group of investigators in charge of his files eventually grasped how he classified the cases, suspects, leads, and evidence. It was an immense compilation that was organized with a master folder for each type of crime, and sub-folders inside the large one for each case. He had kept notes from old investigations, some of which had been successfully closed, and some that remained unsolved.

There was also a bright yellow binder labeled "Masquerade," clearly containing current, active intelligence about a ring of corporate thieves. There were sticky notes indicating he dates when he had discussed these findings with his FBI, even CEA counterparts. A compact disk was secured to the notes with a large clip.

The investigators surmised that "Masquerade" held details of immediate interest that might be relevant. Harry apparently had imagination, they gathered, based on how he had labeled the files. It had already been established that the bombing had been a targeted killing, but the intended target was still not fully determined.

They were re-examining the entire footage of the day of the attack. There were cell phone videos, photos, and street camera pictures.

Esmeralda was called back upstairs. In the elevator she noticed again the freckled young man, who was having a lively conversation with an older woman. He stopped briefly when he saw her. They both looked away after their eyes met, and she tried to remember where she had seen him before.

John Pope was waiting for her this time.

"Ms. Santoro," he started, "since you were present at the scene of the bombing, we will need your help." He showed her into the adjoining room and pointed to a desk with a large computer monitor.

"These are the photos we have from the scene. Please examine them carefully, to see if anybody looks familiar," the investigator told her. "We need a fresh set of eyes to scan these images. Take your time to study every person in every corner. The technician will sit with you to assist with the photos."

Esmeralda sat at the computer screen and peered at each of the pictures, some of which were hazy, blurred by of the smoke. Others were poor because the phones had not been held steady.

When she first scrutinized the shots, she concentrated on the immediate area in front of the restaurant, where the bedlam happened. But one of the videos was aimed at a cluster of shops across the street, and she caught a glimpse of a figure. It was moving away fast from a corner of an office complex to a side street.

"Can you freeze this frame, please," she asked the technician. The image was somewhat fuzzy, but she could not mistake the blond curly hair.

"I think I know this person!" she blurted. "It's Brent, the guy who has been trying to follow me!"

Everyone turned to look at her in silence.

"I told Judy about him, and I thought she passed it on to you," she stuttered and blushed, unsure of what she might have gotten herself into.

She was asked to step over to another desk to describe what she knew about the fellow, and where the details came from. When she mentioned Lexi, they demanded her full name and phone number, and told Esmeralda to go back to her own desk and avoid mentioning Brent to anyone. She trembled when she left the third-floor office.

Some pieces of the puzzle began to fit into place. The advanced facial recognition tool discovered his two aliases: Donald English and Patrick Fox. He had graduated from high school as Patrick Fox, then assumed a new identity in college, which he kept. The third alias was used for some of his money schemes.

The forensic accountants entered the probe. It was challenging to track all the money dealings in which he had been involved, but it was evident that he had stolen funds from clients' accounts. They clearly saw a connection between him and the bomb attack--his presence at the scene, and his attempts to find Esmeralda. The FBI had now identified a potential suspect in the case.

Esmeralda was summoned to the third floor for the third time.

"We now consider Brent Bushnell a person of interest," John Pope told her. "Let us know immediately if you see him again." The man gave her his personal phone number.

"You can text or call me at this number any time, day or night. By the way, Ms. Santoro, you are not in trouble, or under any investigation. You've been very helpful, and we plan to call on you for future assistance. Do you understand?"

She was speechless, unable to find any words to say to the man. She nodded and left to go back downstairs.

Lexi called her that evening, her voice frantic.

"Somebody from the FBI showed up at my apartment and grilled me about Brent. Do you know anything about it?"

"Maybe," she said quietly. "I can't talk about it, but don't worry. You are not in trouble."

"What's going on? Do they think I'm somehow connected to whatever is going on?" Esmeralda could still hear her friend's panic over the phone.

"I am sorry, I don't know anything about it, Lexi. Again, I am positive that you are not in any trouble. Let's meet later this week, okay?"

Lexi hung up, and Esmeralda, had to force herself not to cry. There was too much tension in the conversation, and she tried to reassure herself that Lexi was not blaming her for what was happening.

That night, lying awake in bed, all at once it came back to her. She remembered where she had first seen the freckled guy. It was at Harry's funeral. He was standing with the family, and looked particularly mournful waiting in line to pour dirt on the coffin. The instant recollection brought a sort of fondness, an imaginary bond with him. Something told her to be friendlier toward him if she sees him again. If he had been close to Harry, it might not be a bad idea to get to know him.

Finding Lady Windsor

Like the other people searching for pets, Celeste was heart-broken and concerned over her missing dog. While she had indeed developed a connection with Lady Windsor, she was far more anxious to find the dog's collar. Unlike the others, however, she had no pictures of her beloved canine, and explained that many of her cell photos were accidentally deleted.

She went to a few shelters where surviving pets had been taken. It was sad to see the forlorn looks of the displaced animals, some lying down while others were pushing against the wall of the cage. Lady Windsor was standing in a cage among larger dogs, and seemed to have maintained her spunk. She jumped up when she spotted her mistress.

"There's my dog!" she cried and motioned to the young woman in charge to let the Bassett Hound out. Lady Windsor jumped on her, nearly knocking her to the floor, but eventually gave in to being hugged. Her fur was scorched in a few places and she was thinner. The worst part was that her collar was missing, and Celeste could barely contain her anguish. She nodded her head in gratitude on her way out to her car.

She laid out a dish of food and some water for Lady Windsor, who ate eagerly. Then, sitting at the desktop computer, she pulled out the index card from her wallet. That was the only other place where her account numbers were recorded. She entered one of the passwords written on the card. It took a few minutes for her to log on to one of her accounts, which she remembered contained approximately $250,000. Her breath stopped when she saw the balance of $5.00—five dollars. It must be an error, she thought, and decided to investigate later.

She began to have creeping thoughts about Brent. Had he somehow gained access to her financial data, and was that even possible? She had not heard from him after their last communication about stopping Harry's co-workers.

With shaking fingers, she typed another password to access a bank account in Athens. The unbelievable words on the screen were "ACCESS DENIED," with a few words in Greek alphabet below. I must have mistyped, she thought in frustration, and tried again. The two words reappeared, and she burst into a gut-wrenching sob. She then remembered in horror that when she had moved some funds between banks, she neglected to update the account numbers on the card. Perhaps, she thought, her next step should be to enter all the Social Security numbers she had previously used to attempt to gain access to her various holdings.

She sat motionless at the computer, staring at nothing. She couldn't bring herself to check any of the other bank websites. She suspected that her entire fortune was gone, and contemplated her next steps. Who were the main suspects? Brent topped her list, with Thomas right behind him. He had always known how to embezzle money. Obviously, contacting the police or any other law enforcement agencies was out of the question. She knew she was on her own, alone in the world, just like young Maddie so many years ago. What could have happened? She agonized for hours over any possible missteps she had made, or details she accidentally disclosed.

Later that evening her thoughts went back to Steve, and she took his cell phone from the drawer where she had stashed it. Resting in bed, she closed her eyes and briefly relived Steve's kisses on her neck and breasts, and how his fingers traveled down her body... She abruptly stopped herself, powered on his cell phone and tried to find his photos, hoping to see a few from their good times together. She found none; it appeared that the entire content had been erased. Cold perspiration crept over her when she tapped the email inbox icon. The email password had been changed. She tried a few likely passwords, but nothing moved.

Celeste sensed in despair that she had been abandoned and swindled by everyone she had ever known. She could not think of a single friend in the world whom she could reach out to. She lay in bed, frozen, and remained there all night. It didn't matter that she left the lights on; sleep was impossible.

When morning came, she remained in bed, not moving, eyes open, and considered the possibility that her life was over. Maybe her father had been right that she had a crappy nature, and perhaps that was why she had no money or friends. After all, was there anyone who liked her, she pondered, and then convinced herself that dying was not a bad option—she would no longer have to think about anything. There wouldn't be any consequences to face. She got up once to use the bathroom, and put out a dish of food for Lady Windsor. Then she lay back down until she eventually drifted off to asleep.

Bill

Esmeralda was in the cafeteria buffet line, trying to choose between a pasta dish and a sandwich. The person behind her tapped her on the shoulder and she quickly turned around. It was the freckled guy from the elevator.

"Hi," he said with a bashful smile, "I recommend the pasta."

"Oh," she replied awkwardly. "Thanks, I'll try it."

"By the way, I am Bill. I want to introduce myself, because we keep bumping into each other." He was definitely shy and a bit hesitant, she thought.

"Nice to meet you. I am Esmeralda."

As if by agreement, they walked to a table and sat down together.

"I remember you from Harry's funeral," she said. "Were you related?"

"Yes, we were," he said, looking away for a moment. "He was my uncle."

"Oh, I am very, very sorry. I miss Harry a lot. His desk was more or less across from mine, and we worked together. He was my mentor."

"You obviously knew him well. Uncle Harry was kind, knowledgeable, down to earth—all those things. I miss him too."

"So, where do you work here at the FBI?" she asked, changing the subject.

"I am in the organized crime investigation unit. Just started there a year-and-a-half ago. Still learning the ropes. How about you? You look very young to be working here."

"I am just a college intern," she blushed in spite of herself. "I work in the Financial Crimes Unit."

"Really?" he looked at her in obvious amazement. "Financial Crimes is quite a place for a college intern. That's pretty impressive!"

"Oh, not at all. I do a lot of paperwork, not solving any crimes. By the way, my friends call me Esme."

"I saw you going up to the third floor a couple of times, and that is a big deal. I mean, not everybody gets to go there. Those guys work on high profile murders. But I understand if you can't talk about it."

They finished eating and walked out together.

"You know, your uncle was very special to me. Do you think you can tell me a little about him some time?" she asked on their way out.

"Give me your phone number, and I'll call you to figure out a good time to talk," he looked at her. His eyes lingered a little too long, and she felt her face flush again.

They exchanged numbers before Esmeralda went back to her desk. There was something special about this guy, she thought; no surprise that he was related to Harry.

Judy called her over to her desk.

"Esme, you should know that the boys upstairs have eyes on our friend Brent."

"What does that mean? And by the way, he is not my friend."

"I don't have the exact details, but let's say they now know who and where he is, with most of it coming from you. They are interested in him in connection to the bombing."

She shuddered at the thought that she had bantered and danced with the monster who could have perpetrated the horrid act.

The following week at nine in the evening Bill called.

"Hi Esme," he sounded shy. "I hope I'm not calling too late"

"Not at all," she replied warmly. "I am glad you called." She wondered if she sounded overly friendly.

"Do you want to meet for dinner sometime?"

They scheduled dinner in a steakhouse in downtown Los Angeles. It was going to be a long drive, but she agreed immediately.

Esmeralda recognized that she was falling for the young man whom she hardly knew, and much too fast. She could not stop thinking about him until their date.

He was in the front area when she arrived, and they waited for the host to seat them. He started talking as soon as they sat down.

"It was my uncle who got me my job with the Bureau," he said with his eyes downcast. "I was kind of a mess before that."

"He was the kind of man who looked after others," she replied.

"Tell me a little bit about yourself," Bill said, a bit too abruptly. "What's your story? How did you get to become an FBI intern?"

She was taken aback, and shot a glance at him before speaking. His awkwardness was somehow endearing to her.

"It's a pretty long story, you know... But here is the short version: I left El Salvador when I was a little under sixteen. I sneaked across the border, completely illegal. But I was very lucky; I had help from some very kind people, found work, and later got my high school diploma. After that, believe it or not, I ended up helping the FBI solve a human trafficking gang."

"Are you serious?" He leaned forward and stared at her. "How did that happen?"

"It's not an adventure I am proud of. My two brothers had always been up to no good, and one of them got involved in a trafficking operation. They thought that since I was his sister, I would be more likely to connect with him. It was dangerous and very scary, but it worked. An FBI agent, Ms. Fields, liked what I did, and eventually found an internship for me. Since then, it's been my dream to work in law enforcement someday."

"This is amazing, actually unbelievable. What about your mom and dad?"

"They both died," Esmeralda swallowed hard. "I ran away by myself, and looking back, I can't believe it worked out for me. As I said, I was very lucky."

They ordered dinner after the waiter came to their table a second time.

Bill started, "You sound a lot like my Grandma Helena. She also escaped all by herself."

"Seriously? From where?"

"From Nazi Germany. She was a Holocaust survivor."

Esmeralda felt a chill go through her whole body. Her knowledge about the Holocaust and World War II was limited, but she had read about what had happened to millions of people in Europe.

"There was a ship named the St. Louis that was carrying Jewish refugees from Hamburg, Germany to Cuba. The only reason Grandma got on the ship was that another person, who had a ticket, was hurt in an accident and couldn't go. She somehow got this person's papers and used her name to board the ship. She was just a teenager."

"Where were her parents?" She asked.

"Her parents and brother were taken to concentration camps and exterminated in the gas chambers." His eyes looked away for a moment, and she saw he was clenching his teeth.

"I can't believe that people actually went through something like this," she said, shaking her head. "My escape was nothing by comparison."

Their food came, and Bill stopped. Esmeralda wanted to change the conversation, but then felt it would be wrong to trivialize the moment.

"Can you tell me your grandma's story? I mean, how she came here..." She couldn't stop herself from asking.

"You should really hear it from her. She is in her nineties, and her health isn't so good any more, but her mind is incredible. She has a flawless memory. I could introduce you to her so she can tell you about it. I mean, we can go visit her together, if you're interested."

She stared at him, wondering where it was leading.

"I would love to meet your grandma and hear about her journey. Are you positive she will want to talk to me?"

"Grandma Helena loves people, and she gets pretty lonely these days. By the way, she is not an ordinary woman. She studied to become a licensed social worker, and then opened her own agency. She dedicated her career to helping people. So, yes, I am sure she'll be happy to meet you and talk to you."

They paid and walked outside.

The two started to meet for lunch in the cafeteria every day. She puzzled over how destiny worked its magic to create this friendship. She recognized that they were kindred souls, and became fixated on meeting his grandmother. She tried to visualize the old lady in her mind, but was never able to.

A few weeks later he told her he had set a date for a visit.

Searching for Answers

Celeste woke up and sat in bed, hungry and thirsty. She took a bottle of water and drank it, then showered and put on clean clothes. She slowly went to the kitchen, brewed coffee, and prepared toast and eggs. Her composure returned, which allowed her to start contemplating the necessary steps to try to recover her assets.

She had no idea of Brent's whereabouts, and Steve was gone. The only person left whom she could contact was her former partner Thomas, who certainly did not sound friendly when they had last spoken. She decided that her best option was to show humility and ask for his help. She called him mid-morning. The call went directly to his voicemail, and she left a message.

"Hi Thomas, it's Celeste. I know you don't want to hear from me, but I really need your help. This has nothing to do with our past business together. I am turning to you as my old friend. Please call me back."

She took Lady Windsor outside for a walk. It was painful to see the aftermath of the fire around her. A few houses were reduced to piles of burned debris, some with chimneys that still stood. Other homes remained whole, but covered with ash and soot. She turned around to look at her own house, and saw that it, too, was dark and sooty. She still needed to contact her insurance company to see about covering the cleanup.

Thomas called her an hour later.

"Hey, thank you for calling me back," she said, fighting unsuccessfully to hide her anxiety. "Can we meet somewhere for coffee, dinner, whatever works for you?"

"Hi," he replied, and thought she could hear concern in his voice. "Are you all right? You don't sound so good."

"I'm okay, but I want to talk in person, face-to-face, not over the phone."

They agreed to meet that evening in a deli near his office in Los Angeles. She left the dog outside and prepared for the two-and-a-half-hour trip. Driving helped clear her head, and when she saw that she was early, she pulled up to a McDonald's and went in for a soft drink. She needed to kill some time before their seven P.M meeting time.

Finally, Celeste arrived at the deli and waited. Her heart pounded when Thomas entered. This was her new "normal," feeling afraid and powerless.

"Hey Thomas!" she got up and hugged him. "I am so glad to see you."

He hugged her weakly, they went to order sandwiches, and found a table.

"What's going on?" he asked her as soon as they sat down. He was definitely distant, even aloof, she observed. "You've never been someone who needs help. You always figure out ways to get around everything."

"Well, here is a brief summary: I'm sure you heard about the Tehachapi wildfire, which literally happened on our doorstep. Steve and I were ordered to evacuate. I don't remember clearly what followed; by sheer miracle I was rescued by a helicopter, but he didn't make it."

"Oh," He cupped his mouth with his hand. "I am so sorry. I had no idea!" He softened.

"I know... I haven't had time to tell anybody. But there is something I need to confess to you, unrelated to the fire. You're not going to like it."

He took a deep breath as he looked at her, and then their order number was announced.

Celeste got up and brought the food to the table, but made no move to touch her plate.

"First of all, you need to know that I decided to stop making any more slippery investments. I get a feeling that my luck is about to run out and that some government agency is possibly poking into my business. But before I came to this decision, when I was still up to my old ways, I needed somebody to work with, since you were out of the picture. You once mentioned to me that you had an assistant named Brent. To make a long story short, I tracked him down and hired him."

"You're kidding me!" Thomas' voice rose, and Celeste instinctively reached over and touched his arm.

"Please listen to me." She swallowed hard, visibly holding back tears, "Brent doesn't know who I am, what my name is, or where I live. My identity was a code, and we only communicated electronically, via encrypted email messages. I needed to clean up some money that I've accumulated. He made a couple of good purchases for me, and I paid him very well. Then he let it slip that he bought himself a beautiful beach front home somewhere in Southern California. This is after I had warned him not to flaunt his money, and to keep a low profile."

"So, what happened?" he took a bite from his sandwich. "You're not eating."

"Well," Celeste looked at her sandwich without interest, "he disappeared, and honestly, I'm not sure if he is dead or alive. After being stuck three days in a Red Cross shelter, I came back home to find out that the records of all my assets disappeared.

Steve must have put a strong firewall on his phone, which makes it impossible for me to access anything on it. Not even his emails. My laptop disappeared with him, and so did the two thumb drives where I stored the information. I'm just trying to keep what's mine and not have it stolen from me!"

"What are you saying? Was Steve somehow involved in this? Do you think your husband stole your data?"

"I'm not clear about anything, but you didn't hear the worst part. I thought I was lucky that I found the small index card where I had written down my passwords. But when I entered them into the home computer, I found out that all my bank accounts have been cleaned out. I have no cash, and I'm terrified that somebody is out there to hurt me."

"If you don't mind my asking, what have you done with all this wealth over the years, other than stash it in different banks and real estate? Are you enjoying any of it?"

Celeste stared at him. "What do you mean, enjoying it? I've been building my fortune!"

"Look, in the past when we worked together, you ran the show, told me what to do, and I pretty much obliged. So now it's my turn to tell you: I strongly agree that you must walk away from all the underhanded business and clean up. It's a lot safer, and you won't have to keep looking over your shoulder."

She listened quietly and said nothing.

"You know," he continued, "I can try to help you get a position in my firm if you want. Why don't you forget about this ill-gotten fortune? You haven't even benefited from the money; it was all only on paper! You're smart enough to know there's a good chance the IRS or FBI will eventually catch up with you, right? If the assets are gone, maybe it's a good thing, and they won't find anything to pin on you."

"This time, Thomas, the only thing I'm asking you is if you can help me find Brent," she was close to tears. "I'm no longer being bitchy and arrogant. I am now poor, worried and scared."

There was some emotion in Thomas' face when he first answered, and he did not make eye contact.

"Brent resigned from our company months ago, and I haven't kept in touch with him," he said, and then looked directly at her. "Goodness, Celeste, please think about what I just said. I'll see if I can track down Brent, but no promises. I am really sorry about Steve. I'll be in touch."

She left her uneaten food on the table, and drove back to Bakersfield in the dark, her mood bleaker than before. She was doubtful that Thomas would come through with anything helpful.

Helena's Tale

Bill and Esmeralda waited for Grandma Helena to answer the door. She was taken by surprise to see the petite, white haired woman with bright eyes. A beautiful and dignified lady, she immediately concluded.

"Welcome to my home, young lady," she spoke with a trace of a German accent. "Can I get you and Billy anything?

"No, thank you, Grandma Helena," Bill said and helped her to a recliner. "I brought a friend who wants to meet you and hear about your life journey. Her name is Esmeralda, and she also escaped to America, like you."

The room was bright, with sunlight streaming in through the window. There were photos on one wall, and a few certificates on the other.

Esmeralda briefly recounted her journey from El Salvador through Mexico and into the California desert. She told her about the elderly couple who had found her and taken her in, and how she had gotten to where she was.

"You know, "Helena said with a serious expression, "you sound like my kind of girl. I will tell you my story, but it's a long one,"

"Oh, please…" she answered eagerly.

Helena leaned back for a moment before speaking.

"In 1938 it was clear that things were getting very bad for Jewish people. Hitler ordered Jewish businesses to close, our people were fired from their positions, many of them high level judges, lawyers, accountants. We talked about it at home, and my parents spoke with my aunt and uncle about leaving Germany. They kept talking, but I was worried they were waiting too long. I was very scared that by the time they were ready to pack up and go, they wouldn't be allowed to leave. I begged them to listen to me, but nothing helped.

Then Kristallnacht happened. Germans smashed windows and broke into synagogues and shops all over Germany. My mother, who had always looked up to my father, was crying. I cooked up a secret plan and told my best friend Erna about it. I decided I had to leave. I was sixteen, and thought of myself as grown up and independent. Still, it took me a few months to work up the courage. In May, 1939 I heard that there was a ship sailing from Hamburg to Cuba with Jewish refugees. I told my parents that if they weren't coming, I was leaving the next day, but they dismissed me. Still, my father must have had an inkling that I might just be crazy enough to do it, and gave me and Herbert, my brother, each, an envelope with U.S dollars. 'Keep it in a safe place,' he told us.

"Then, very early the next morning, before daylight, I left a note saying that I was going to get on the SS St. Louis that was taking Jews to Cuba, and that I would write to them as soon as possible. I sneaked out with a small bag, and started walking. My heart beat so fast and hard, I thought it was going to jump out of my chest, but I kept moving towards the railway station.

"I saw men in uniform at the station, so I ducked into the public bathroom and waited. I sat in one of the toilet stalls for a long time until I heard a train coming. I figured there would be people coming off the train, a chance for me to blend in. I tore off the hideous yellow star from my jacket, bolted out and reached a nearby field. Unfortunately, somebody must have noticed me and began firing. I was so terrified, that I stumbled and fell down. I lay face down, frozen, holding my breath, waiting for another bullet. The shooter must have thought he killed me, so the firing stopped. I kept on walking for hours, and finally stopped to eat a sandwich and a piece of chocolate I had packed. Then I decided to rest and wait until dark.

"At dusk, I continued until I reached a nearby city, I don't remember which one, and waited till morning in a small bus station. I was quite pretty and good at connecting with people. When I finally came to Hamburg, I walked into a small, crowded office. Posted on a wall I saw the list of the passengers who had travel documents."

Esmeralda stopped her, "But, wait... How did you manage to reach Hamburg?"

"Oh, yes, I forgot that part. Very early in the morning, I ventured out of the bus stop. On the side of the street a farmer and his son had just finished loading produce on a cart with a horse. When they saw me standing on the side of the road, the man yelled from the cart: 'Are you lost?' I told him I had to go to Hamburg to visit my sick cousin, so they let me climb on. I had to squeeze myself between two big crates, and two days later they dropped me off a couple of miles from the Hamburg port. Between the two days, overnight, I slept fitfully in a barn, and my whole body hurt the next day. It was not a quick or comfortable ride; this was a horse pulling a cart, and we stopped for breaks on the way, which took more time."

"Couldn't you have taken the train to Hamburg?" Esmeralda asked.

"It was too risky to go by train. I wanted to remain as invisible as possible."

She went on, "I dozed off in the cart most of the time, which was good. Back then you had to be careful not to say too much about yourself to strangers, even to good-hearted ones. After they dropped me off, it took me over an hour to find the huge port and look for the dock.

"There was quite a bit of commotion, and above the noise I overheard that a young girl was injured and wasn't allowed to board. The girl's mother was hysterical, and the papers she was holding fell to the floor. I bent down, grabbed the papers, arranged them and handed them back to the crying mother. Except that I kept the ticket belonging to the injured daughter and slipped it into my pocket. The poor mother and I both realized the girl wouldn't be allowed to board the ship. She had to go to a hospital, and who knows what happened to her afterwards."

"Well, here was the St. Louis. I climbed aboard the ship, and showed the ticket to an absent-minded clerk. He asked where the rest of my documents were, and I mumbled sheepishly that I had them in my suitcase. Of course, there was no suitcase, but he waved me off, and I went straight to my cabin, so exhausted, that I immediately fell asleep on my bunk and woke up when the ship was already at sea. I was very relieved, figuring that even if they found out that I had no papers, they weren't going to throw me into the ocean. So, I washed my face, combed my hair, and came up to the deck to look at the sea and chat with other passengers. Looking back, it's hard to believe that I was so fearless. But, I guess, I was only sixteen. It didn't take long for a handsome sailor with reddish hair named Hugo to start flirting with me. I was lonely, enjoyed the attention, and soon a romance developed between us.

"I had never had a boyfriend before, so this first love was very exciting to me. We hid in small places on the ship, we laughed at each other's jokes, and had some intimate moments. Hugo was a sweet young man who dreamed about becoming a captain of a big commercial ship. He had wanderlust and didn't like the idea of settling down anywhere.

"All of us, refugees, were very upbeat, relieved that we escaped Germany, and had a few celebrations on board. The sad news came when the St. Louis finally arrived in Havana, and wasn't allowed to dock. They refused to let us enter, so our ship did not stop at the pier, but anchored about eight hundred feet back in the water. The captain was a good man who wanted to help us, so he decided to sail to Miami. The hope was that the United States would let us in, but again, all the behind-the-scenes negotiations failed and we were turned away.

"The St. Louis finally had to sail back to Europe, and eventually a few European countries took in most of the refugees. But as we approached Miami, the minute I saw the lights of America, I told Hugo I had to get off the ship, because there was no going back for me. We were anchored quite a distance from the pier, and Hugo was terrified, telling me I wouldn't survive such a long swim. I was undeterred, so he found me a sailor's uniform and cap, which were too big, but I put them on. We hugged and said goodbye; we knew it was unlikely that we would see each other again. I then quietly slid myself off the deck. It was scary... The water seemed so far down below the ship, but I made it and swam to shore. That's how Billy's Grandma Helena, wet and exhausted, entered the United States."

Esmeralda wanted to burst into applause, but thought it was inappropriate. What courage this small woman had...

"I found a hidden spot on the dock and sat there, waiting for my clothes to dry. When I finally watched the ship drift away, I started crying and couldn't stop. Would you believe it was the first time I cried since I left my parents and brother behind? I wept for the people I got to know who stayed on, all those who had to keep looking for a safe place. Once the floodgates opened and the tears came, I finally allowed myself to cry about my family. I missed them so much.

"The next morning, I used a few of my dollars to buy a roll, some cheese and simple clothes at a store called Woolworths. I immediately looked for work as a maid and, even with my poor English, got a job working for a very nice family. I sent home a telegram that I arrived in Miami, asked when they would be able to leave, and waited for a reply.

"Then... Now that my grandchildren are all grown up, I can be open about what happened next..." She glanced at her grandson before continuing. "Soon afterwards I found out I was pregnant. I couldn't believe it; I was shocked and scared, but thanks to the kind people I worked for, I gave birth to a healthy baby—Billy's father Albert."

The woman stopped talking, the bright eyes looking away, seemingly searching for something far and invisible. Bill blushed and turned his gaze to the window.

"Did you ever find out what happened to your parents and brother?" Esmeralda asked.

"After a few anxious months, a telegram came. My father and brother were taken first, and then my mother. It said that Father Otto at the Catholic church had something important for me. The last words my mother wrote were, 'you were the smart one, darling.' It broke my heart and I cried that whole night. I never heard from them again. I found out later that they died in one of the gas chambers in the Buchenwald camp system. It was a big concentration camp with a few sub-camps nearby."

"And what happened your parents' and uncle's property?" Esmeralda could not stop herself.

"In 1938 all the Jews were ordered to register their assets with the German government. It included everything they owned—businesses, bonds, homes, and everything else. Of course, the Germans stole all those assets. My father and uncle had seen it coming for some time, so they promptly began to convert most of their holdings to diamonds. They had to make separate arrangements with different individuals until pretty much everything was sold. The idea was to make sure were going to have something, a way to survive in case we got out. Our parents told my brother and me about the diamonds, but it didn't help in the end. I wish I had them on me when I ran away, but my escape was something that nobody had expected.

"As the danger grew, my uncle stashed the diamonds in a small sturdy bag and put our names on a piece of paper inside. Our family name was Berger. For years, my parents had been sending my brother to bring food to the poor people in the nearby church. My uncle said that he'd given the diamond bag for safekeeping to the Catholic priest who had always been very grateful to us. The priest showed my uncle a small hole in the inside wall of the church, and promised to hide the stash there. Nobody knows what happened to the diamonds. They were nowhere to be found after the war.

"Unfortunately, I was never one to search the past, so I decided to put the sadness behind me and better myself. I never tried to reach Father Otto, and chose to assume that the diamonds didn't actually exist. I told myself they didn't matter to me. And I swore to myself to never speak that cursed language, German, ever again."

Esmeralda was quiet, and barely kept herself from crying.

"Tell her about Grandpa Villy," Bill said after a long silence.

"Villy, or William, had it easier because he had immigrated to America a few years earlier with his whole family. They had sponsors and were able to get visas. When my Albert was two years old, a friend invited me to a small party and that's when I met Villy.

"We fell in love very quickly, and got married. After he finished medical school we moved from Miami to Los Angeles, then in time we had two more wonderful children, Harry and Rebecca. Villy opened a gynecology practice, and we had a marvelous life. But then... a tragedy so unspeakable happened to us."

Esmeralda held her breath, and Bill moved his chair next to Grandma Helena and took her hand. The old woman's animated face changed, and she stopped, as if trying to remember something, then continued.

"Our little girl, Rebecca, was too beautiful for her own good," she said and shook her head. "People were always looking at her. She was a cheerful, rambunctious child, very active, and liked to play outside with her friends. I always worried about her because she enjoyed talking to everybody, even strangers. She brought a lot of joy to all of us, until one day, our Rebecca disappeared. It changed our lives forever."

"What do you mean, 'disappeared?'" Esmeralda asked.

"She just vanished, and we never saw her again. The police, along with many of our neighbors, searched everywhere and came up with nothing. All we could assume was that somebody kidnapped her. Our daughter was simply gone. Villy was never the same after that. He couldn't get over the loss of his little girl. He passed away too soon, some years ago.

"Albert, our oldest, tried for years to find any trace of his little sister Rebecca, but nothing worked. A few years later he contacted the FBI, but they were not interested. A few years later, the police agreed to reopen the case to go back to search for clues, but they never got anywhere."

"I can't believe it," Esmeralda said quietly. "This was too much. After all that you had been through..."

"It's a good thing that your grandpa Villy didn't have to live through our son Harry's murder," she looked at her grandson. "Harry was such a good person. Why did he have to die?" She was choking on invisible tears. "Of my three children, only Albert is still with us."

Both of them rose from their chairs, and Bill reached over to his grandmother to help her get out of her recliner. He hugged her.

Grandma Helena composed herself and addressed her young guest. "My dear girl, perhaps you and I are made of the same cloth. We both know how to get past hard times. I think that's why I am still here and Villy is gone. He was weaker than me. It's important to stay strong."

"Thank you so much for telling me about your life," she said and took the old woman's hand. "You are an incredible person. It am very honored that I met you."

"I could tell this was hard for you," Bill told her when they were back in his car.

"Yes... I shouldn't have cried. I have always been very tough, but this incredible tragedy, together with Harry's death, was so difficult to hear. Your Grandma is truly extraordinary. She calls you 'Billy;' how sweet.

"Please don't call me Billy, okay?"

He dropped her off and Esmeralda walked to her apartment, mournful, but determined to try to help in apprehending the murderer. It would be her way to honor the remarkable woman and the loved ones she lost.

The Screws Tighten

The investigators on the third floor, who had been pre-occupied with the bombing case, now joined forces with the Financial Crimes Unit. It turned out that Harry was close to discovering a money laundering operation run by persons who used code names. It appeared that somebody wanted him out of the picture, so they knew they had several dots to connect.

The first individual who was caught in the FBI net was Brent Bushnell, aka Patrick Fox and Donald English. An IRS flag pointed to a cash purchase of a luxury home with funds that could not be tracked. Based on his declared income, it was unlikely that he had the resources to buy this house. The trail of deposits, withdrawals, and incoming and outgoing wire transfers in Brent's bank accounts indicated that he had been working with another individual or entity.

The technician who probed the convoluted money trail encountered a black hole when searching parties involved. All the Social Security numbers appeared to be fake, and no names popped up. A data analyst named Leslie was called in to break into Mr. Bushnell's online activities, and she discovered encrypted email communications. The messages were too insulated for her to be able to breach them. She did, however, detect the code name "Agent M," which set her on a course to identify this individual.

"The big problem is that Brent Bushnell has been using a burner phone, which we can't track," Leslie told her superior. "The only way I can try to find Agent M is to try to send some kind of message to this nameless associate, impersonating Mr. Bushnell."

"You have my authorization to go ahead," John Pope told her. "Use any means to break into their correspondence. When we find the actors behind the money, it will most likely lead us to the bomb plotters."

Leslie tried unsuccessfully to penetrate the encryption code to send out email messages. Then she decided to search Brent's email history to find contacts who might point her in the right direction. Older correspondence with a certain individual caught her eye, which led her to Thomas Snow. It was a simple task to call or email Mr. Snow, but she was not an investigator and that was not her task. As soon as she had identified the contact, she sent it on to John Pope, who would take over.

Pope remembered having met Lexi and being impressed with her. Before sending out any warning flags to his colleagues, he decided to reach out to her.

"Hello, Lexi," he began in a friendly tone after she picked up. "This is John Pope from the FBI. I hope you can help me."

"Okay," she replied in a weak voice, "If you guarantee me that I won't get myself into a bad situation, I'll try to help."

He scheduled a meeting with her at five in the afternoon at a Starbucks. Lexi arrived at a quarter to five and was a bit startled to see John Pope seated at a small table with a laptop. She was dressed professionally in a black pant suit and a white blouse, and checked her makeup in her compact mirror. Then she approached slowly, waiting for him to notice her.

"Oh, good afternoon, Lexi," he said after raising his head from the screen. She was convinced the man had never learned to smile. "Thank you for meeting me; please sit down. Can I get you something to eat or drink?"

"Coffee will be nice. Just black, please," she said after sitting down. *If he wants my help, he should do something nice for me,* she thought while waiting for him to bring the coffee.

"Lexi," Pope started, "you described to me Brent Bushnell as a shady and potentially dishonest person. Remember?"

"Yes, and I still believe him to be shady and dishonest. What's going on?"

"We've been investigating Mr. Bushnell, but since this is an ongoing case, I can't give you any details. I want to ask for your help. Will you be willing to contact him to try to get some information that we need?"

"I doubt he'll tell me anything useful," she replied nonchalantly.

"Our profilers believe that he likes to show off to certain people to impress them, so that's how we want to approach this. We need to obtain details on who he's been working with for the past year. I will give you some talking points."

"I guess I can try," Lexi replied after hesitating briefly. "Tell me what you're looking for, and I will do what I can. But there's no way I'm sleeping with him."

Lexi had already gotten over her initial jitters over talking to the FBI, and regretted that she had been so harsh with Esmeralda. In hindsight she recognized they were both helping solve a mass murder, and that she had not been implicated or suspected in any crime. She became enthusiastic about her assignment. It seemed thrilling to help catch Brent in one of his devious schemes. After leaving Starbucks she called Esmeralda.

"Hey," she said to the voicemail, "give me a call. I miss you."

When Esmeralda called back later that evening the two spoke for a long time, and set a date to celebrate Lexi's approaching birthday.

Trying to Pick up the Pieces

The interior and exterior of Celeste's house were being painted as part of repairing the fire damage. She did not want to move to a temporary location and remained in the home while the work was being done. Her distress over her missing funds had lessened a bit after she came upon one money market account that had not been emptied.

She was shocked to discover that this small nest egg was registered under her original Social Security number. She stumbled upon it when she searched for her assets under every ID number she could remember, and found that it was registered in her childhood name Maddie Ellis. She immediately cashed and closed the account, and placed the currency in a metal toolbox in a dresser drawer. It was a relatively small amount, about $130,000, that she could use for her immediate expenses.

She asked herself why she had decided to change her name to Celeste Butler back then. She recalled that it was one of the steps she had taken to free herself from her father's control. Perhaps now, she considered, would be a good time to go back to being Maddie. It might constitute a rebirth for her, an escape from the dreadful present into a new future. It was definitely food for thought, she figured, but decided to wait before taking further steps.

As she suspected, she did not hear from Thomas, but was ready to move on. Just when she began to consider looking for work in the financial industry, a registered letter arrived. It was a request from an insurer's fraud investigation department to provide documentation related to a life insurance claim she had filed and collected. The minute she finished reading the letter, her head felt wobbly and she sat down to steady herself. It read like a summons to appear in court, and every part of her body shivered. She sat down at her desk to search for any records she had saved relating to the particular policy and the payout. It had been three years since she received the proceeds.

She located copies of the original application and the documents she had provided to claim the proceeds, but nothing else. The letter requested proof of her insurable interest in the policy. It meant that she was required to present evidence of a familial or economic dependence on the insured party, the fabricated deceased. According to the application, which she had submitted under an alias, the coverage was written for a non-existent female. It was a relatively small plan, for $150,000, which had not required a physical exam, and the blood and urine samples Celeste provided were her own. The letter stated there was a 30-day deadline for providing the requested details.

Celeste was dumbfounded that she had been tracked down as soon as her former name surfaced. Where did they find her Bakersfield address, and how did they link the life insurance policy to her? She feared that more pieces of her world were beginning to crumble, and that through a domino effect, her illicit money trail would be discovered. Maybe I have it coming, she thought, even considering the option of confessing all her fraudulent life insurance transactions. But then, she did not have the resources to repay the damage, or even the fines she might face. Could prison be in her future?

By entering her previous SSN, and thereby discovering the small money market account, she had unwittingly revealed her original identity. Within three weeks she began receiving mail addressed to Maddie Ellis. Most of it consisted of generic advertising flyers, but one letter gave her pause. She thought she was hallucinating when she saw it had been forwarded to her from her childhood home address. She lay it on her desk, unopened, while working on a response to the life insurance fraud inquiry.

She began preparing her reply on a scratch pad. She chose to claim that the insurance probe had nothing to do with her. They had mistaken her for someone else, she wrote, since she, Celeste Butler, was not familiar with the transaction. Worst case, she would state that she had forgotten about the insurance policy. After all, neither the deceased, who had been the named insured, nor the beneficiaries, matched her personal records or details.

Stolen Treasures

In April of 1945 World War II was ending. Jack Ellis was an enlisted soldier in the 4th armored division, and like his army buddies, he felt the relief that came from the prospect of going home. There was now real hope and great euphoria that Germany had surrendered. The immediate mission at that point was the liberation of inmates from concentration camps.

On April 4, his entire company marched into a what looked like a hell hole named Ohrdruf Concentration Camp in Germany. When Jack with two other men stopped near a mound of dead naked bodies, he excused himself and turned into a corner to throw up. The stench and horror were more than he thought he could bear, so he slowly walked away and stood outside the gate. On the battlefront he had witnessed his share of death, maimed bodies and suffering, but nothing had prepared him for this place of horror.

The nausea abated, but Jack could not quite bring himself to re-enter the gate, as a wave of rage crept over him. He closed his eyes briefly and waited until his stomach relaxed, then forced himself to think about his fiancée in California for a minute. He realized it was time to go back and face the ghastly reality, and started to walk back.

It was then that he saw a man dressed in black wave his arm to get his attention. He was an older fellow who tried to walk hurriedly despite a limp. Jack briefly weighed if he should go back to join his unit, but remained and waited for the man to reach him. When the stranger came closer, he noticed the priest's collar around his neck.

"American soldiers?" the stranger asked breathlessly with a heavy German accent.

"Yes, father. We are here to liberate this camp."

Jack glanced over to the dilapidated barracks inside the camp and saw emaciated men coming out. The Americans supported some of the inmates who were too weak to walk, and he steeled himself for the prospect of joining them. It was going to be one of the most horrific days of his life, Jack knew, but he wanted to take part in giving some minimal kindness to the survivors.

"Please halt. I have something to give you," the priest said when he came closer. He held a small brown pouch tightly between his hands.

"This belonged to a Jewish family from Weimar," he said, still breathing heavily, and held out his hand that held the pouch. "Their name was Berger, truly very charitable people. They asked me to hide this small bag for them until they came back. Sadly, I believe they died here." He stopped for a moment. "But I believe their girl, Helena, slipped away to America. Their name is written inside. They were my very good friends."

Jack listened to him quietly while glancing sideways to look at his comrades inside the camp.

"What is your name, young man?" the priest asked, his breath calmer.

"Jack Ellis."

"When you go back, Jack, will you please take this to the..." He removed a slip of paper from his pocket and read, 'American Jewish Joint Distribution Committee?' They will hopefully know where to find Helena Berger."

"What distribution committee?" Jack asked uncomfortably, shifting his feet. The idea of carrying a family heirloom to the States seemed burdensome to him. He wanted to turn around to join his buddies.

"Are you a good man?" The priest asked.

"Yes, I'm a good man," he replied indignantly. "That's why I am here to help these miserable people."

"This contains something very important," the priest held up the sac, which was closed tightly with a drawstring. "So, if you are a good man you will take it to this office, yes?" He loosened the pouch and pushed inside the slip of paper with the name of the organization. After pulling it shut again, he handed it to the soldier.

"Yes, I will."

"You must promise in the name of God, Jack Ellis" the priest pleaded. "Please."

"I promise," the soldier said and took the small satchel. The two gazed at each other for a few seconds, before each turned away. Jack stuffed the pouch in his pants pocket before entering the disarray inside, beyond the barbed wire fence. When he turned his head back, the priest was gone.

Jack had been a gifted pupil at school, and a voracious reader. The war and his parents' meager circumstances prevented him from reaching his dream of attending college to become a history teacher. The horrors of the war haunted him for his entire tour, although he had always fought to erase the troubling images from his memory. He willed himself to focus on returning to the love of his life in southern California.

One month later, Jack Ellis came back home to his sweetheart, Deborah, and married her a few months later. Still shell-shocked from the war, he spent hours at home and busied himself with organizing their apartment. His new bride continued her teaching job, giving him time to be alone with his thoughts and memories.

He had forgotten about the German priest and his own promise to deliver an old pouch to some unfamiliar organization. The small brown bag remained in a backpack filled with items he had brought home from the war, which he had kept unopened.

It was only when their child was born that Jack came out of his gloom. It was a baby boy whom they named Titus. He then took a job working for a construction contractor who built apartments. He started as a lowly laborer, doing the demanding work of carrying materials, clearing the grounds, and anything else the job required. Jack eventually imagined his own future of becoming a contractor, and wanted to learn the business from the ground up.

Over the years, Jack noticed that his son was a troubled child. He skipped school whenever possible, and only studied math, the one subject he liked. Titus graduated from high school only thanks to his mother's connections with the school principal. With no other children, the Ellis home was not a happy one. Jack's dream to become a contractor had never materialized, and his health began to deteriorate. Soon after he reached sixty, he knew he did not have a long time to live; he suffered from an incurable blood disease.

On a rainy Saturday he decided to go through all his mementos and miscellaneous items he had brought back from the war. He arranged a few objects on the coffee table—a beer mug, a bottle opener, socks. At the bottom of the old backpack he noticed the brown sack that the priest had given him. When he opened the small sack for the first time, his mouth fell open. It held a cache of diamonds, and he pulled out a few. The stones sparkled in the light, creating small rainbows on the wall, and he stared at them for a few moments before putting them back. He then carefully pulled out the small slips of paper, one with the names of the families, and the other with the name of the organization he had promised to bring them to.

Jack kept looking at the treasure he discovered, all at once overcome by guilt. He had forgotten about the priest and the brown bag from all those years ago, and had gone on with building his own life. Was he being punished after all this time? Was that why he was afflicted with a terminal illness? Jack had never been a man of faith, but he remembered he had made the promise in the name of God...

With both hands holding his head, he struggled to come up with an idea of how to get the heirloom to its rightful owner. Slowly, painfully, he came to a tentative decision.

"Titus," he told his son over the phone. "I need you to come over; there is something important I want to talk to you about." Titus had moved out and lived in a rented apartment on the other side of town.

"All right, I'll be there Friday," his son said. "Maybe ask Mom to make stuffed cabbage for dinner."

"I'll ask her. Son, you'll come Friday, right?"

"Yeah, I'll be there."

The Net Tightens

The investigators on the third floor of the FBI building caught up with Brent. A young female undercover field agent began chatting with him in a coffee shop, and Brent took the bait. They sat down, had coffee, and agreed to meet the following evening for drinks.

They met in a noisy steak house, and Brent looked mesmerized.

"I feel like we've known each other all our lives," he said and took her hand.

"Oh, I feel the same way," she agreed with a shy smile.

They drank and chatted, until it was time to leave. While they had been sitting, she noticed that Brent's wallet was in the inside pocket of his blazer, which he hung on his chair. While he was gone to the bathroom, she covertly attached a listening tiny tracking device to the wallet.

He opened his car door to let her in, and walked over to the driver's side. That gave the agent an opportunity to plant another GPS transmitter under the passenger seat. Since she seemed willing, he started driving towards his beautiful home, hoping to spend a romantic night. However, the young woman suddenly felt ill.

"I am so sorry," she said, holding her stomach, "I'd better go home. I think I'm getting the flu."

"How will you get home?" he asked her. "Do you want me to drive you?"

"No, thank you; I'll call my roommate. I don't live too far."

He opened her car door for her, and hugged her when she stepped out.

"Give me your number and I'll call you in a couple of days, okay?" she said quietly, then typed his phone number into her phone, and walked away.

"I think we can track him now," she said into a microphone in her bra. "We can find him on foot and in his car."

When Brent turned on his computer soon after coming home, he noticed an email from an unfamiliar source. The subject line intrigued him, so he opened the message.

"Hello Brent," he read, "my name is Steve, and it turns out we are both working for the same boss. We need to talk. Can we meet some time?"

Steve decided to seek out Brent after he discovered that he had had a hand in Celeste's transactions. He had silently been seething for some time, while feigning admiration for her. Over the years since they were married, his high esteem for Celeste had diminished. His resentment toward her had gradually grown, mainly because he was sure she considered him far beneath her. He was fully aware that his expertise, even his basic knowledge, in the areas of finance or investments, including real estate, were close to zero.

"There are courses in finance and business at the community college here," she told him several times when she observed his frustration. "You should sign up, and once you get a good handle on some basics, we can work together."

He hated himself for not having taken her advice to enroll in a class. It was easier to despise her for thinking she was so superior to him, and to hatch plans to crush her. He knew that his wife had been keeping vital details from him and only let him in on the general ideas of her enterprise.

The wildfire was his perfect opportunity. When he first noticed the orange haze on the hills, he knew they would have to evacuate. Over time, he had befriended a fellow hiker's teenage son who excelled at debugging and restoring software systems. Having no technology skills himself, Steve hired him to penetrate his wife's banking files. The young man patiently showed him how to perform a few computer tricks. Steve had been preparing the groundwork for some time, so he was ready. Before waking up his wife, he spent less than fifteen minutes accessing all their accounts. He changed the passwords and moved the funds to his own CD's that he had set up days earlier. He also blocked her path to the real estate records.

As a hiker, Steve had always kept useful tools in his car, and had placed the laptop in a waterproof side bag. After they abandoned the vehicle, he crossed over to the opposite side of the pond from where Celeste was. A physically fit man, he climbed up a tree in a grove that had escaped the fire. After he watched the helicopter pick up Celeste, he came down and waited at the foot of the tree at the edge of the water. The ground under the tree was parched, not burnt, and somehow remained segregated from the trajectory of the flames. He was wearing his brown leather hiking boots, ready to walk away as soon as he could.

He remembered to discard his mobile phone by the pond, so that he would be presumed dead or missing. While still at home waiting for Celeste, having cloned a new phone, he had installed firewalls and strong passwords on it, making it impossible for anyone to find anything on it. He then tried to erase his phone, just in case it might be recovered. It was payback that he decided his wife definitely had coming, for always keeping him in the dark. He wondered how she would cope with the aftermath of frustration and helplessness, with no access to any of her records, and her two thumb drives stashed in his bag.

Brent decided to be cautious with the unknown Steve. It might be a trap, he thought, but went ahead and replied.

"I have no idea who you are or who you think I work for. Please send me some proof that it will be in my interest to meet you."

"Email is not safe," Steve responded. "Your employer would second this motion."

"No cellular phones or recording devices," Brent wrote. "We meet in a park somewhere."

"I am down in San Diego," the response came. "Balboa Park, meet me tomorrow at 3 at the entrance to the botanical center. I'll buy you a beer."

The bug in the young man's wallet allowed the team in the third-floor office to hear the conversation clearly. They decided to wait before apprehending either man until they had substantial evidence of dirty money transactions. They needed facts and figures, and for that to occur, someone had to gain Brent's trust. Just in case, an agent was assigned to watch the meeting at Balboa Park.

Lexi was given two optional paths to reach Brent. One was to show interest in his success; the other was to flirt with him and feign romantic feelings. She, too, was equipped with a microphone.

"Hi," she said when her call went to Brent's voice mail. "Lexi here. I think we parted on a sour note, and I want to make it right. Call me."

Two days later he called her back.

"Wow, Lexi. I didn't think you wanted to see me again. Is everything good?"

"Yeah," she replied in a flirtatious tone. "I was having a very bad day when we last talked, and I want to make it up to you. I think that maybe we should get together..."

Brent did not go to San Diego. Something seemed off. I smell a rat, he told himself, possibly a government snitch... He decided to ignore any messages from the obscure Steve. To the FBI it was irrelevant that the two had not met—they had a fresh lead in their sights, a man who called himself Steve. Leslie the analyst was assigned the duty of tracking down this person, and now the two units—Financial Crimes along with Domestic Terrorism—drew up the blueprint of a joint operation.

The Girls

Esmeralda asked for a longer break, so she could meet Lexi for lunch to celebrate her birthday. The occasion, however, was overshadowed by their conversation about the FBI probe. She listened to the details of her friend's assignment with Brent, which worried her. It brought back memories from years ago when she assisted in apprehending a human trafficker who turned out to be her own rogue brother. Going under cover was always risky, and she talked about it to her friend.

"it will be hard to remember what to say and what not to," she told Lexi. "I imagine it's even harder when you're not trained for the assignment."

Her friend replied confidently, "All they want me to get from Brent is the identity of the person, or persons, he's been working for. I think I can bluff my way by telling him I want to learn from his success. Mr. Pope told me that the behavioral analysts believe the guy's ego has to be stroked. As if I didn't know."

"Yes," Esmeralda chimed in. "from the short time I spent talking to him, that sounds right. So, you have to admire his achievements, accomplishments, or anything else he brags about."

Lexi was quiet for a few seconds, then put on her "dumb blonde" face and cooed, "Oh, what a genius you are, Brent... I know you cheat and steal, but I'll totally ignore that for now..."

Esmeralda laughed. "Call me any time, you hear?" she looked at her friend intently. "If you get scared, or you need perking up, I'll be here."

"Mr. Pope gave me his personal cell number, and said I can call him any time too. Once I go over all the talking points they gave me, I think I can improvise the rest. I'll be all right."

Lexi was ready when Brent called back.

"Hey, how is it going?" she asked with a smile that she hoped came through over the phone. "What have you been up to?"

"Well, I'm taking a break from work for a while. I figured I can use some down time, so there's nothing special going on. I was a little baffled when I got your call. I was pretty sure you didn't want to have anything to do with me."

"You know, I was just going through a bad situation at work. Somebody in our office, who I always thought was straight and honest, was fired for sharing company secrets. It put everybody on edge, and that's why I just wasn't myself. I'm definitely over it now and I am very sorry. How about meeting for a drink later?"

"Why don't you come over to the house?" he suggested. "We can have drinks here."

It was a Saturday afternoon. In Brent's modern den, Lexi went along with his chatter, and asked questions when the timing seemed right.

"How about a glass of wine?" he offered and went to his liquor cabinet.

"Not now, thanks," she said pleasantly. "Maybe a little later."

Lexi was on a mission and wanted to stay sharp. She had memorized the "triggers," or talking points given her by John Pope, and was ready to use them. The end goal was to surreptitiously insert a thumb drive into Brent's computer, copy the content, and remove it before getting caught. The transfer of his files, she was told, would take up to two minutes.

She said casually, "I could use a cup of tea or coffee if it's okay."

"Sure," he said, taken aback. "No problem. I can get coffee started." He went into the kitchen, and she pushed the small device into a port in the back of the desktop computer. He was back before she had a chance to type the code on the keyboard.

"This is such a great house," she cooed. "How did you find it?"

"I have very good contacts, and a realtor I know clued me in on it. There were multiple bids on it, but I came in with a full cash offer, so I got it."

The coffee machine beeped and he went back to the kitchen. Quickly, she typed the needed code, and watched the screen anxiously. A message appeared on the screen, "Uploading to external drive." Hopefully, she prayed, it will take two minutes for him to pour and bring over the beverages. She let out a breath she didn't know she'd been holding when the message "Transfer complete" appeared, which meant the deed was done. Just as she reached to pull out the thumb drive, Brent appeared with two mugs of coffee. She clicked Escape on the keyboard for the screen to change, and hoped he didn't notice.

"I've got it, no worries," he said and placed the beverages on the table. "Just relax." Thankfully, he thought she was trying to grab one of the mugs to help him. She casually walked over to the couch, sat next to him, and they drank their coffee, chatting about the day's news.

Lexi got up, gradually moved around the room, and seated herself in his office chair. All she needed was a few seconds to pull out the stick in order to slide it into her pocket.

"Do you mind lowering the blinds some," she asked. "The sun is in my eyes."

He rose, lowered the blind, and Lexi had the tiny drive safely in her slacks pocket. She had earlier prepared an outgoing text message to Esmeralda, so all she had to do was press the "send" button. The message said, "Now is the time. Call or text me so I can have an excuse to go." She pressed the button.

Her phone shortly chirped with the reply message from Esmeralda, and Lexi's expression became panicked.

"What's going on, is everything all right?" he asked.

"I have to go; a friend was in a car accident this morning, and I just got a text that she's in the hospital. Thank you so much, Brent. I really had a great time," she said and went to hug him. "I am so sorry; I'll be in touch."

As soon as she was in her car and at a safe distance from the house, she called John Pope.

"Lexi, how are you?" he asked. She detected a bit of warmth, or perhaps concern in his tone, which took her by surprise.

"Mission accomplished," she declared nonchalantly. "Brent was delighted to teach me all his money-making skills, most of which I think are imaginary."

"Yes, and what else?" Pope prodded. He was back to business.

"I have the drive. How do you want me to get it to you?"

"Excellent, Lexi. I'll stop by your apartment in thirty minutes."

Esmeralda had been anxious about Lexi's meeting with Brent. She was concerned about any repercussions that might affect her friend. She also wanted to hear about the outcome— was she successful? She knew about the scheduled "date" between the two, but was not privy to any details. She was a bit envious that her friend, hitherto unknown to the FBI, was actually handed an intriguing assignment. She, on the other hand, had to beg and plead for permission to assist in an in-house investigation.

She finally got a call from Lexi, who asked her to meet after work.

"You can't imagine the rush I felt after I left Brent's house with the flash drive. I don't think I've ever been more excited. He's such a worm... He tried to impress me with phony tricks, as if I'm completely stupid... Just to get me to sleep with him."

"Did he ask any more questions about me?" she asked.

"Not this time. I think his plan is to wear me down with his charm, and then grill me again. The idiot is strategizing."

"Hey, you were so 'cloak and dagger,' I am very impressed."

"Seriously, I have no idea where I found the guts to go through with it. I think it was mainly that I hate what Brent has been doing all his life. Somehow it got personal for me."

"So, can you tell me anything about what happened?"

"Let's say that I handed Mr. Pope what he asked me to get, which was dirt on the guy. Honestly, that's all I can tell you. He stressed over and over not to discuss it with anybody. You know how it goes. Anyway, how are you doing? You look exceptionally happy," Lexi changed the subject.

Esmeralda blushed. "Believe it or not, it probably sounds corny, but I think I'm in love," she said with a smile.

"Oh, my Lord! Who's the lucky guy?"

"It's a long story... Remember Harry, my supervisor, the victim in the bombing? By chance I ran into a guy who turned out to be his nephew. He works in my building, but in a different department. We became friends, and he took me to meet his grandmother, who is the most amazing woman I've ever met. I immediately bonded with her; it's as if they are my blood."

"And you never mentioned any of this to me?" Lexi's eyebrows rose. "What's the name of the nephew?"

"Sorry, Lexi; I should have shared it with you. I just wanted to see if it was going anywhere. His name is Bill. He was named after his grandfather William, who died years ago. I understand he left Germany before the Nazis started persecuting Jews. But Bill's grandma, Helena, when she, her parents and brother were rounded up to go to the death camps, sneaked out right from under their noses. She went through hell, but somehow made it and built a good life and a great family."

"So, tell me a little about you and your new guy."

"We spend a lot of time together. I don't know how or why, but we understand each other, which makes it very comfortable."

"Just comfortable?"

"We connect on many levels, but we're not officially romantic. I think I love him, but I'll have to see how it goes from here."

"If it's meant to be, it will happen, and it sounds to me like it will work out between you. I think it's good to be friends before you become lovers. You get to know each other first, and it's nice that he took you to meet his grandma. It sounds like he appreciates family."

"Having listened to this lady is pushing me to see how I can help find these killers. I hope they solve Harry's murder while Grandma Helena is still alive. He was her own son, and she deserves to learn the truth. What an amazing lady... She is in her nineties, and still very sharp.

Lexi heard a chirp on her phone. It was a text from Brent.

"Hey, can we get together for dinner and also invite Esme to join us?"

"See," Lexi showed Esmeralda the phone. "it didn't take him long. He still wants to find out details about your work. He's getting desperate."

"Judy in my office told me that he is most likely fishing for information. In a video of the explosion, I caught an image of him standing across the street. That's why our guys are after him—he probably knows something about what happened."

"I don't think you should go to meet him," Lexi said. "He may put something in your drink."

"Don't worry, it's not going to happen. Tell him you can't get hold of me or that I'm out of town, or anything else you can think of. I am terrified of him."

"Keep me posted on what happens with Bill... You deserve to have love in your life. I hope you two will become a couple."

A Birthday Party

Grandma Helena invited Esmeralda and Bill to her own birthday celebration. It included his parents, cousins, and a few elderly friends. He introduced his date as his "friend from work at the Bureau." She met Albert, his father, a somewhat portly man with reddish hair turning silver, and blue eyes. His mother, Annie, a petite dark-haired woman, was friendly but kept glancing at the pretty Hispanic guest throughout the evening.

Esmeralda was happy for the chance to talk with Albert, so she could learn more about their history.

"My mother Helena's family, the Bergers, were well connected and affluent," he told her. "They had a successful business and worked hard. Rumors came that the SS government planned to confiscate all assets owned by Jews. Mother said that her father and uncle were able to trade their holdings—bank accounts and real estate--for diamonds. She remembers that her uncle had asked a Catholic priest, his close friend, to hide this cache until they would be able to come back for it."

"Did anybody try to find the priest later?" Esmeralda asked.

"A few years ago, I finally worked up the courage to fly to Germany, something I thought I was never going to do. I went back to Weimar, where they had lived, found their old home, and went there to try to find some remnant from their lives. Anything. The people who live there now knew nothing about the former owners. They said they were very sorry about what happened to the nice families who had lived there, but had never found anything that had belonged to them."

Bill said, "What's a shame, to work hard and build a nice life, only to have all of it erased like that."

"But then, at the last minute," Albert continued, "this German woman remembered to give me a photograph of two men that she had found in the attic. One of them was my uncle, and the other a priest. I was convinced this was the man who had the stash, or at least knew where it was."

One of the older guests, who had been listening quietly, spoke. "I've read that quite a few clergymen had gone out of their way to help Jewish people. Some even hid children, which put them at great personal risk."

"Next, I went to visit the old church in Weimar," Albert went on, "and showed the photo to the woman in the reception area. She recognized the man, whom she called Father Otto. Unfortunately, I was too late, because he had died a few years earlier, and a new priest had taken over. I returned the next day and asked the young priest if he had heard about the hidden stash. He said that sadly, he knew nothing about the Berger family or the diamonds. I knew I was too late, and came to the conclusion that we should forget about it, so I flew back home. I wish I had gone there ten years earlier, but Germany had never been on my wish list of travel destinations."

"Could it be that the story about this missing treasure is all fiction, and never happened?" a close family friend whispered quietly to Albert. "It's possible that Helena had heard people talking about the idea of trading assets for diamonds, but her parents hadn't gotten to do it. After all, she was just a young girl back then."

Grandma Helena stood up and clapped her hands.

"We have a birthday cake," she announced. "Let's stop talking about the past and have some fun!"

One of the women brought out a cake, placed it on the coffee table, while another guest brought paper plates. There was coffee and tea, and the mood changed. Somebody started singing "Happy Birthday" and everyone joined in, watching Helena beam in joy.

Esmeralda had hoped to have had a chance to hear more from the old lady, but it was not to be. Her son Albert led Grandma Helena back to her recliner, where she dozed off, and the guests left.

"Uncle Harry was a quiet man," Bill said later. "He was very smart and knowledgeable, but wasn't a big talker. My dad is the opposite. He's not shy, and can express himself well. He was always picked to speak at company functions when he was an engineering manager."

"He seems very genuine to me. I like your father," she replied.

The Bequest

Celeste was getting ready to walk Lady Windsor when she noticed the mailman come to the house and then heard the doorbell. Her heart pounding with fear of another blow, she answered the door.

"I have a piece of registered mail for you that needs your signature," the man said and gave her a small slip of paper. She signed it, handed it back to him, and took the envelope. "Sorry, Lady Windsor", she said to the dog who was wagging her tail, "We'll go later. I have to see what this letter is about."

Her head spun when she read the official notification that came from an attorney, and she bent her head down to keep from passing out. It was addressed to Maddie Ellis, informing her that her father, Titus Ellis and brother, David Ellis, were deceased. They had been killed in a car accident nearly two years earlier when Titus had apparently fallen asleep at the wheel and lost control. The out-of-control vehicle collided head-on with an oil tanker, which ignited an inferno. The tanker driver had survived, but Titus and his passenger had not. The letter stated that the estate had been frozen since no next of kin had been found, and was about to be turned over to the state of California. Her identity, that of Maddie Ellis, had just been discovered when they launched one last attempt to locate her. Being the sole survivor and heir, Celeste was now the recipient of her father's estate.

It had been twenty years since she had seen or spoken to either her father or brother, and she sat at her kitchen table, frozen. Eventually, the tears came. She didn't know what she was crying about more: her life of complete estrangement, the lack of any family, or the news that they were dead. Maybe, she thought, what hurt most was having cut contact with David. After all, her brother was just a kid when she left. She saw that the dog had come over and was looking up at her sadly, so she picked her up and put her in her lap.

The letter included the address and phone number for the lawyer, with a request that she contact him immediately. Go figure, she thought. Her awful father, about whom she had vowed to forget, had left her his estate. She wondered if there was anything substantial in the bequest. It was still early enough in the day, the attorney was located in her time zone in San Francisco, so she decided to make the call.

Celeste steeled herself to sound strong and professional and dialed the number. Subconsciously, she held her breath until a woman's voice answered.

"Hello, my name is Maddie Ellis." She could barely mouth the name. "I got a letter about an estate I inherited from my father, Titus Ellis. I was asked to call your office right away."

"Yes, ma'am, please hold on. I will get Mr. Fisher on the phone."

"Ms. Ellis," a booming man's voice came on. "I am very glad to finally hear from you. May I ask where you have been for the past couple of years? We've been searching for you since your father and brother passed away."

"I've been out of the country for some time," she made up the facts as she spoke. "I am sorry you had a hard time finding me, but here I am."

"Ms. Ellis, Where is your current residence?" She was sure he didn't believe her tale about having been overseas.

"I live in Bakersfield, California." He knows my address, her logic told her, because that was where his letter had been mailed. So why is he asking?

"How soon can you come to San Francisco?"

"I can be there tomorrow."

Celeste went outside again to walk Lady Windsor. The dog had to stay with a neighbor the next day until she returned, and needed the exercise. Endless thoughts filled her head while walking. How did she turn out to be so lonely? Was there anyone she could talk to, pour her heart out to? She had no relatives, and no friends, not even from her youth. Then she reassured herself that she had always been self-reliant, and that perhaps this was a defining moment for her. A turning point, maybe.

When she entered the house, she prepared a business suit and high heeled shoes to wear the next day. Appearances were important, and she wanted Mr. Fisher, the lawyer, to view her as a savvy, elegant woman. Looking attractive, too, wouldn't hurt. She looked in the mirror and put her hand through her hair, then shook her head in disgust. It's time to fix me up, she told herself, and drove to a nearby beauty salon.

"Please do something with my hair. I have an important meeting tomorrow, so I need to look professional," she told the beautician.

An Unforgiving Past

Jack was torn about how to approach Titus about the treasure he had rediscovered. He told Deborah about the small sack of loose diamonds. "It was wrong of me to forget about it when I came back from the war."

She sat down on the sofa next to him. She noticed the peeling paint on the window frame, and thought about how much her husband could have done to update the house. He was a carpenter, but had never been interested in home improvement projects.

"You were not yourself when you came back," Deborah finally said. "The war did bad things to you, so don't blame yourself. The good news is that you found it now."

"But what should I do with it at this time? I am sick; it's too late for me to figure out where to take it."

"When you find money and you don't know who it belongs to," she suggested, "you take it to the police."

"No, this is not like that. These diamonds need to go to a specific organization that will locate the original owner. It's the Jewish Joint Distribution Committee, or JDC for short."

"What if there is nobody left? The Nazis might have killed them all."

"I remember the priest saying that a girl from that family came to the United States. The name is Berger. I just looked at the notes in the bag. I have to try to keep my word."

"Why don't you talk to Titus about it. It's time he did something important." His wife patted his arm and left the room. Although Jack had already asked his son to come by, he was still not sure what to tell him.

It occurred to him that he had never measured up to what he should have been to Deborah, and that she had never complained. Through the years, she had been his quiet partner and solid shield. Oddly, his wife had never spoken about her childhood, and now, with his end looming, he felt an urgent need to ask her about it.

"I have to go to bed," Jack said after they finished supper, "but will you please remind me to ask you something tomorrow." He then shuffled over to the bedroom and went to sleep.

"I can show you some family photos that I kept," she told him the following day. "There isn't much there, because my parents never talked about their past in Russia. They insisted that we were Americans, but my father made sure I knew that I was named after his mother."

She placed before him a large envelope with a few photographs he had never seen before. They were of people from what seemed a bygone era, unsmiling, and dressed in dark, conservative attire.

"I can't tell you for sure who each one of them is," Deborah said. "I happened to see this envelope when I was clearing out my mother's apartment."

"What was it like growing up with these people?" Jack asked.

"My childhood was boring. I was a single child to parents who worked twelve-hour days, and was not allowed to leave our apartment. I liked reading and doing homework. They argued all the time, but I learned to tune them out and read my books. My freedom came only when I turned eighteen and started my studies to become a teacher. When I was little, we had a few simple celebrations that I remember vaguely, but, for some reason, they've always brought me sad memories."

"What kind of celebrations?" Jack asked, suddenly eager to hear about his wife's past.

"My mother liked to light candles sometimes, which was a Jewish custom. But..."

Jack looked incredulous. "I can't believe that you never told me you were Jewish," he interrupted. "Why?"

"My mother had constantly drilled into me to forget about it. She was an avowed socialist who was inspired by Communist ideology. She always said that religion is not logical, and that all is does is prevent people from having practical, productive lives. Anyway, after my father left us, she stopped lighting candles and never mentioned our faith or culture."

"Your mother passed away while I was away during the war, so I didn't get to meet her. I knew that your parents had divorced, but do you have any idea why your father left?"

"When I was about ten or eleven, my mother told me that my father went away and wasn't coming back. She never explained, and I never saw him again. Looking back, I sense that he tried to keep our traditions, but she wanted none of it. When I grew up, I put my uneventful childhood in the past, trying to focus on the present. I was overjoyed to marry you after you finally came back in one piece. You were smart and handsome, we've always been able to have interesting talks, and things have been good. You gave me a nice life."

"If I had known that you were born and raised as a Jew, I'm quite certain I would have tried to have more family traditions. We might have raised Titus with some faith, better values. Look at him..."

"Titus will find his way in the world. We should keep him out of this conversation," she said.

"A lot of missed opportunities," Jack said sadly, his eyes down.

"It's all in the past now, Jack," Deborah said sadly. "I probably should have told you... But, somewhere deep inside, I think I was afraid you would have rejected me if you had known."

"Never!" he exclaimed. "But the fault lies with me too. It was I who should have tried to find out more about you back then, after the war. But I was a mess, just so happy to come back. I failed you, Deborah. I am sorry," he said and put his arm around her. "You deserved more than what I've given you."

"Please stop, Jack," she said. "You are a good man, and we always loved each other. But remember, you are not well, and all I want you now to do is take care of yourself."

"Your parents must have run away from Russia because of religious persecution. Think about the similarity; this little sack with precious stones belonged to people who were murdered just because they were Jews. They couldn't get out. If it turns out that their daughter is living here in the States, we must do whatever we can to find her. Do you agree?"

"Definitely." She stopped, gazing somewhere far away. "You are putting things in new perspective for me. It just occurred to me that I probably betrayed my father and grandparents by denying who I was." They were both silent for a moment. "When I was teaching fifth grade years ago, I befriended one of the other teachers. She was always open and proud of her Judaism, but I never let on who I was. I can see how foolish I had been at that time."

"It was your mother who indoctrinated you, so don't be so hard on yourself," Jack said. "She shouldn't have instilled those ideas in you. She should have encouraged you to learn about who you were, so you could decide for yourself. This is not Russia. Religious practice is acceptable and respected in America.

"I'm convinced that my father was a big missing piece in my life. I wish I could have maintained some contact with him. Back then, I didn't feel strong or independent enough to look for him. I was just a little girl. When I asked my mother where he had gone, she strongly told me not to think or talk about him, because he was a bad person. I didn't really believe her, but couldn't think of anything I could do about it, so I left it alone."

"When I tell Titus about the Berger family's nest egg, it may be helpful to tell him about your heritage. Your childhood history may mean something to him. What do you think?"

Deborah replied, "I don't see our son getting softer when he suddenly learns that his mother was Jewish. You know how harsh Titus can be; he would most likely taunt me forever for failing to tell him about it. Let's keep it simple for him."

"Titus is coming over this Friday," Jack said as he stood up slowly, "so I'll talk to him about contacting the JDC about the stash of diamonds. Don't forget to make his favorite stuffed cabbage."

Keeping the Promise

Jack had just gotten up from a nap when his son walked in. The two had never formed a close relationship, and he always questioned himself if he should have done better in raising his son. They were quite different—Jack had always been conservative and thrifty, working hard to support his family. Titus was adventurous, went from one job to another, and had little or no money.

"Hi Pop," the younger man said and sat down next to his father.

"Hi son," Jack replied with a feeble smile. He was sitting on the sofa, lethargic and out of sorts. "So how are you doing these days? Where do you work?" He couldn't see his son's expression in the dim light of an old standing lamp.

"I just got my real estate license, so that's what I'm getting into," Titus was animated. "I signed up with a broker, and I have a good feeling about it. I'm not cut out to work for somebody else. I want to be my own boss."

His father's face showed a positive reaction, and he nodded. "Well, I wish you success. Lots of people are buying and selling homes. You just need to have the right personality."

"No, Pop, I don't want to be a realtor who works with home buyers or sellers. I want to buy homes for myself, fix them up, then either sell or rent them out."

Jack needed to get to the point.

"Look, I have to tell you about something that happened to me at the end of World War Two. This is a serious matter, so it's important that you pay attention." His son straightened up and looked at him.

"You know about what happened during the Holocaust, right? Jewish people were taken on trains to concentration camps, and everything they owned was stolen from them."

"You mean, the Nazis robbed them?"

"That's exactly what I mean. I never told you this, but our whole regiment went into one of the death camps to bring out the inmates who survived. We came to liberate them. You can't imagine how unspeakable it was to see what the Germans did to these poor people."

Titus looked at his father and listened.

"I had walked out of the camp for a moment to get over the shock of what I saw, and that's when a Catholic priest spotted me and came over. He told me about a family who had something valuable that they had to hide from the Germans. So, before they were taken away, they gave the priest a small bag, more like a pouch, and asked him to see that it gets to a relative in case they didn't make it. You understand, right?"

Titus nodded.

"Well, the whole family was killed, except one daughter, who got out and presumably made it to America. The priest handed me the pouch. He made me promise to do whatever it took to deliver it to a certain institution, which specializes in locating missing survivors. Surely, these people believed that this organization would be able to track down the daughter and make sure she receives it."

"Wow...did you ever take it to them?"

Jack stopped and closed his eyes briefly before continuing. "The name is 'American Jewish Joint Distribution

Committee.' The thing is, when I came back from the war I was in pretty bad shape. I couldn't work or concentrate on anything. I didn't want to open my bag of stuff that I brought back, and over the years I'd forgotten it even existed. When you were born, I got myself together and started to think seriously about earning a living to support your mother and you. Anyway, long story short, I just now discovered it when I came across my old backpack."

"Okay," Titus asked, "then, is it too late to take it to them now?"

"That's where I need your help. My health is bad, and I'm not going to last much longer. I want to make sure that these people's daughter—her name was Helena Berger—will get this bag. It contains important things. He read aloud the name of the joint distribution committee again from a piece of paper. "Can you get in touch with them to see if they have any information about this woman?"

"How will I find this committee?"

"I looked them up in the phone book, and it listed an address in New York City. I also found their phone number." "Son, this is very important to me. You should give them a call, and maybe fly back east. I'll pay for your ticket. Can I have your word that you'll do it? I will die in peace if I know this finally reached the right people."

"Okay, Pop," Titus said and looked at his father sadly. "Whatever this thing is, I'll make sure this outfit will get it."

"Please call them, and if they ask you to come in person, remember, I'll pay for an airplane ticket."

Jack showed his son the brown sack, slowly pulled out the small yellowed notes with the names of the families and showed them to him. He was careful not to let Titus see the diamonds inside. "There were two families by the last name of

Berger, obviously related, but it's not clear which one the daughter belonged to. Here is the contact number of the Distribution Committee." Jack wrote down the details on a sheet of paper and handed it over. He then carefully put the papers back in the sack and closed it tightly before returning it to a dresser drawer. "As soon as you find out that they have any information about Ms. Berger, let me know. Then we can figure out our next steps."

Titus went to the kitchen to see his mother. The table was set for three, and they sat down to eat.

"Mom, the cabbage is so good," Titus said, his mouth full. "It's been a while since I was here to have it."

"It would be nice for you to come over more often," Deborah replied, but she seemed distracted. Jack was quiet, and other than the clatter of silverware against the plates, nothing more was said.

San Francisco

San Francisco was cold, but the sky was a deep blue, and Celeste savored it. She arrived early at the address of Fisher and Associates, kept her sneakers on, and walked around the block before stopping for coffee and a bagel. She had done some online research about the accident that killed her father and brother. She had scoured for information on the type of work or business they were involved in. It turned out that her father, Titus, had bought a Ford dealership and that her brother David, who had remained single, ran the office.

Celeste checked her newly coiffed hair and makeup in the rearview mirror, then changed into her high heels before heading to the law office. She brought her birth certificate, the only authentic document which proved who she was. All her other forms of identification were under the name of Celeste Butler, with no mention of Maddie Ellis. She thought of some explanations she could provide, but knew she was walking into the unknown. It would be challenging, if not impossible, to explain the lack of any bank records under her childhood name. She anxiously hoped not be questioned about it.

She entered a reception area and was asked to sit down and wait for Mr. Fisher, who was on a phone call. About fifteen minutes later a receptionist led her to the attorney's private office. Mr. Fisher was a tall, handsome man with graying temples, and he rose from his chair to greet her. She scanned the contemporary decor; there were no family pictures, only certificates and diplomas on the walls.

"Hello, Ms. Ellis," he said with his booming voice. "I should say, the elusive Ms. Ellis, right? Please have a seat."

She smiled and sat at his desk across from him.

"Ms. Ellis," Fisher started, "let me first say that I am sincerely sorry for your loss."

"Thank you," she said with downcast eyes. She found him quite likeable.

"I'll get to business. Did you bring any identification with you?"

"All my documents were destroyed in the Tehachapi fire not too long ago," she had practiced this. "The only thing I have is my birth certificate."

"I wasn't aware you lost your home in the fire," the lawyer said. "That's very tragic."

She knew she had to improvise.

"My house wasn't a total loss, but there was a lot of damage. I'm embarrassed to say that my papers were stored in a cardboard box in the garage, where much of my stuff was reduced to ashes. The fire was the most upsetting experience I ever had." She handed him the document, and he looked at it briefly.

"Ms. Ellis, I don't know how much contact you had with your father, but he left behind a substantial estate."

"I'm afraid we had a falling out years ago, and now I regret that I never reached out to him. I didn't know he and David were gone." In spite of Celeste's resolve to show resilience, she broke into tears.

"It's very sad. Broken family ties..." Fisher said and handed her a box of tissue.

"I became so very sure of myself, not thinking that I needed anybody. But I see now that family is important, and unfortunately, my father and brother were all I had." I'm talking too much, she thought, and stopped.

"Titus Ellis' will listed your brother David and you as his heirs."

"Was he married when he died?" she asked.

"Your father was divorced." He pointed to a sheet of paper on his desk. "Please take a look at the list of his assets. His executor and trustee oversaw the sale of his car dealership. At this point, everything has been liquidated and the proceeds were invested in a low risk brokerage account. Apparently, close to 2.5 million dollars in cash was found in a trunk in his home, which is included in the estate."

"What was he doing with so much currency?" she asked.

"This was actually investigated by the IRS on suspicion of illegal activity or money laundering, but there was no evidence of any of that. You are fortunate, to receive this inheritance without complications. Sometimes there are liens and judgments against estates, but this is, from what I see, free and clear."

Celeste froze for a moment, trying to assimilate the sudden shift in her fortunes. The wealth she had accumulated illegally had been stolen from her, but now she was inheriting legitimate money. It seemed more than she could comprehend, but she instantly collected herself.

"What are my next steps?"

"I need you to sign a few legal forms, which I will notarize. Then you'll need to provide me with the name of a bank or brokerage to where the funds can be transferred on your behalf."

"Is it possible to get the existing brokerage account retitled to my name?" she asked. "It will be easier for me than having to set up something new."

"I will look into it for you. It may be impossible, since your financial and credit history are nonexistent. Let's finish the signing and notarization; then we can continue from there."

She took copies of the documents she signed and went to her car for the drive back to Bakersfield. She knew what she had to do--go back to being Maddie, thus putting the past behind her. There would still be complications—the house was still owned by Steve and Celeste Butler, so that selling it under Maddie Ellis appeared impossible. Until the sale of the house she would have to endure a double identity.

Celeste fully comprehended that having two names was a double-edged sword. The life insurer demanded more details from her, and they had identified her as Maddie Ellis. For better or worse, it appeared that this was who she was meant to be.

Titus

The worst problem Titus had was his short temper. After too many breakups to remember, he decided that he needed to make a change. He worked on his self-control, and resolved to find a woman who would agree to marry him.

Less than two weeks after the conversation with his father about contacting a certain organization and trying to locate a woman named Helena, Jack was rushed to the hospital. He passed away the next day with Deborah and Titus at his side. After the funeral, Titus' mother tearfully asked him if there were any mementos he wanted from his father. He went through several closets and drawers, choosing a few small items he placed in a paper bag.

In one drawer he noticed the small brown bag. As soon as he pulled it out, he remembered. "I'd better get a hold of these people that Pop asked me to," he thought to himself, and stuffed it in his pocket. Titus had never been outwardly affectionate, but still, he went over to his mother and gave her an awkward hug before leaving.

After Titus left his parents' home with the pouch, he drove back to his small apartment and went to sleep. He planned to buy some professional clothes to be able to begin his real estate venture. He knew he was not sophisticated or knowledgeable enough to pick one good opportunity over the next, but resolved to learn. Like his father years earlier, Titus put the brown sack out of his mind. It remained in the pocket of the old blazer he had worn for his father's service, gone unnoticed again.

It took a year for him to save enough to buy an old home in a growing suburb, and he threw himself into the process of making repairs. He then listed it for rent, found a tenant who seemed stable, and became the proud owner of a rental property. This new status gave him the boost he needed to go out to classy bars to try to meet people. Sally was a lively woman with a college degree who soon became his live-in girlfriend. After they married, Titus gradually became more aggressive towards his wife. Sally took a job as an executive secretary, and they settled into a lifestyle in which they spent little time together.

After his father, Jack, had passed away, Titus rarely called his mother. Soon he and Sally had two children, a boy they named David and a girl, Maddie. It appeared that their family life might be getting happier, and they took the children on a few weekend day trips. Happiness, however, was not in their future.

Shortly after their daughter's first birthday, a 6.5 earthquake struck southern California at 4:30 in the morning. Sally jumped up from her bed, grabbed the girl and ran outside.

"Titus, I've got Maddie! take David outside!" she screamed.

The house shook for what seemed to be several minutes, but the quake had lasted only twenty seconds. The structure only suffered minor cracks, but plates, cups, and glassware had rained down from the kitchen cabinets. The floor was covered with broken china and shards of glass. Titus carried David, who was screaming, back to his bed before marching angrily into the kitchen.

"How could you leave your little boy inside?" He yelled at her.

"I grabbed Maddie and yelled for you to take David," she answered defensively.

"I didn't even hear you, Sally! Plus, you are the mother, and you are responsible for the kids. What kind of parent are you?"

Sally silently started to pick up some of the broken debris and sweep the kitchen floor.

"I am leaving you," she told him later that evening. "I can't take this anymore."

"Oh, no. You're not going to leave me. I'll be the one divorcing you. Pack your things and get out!"

She walked quietly to the bedroom, then came out a half an hour later rolling a suitcase with one hand and carrying Maddie on her other arm. Titus blocked her at the door.

"Leave her here. You're not taking the child!"

"Titus, please move out of the way," she said calmly. "We can figure this out later. Right now, she needs to be with her Mommy."

"Not the kind of Mommy you are!" he shoved her towards the wall and grabbed the child. "Just go!"

Sally walked out, quickly got into her car and backed it out of the garage. She heard a fallen trash can roll down the driveway. Titus ran after her and stood a few feet in front of the vehicle, but she kept driving. He had to jump aside, and remembered in his rage that she had always kept a set of keys in her handbag. He was frustrated, unsure why he had tried to block her when she drove away. How was she supposed to have left without a car? He didn't delve deeply into his senseless action; he was glad his wife was gone.

Titus was the type of person who didn't let anyone win against him. Over the next three months Sally called every few days and tried to reason with him, only to be repeatedly refused and verbally bashed.

"Titus, I'm not interested in anything in the house. You can keep everything. I just want to see the children. Can we work out something like shared custody?"

Sally sank into deep depression. She resigned from her office position and moved away. He did not know, or care about, where she was. He had his children with him, and arranged daycare for them while he was out during the day.

It was two years later when he was going through old clothes he planned to give away. He cursed each time he discovered a piece of her clothing, tossing it into a corner. He was checking the pockets in old slacks and jackets when he came across the small, old brown sack his father had given him. Titus opened the bag in disgust and stopped breathing for a moment when he saw the contents. Were those real diamonds? He stared at them for a while, trying to think of what to do. He decided to go to a jeweler to find out if they were real. He sat down, carefully poured the stones on the bed, and glared. They gleamed brightly in the light.

Titus nervously stuffed the old garments in plastic trash bags and threw them in the bed of his truck. Then, with shaking hands, he carefully poured the glistening gems back into the bag, all except for one. He didn't notice the crumpled slips of paper at the bottom, and rushed to pull out the phone book to find a high-end jewelry store.

The next day he put on dressy slacks and a button-down shirt, and went to the store he chose with the single diamond in his pocket. The jeweler gawked at him when he looked at the stone under his microscope.

"This is a valuable diamond, sir. It is over two carats and the cut looks perfect to me."

"Do you have a rough idea how much it's worth?" he asked, trying his best to sound cordial.

"I can't give you an exact appraisal at this moment, but I am guessing it could be close to a hundred thousand dollars."

Titus knew the man was curious, perhaps even suspicious, but he was not about to give out any details. He took the stone in his hand, thanked the jeweler, and drove back home. He estimated there were about forty of them in the small bag.

He engaged a jewelry broker who, over the next three years, found buyers who paid for the diamonds in cash. Fearful about losing the money, he hid it in a large trunk in his bedroom closet. After Deborah, his mother, died from cancer, Titus inherited his parents' house and both of their retirement accounts. Jack and Deborah had consistently built up their nest egg, and now their son's fortune had grown to several millions.

Meanwhile, the children were growing, and his frustration with them escalated. Raising two kids proved challenging, and he had other plans in mind—he wanted to meet a new woman who could take over the parenting.

Celeste and Maddie

Celeste's mind was in a whirl while she drove back. She figured that it was probably impossible for her to legally change her name. Half of me is an Ellis and the other is a Butler, she thought mournfully. She contemplated the possibility that she might not even be a whole person with real roots.

She needed to establish herself as Maddie Ellis in order to access her father's estate, but still, most of her documents were in Celeste's name. She clearly needed good legal advice, but had no idea who to turn to. Should she list her home for sale under her current name? What about getting a new driver's license? The questions filled her head even after she arrived and took the dog for a walk.

The next morning, she sat down with a cup of coffee and made a decision. She dialed Mr. Fisher's phone number.

"Good morning, Ms. Ellis," he greeted her jovially, which helped put her at ease.

"I wonder if you will be willing to help me with another personal matter. It's unrelated to my inheritance."

"What type of personal matter?" he asked.

"I prefer to talk to you about it in person if it's okay." It occurred to her that he might refuse to see her.

"Ms. Ellis, you may be wasting time to come all the way here if this is something that I don't usually handle."

"I would very much like to meet with you, even if it turns out you can't help me," she pleaded. "It's a very sensitive situation."

His receptionist scheduled an appointment for her for three days later, the following Friday morning, and Celeste began to feel some relief. She was glad that she had some time to put her thoughts together before the meeting.

He greeted her warmly when she was shown to his private office, and motioned for her to sit down.

"So, what brings you here today, Ms. Ellis?" he questioned.

"Please call me Maddie," she said with a smile.

"It's actually good that you came," his expression turned serious. "It turns out that it's impossible to simply retitle the brokerage account in the estate from your father's name to yours. You will have to establish an account yourself, and then the funds will be transferred over. If it helps, I will give you the broker's direct phone number."

"This is where I have a big problem, Mr. Fisher," she started and clasped her hands together. "When I was very young, I made a big mistake, which was followed by more mistakes. I ran away from home when I was fifteen, and when I was old enough to get a driver's license, I decided to change my name. The idea was to disappear from my very abusive father. That's the reason that nobody could find me to notify me that he and my brother died. I changed my Social Security number, became Celeste Butler, and that's who I've been for the past twenty years."

The attorney listened intently. "Just curious; how did you decide on this name?"

"I was young and ambitious, and Celeste sounded to me unique and powerful at the same time. Meanwhile, I got married, and my husband actually took my last name, becoming Steve Butler. He said he had always hated his own name." She stopped for a moment. "Unfortunately, I lost him in the Tehachapi wildfire."

"I am very sorry to hear that," he said quietly. "That's a lot to take in all at once, losing your husband and learning about these other tragic deaths. But, tell me, if you've been living under the name Celeste Butler, what happened that brought the original Maddie Ellis back to life, which enabled us to track you down?"

She was careful not to refer to anything that might hint at her questionable activities, but there was one she thought was harmless. "After Steve died, I searched under both names and SSN's for any sources of money available to me. Somehow, I thought of checking under Maddie with my old SSN, and discovered a money market account that I had forgotten about. I assume that as soon as I went online under my original name, it re-appeared in cyberland. My home, plus this modest bank account comprise my entire net worth."

He listened intently, and was silent for a long moment before speaking.

"So, I understand your dilemma. You have a double identity of sorts. Needless to say, you have to untangle it so you can start using one single name. I will have to think about a way out of this situation. So, yes, I am going to take this on and see where it goes."

Celeste had to contain her relief and elation. She was tempted to reach across the desk and grab his hands in gratitude. He was willing to help her... She had someone on her side, and perhaps she would emerge intact from her chaos.

"Until we decide otherwise, I am going to call you Maddie. I must ask you if there is anything that I need to be aware of? Do you have a criminal record? Any unpaid debts, liens, or judgments against you? Is there anything you are not telling me?"

She mulled it over briefly. "I don't have any debts, and the answer to all the other questions is no."

"Here is the big question: what is the name you want to adopt and use from now on?"

"I actually like the original me. Can I possibly go back to being Maddie? I think it will sort of cleanse my soul."

"I will research how many mountains we'll need to climb. If it looks like it will not work out, I'll let you know and we can think of another option. By the way, I must advise you of my fee schedule, which is $500 per hour."

Her face paled, but she didn't respond.

"I don't mind waiting until you have the proceeds of your father's estate to get paid. You will be in fine shape to cover your legal fees," he said and smiled.

"Certainly," she replied. "I appreciate it very much."

"As I mentioned, I will need to take some time to consider the best route to take in this case. We can communicate electronically, so that you don't have to make the drive from Bakersfield every time we need to talk. There is an approaching deadline for the dissolution of the Ellis estate, so we must proceed quickly. Do you have any questions?"

"Thank you for helping me get out of this situation. The only question I have is how long you expect it will take to finish the process."

"Again, it depends on the hoops we'll have to jump through. I will get to it in the next two days, and barring any unforeseen complications, we are looking at two to three weeks. The main thing I will have to do is to obliterate the name Celeste from all public records. I will contact you with a more accurate timeline once I see that the wheels are in motion."

The Killing of Harry

Harry had been an occasional guest lecturer at a forensic intelligence department in a college in Charles Town, West Virginia. His input about cyber-crime and all manner of financial fraud and corruption was highly regarded by all branches of law enforcement.

Based on a recommendation by his supervisor, Thomas Snow, Brent Bushnell was assigned to attend one of Harry's sessions on the subject of information security. Privately, he was not sure of how riveting the presentation was going to be. Still, he flew to the location and sat among about two hundred FBI and police recruits. He jotted down a few catch phrases that he thought would impress his superiors, and during a break decided to read about the background of the instructor.

He learned that Harry, the speaker, was a Senior Special Agent in Charge, or SAC, who oversaw investigations into financial irregularities. That was valuable knowledge for the young man who had been dabbling in questionable activities. The fact that this senior agent was based in the Los Angeles area was of particular interest to Brent—it was in his own backyard.

Several months later, when Brent found himself working for Agent M, he had received a message from his employer. It stated that the suspected FBI inquiry into their transactions needed to be obstructed. He immediately presumed that the esteemed speaker at the Charles Town college, was the man in charge of this inquiry.

He had never before experienced the excitement that came from the lavish compensation he was receiving. It appealed to his sense of adventure and to his taste for underhanded business practices. He loved the rush he felt from the trust and commitment he was shown, and was determined to prove his worth at every opportunity.

Now he had been assigned to "take care" of the FBI probe into Agent M's empire, and he spent hours, late into the night, pondering his options. He knew he needed help, and finding it was going to be tricky. There was an odd young man he had met in a bar a few months earlier who couldn't stop talking about his skill with remote control gadgets. The guy mentioned toys, machines, household appliances, smart phones, and more.

A few evenings later, Brent noticed the young man again in the same bar. He invited him to join him at a small table, soon to be regaled once more with the glories of remote control.

"You can get a phone to start your car, hack into somebody else's car, make an alarm system go off, even set off explosives," the tall, thin stranger said and drew diagrams on a napkin.

Brent perceived that this person might be able to activate something that would stop Harry in his tracks.

"Can you interfere with computer software using a phone?" he asked.

"I've never done it, but I think I can figure it out. Why do you ask?"

"No reason," Brent backed off. "I am just blown away by all this stuff you say you can do."

"Hey," the young man said and scribbled something on a napkin. "My name is Kyle, and here's my number. If you ever need my help, let me know. I'm always available for side gigs."

"Okay, I'll keep it in mind," Brent said before he left. "See you around."

He drove home, wondering if the guy was reliable enough to be recruited for the mission of disrupting the FBI probe. It might not be easy to pinpoint Harry's office location, but it was doable. The next step, obstructing the investigation, was another matter, for which Kyle's skills might come in handy.

A few days later he walked into the FBI building. A stern looking man behind a counter stopped him.

"I attended a lecture by a Senior Special Agent who works in the Financial Crimes department, and I wonder if there is any way I can meet him in person. He really impressed me."

"I am sorry, sir, but you need a special pass to enter any of the offices."

Brent nodded, then looked around and spotted a sign on a wall with an arrow pointing to the FCD, the department he was asking about. It was the Financial Crimes Department, located on the first floor. He left, and called his new guy. The first step he asked his new cohort to do was to implant a wiretap inside the immediate work area. He offered to pay him $500 for the job.

Kyle did that by remotely disrupting the air conditioning unit in that office, and then impersonating a repairman with a forged ID badge. This enabled him to attach a listening bug to the bottom of Harry's desk. Brent was now able to hear some of the conversations in the office, most of which included terms he could not understand. Occasionally there was casual banter, but he persisted in his attempts to discover the man's schedule.

His target did not keep to a regular time table. He came in at different hours, mostly early, and usually stayed late. He ate lunch in the cafeteria, so Brent never got to see him. Not that he was always on the lookout for his target; he relied on Kyle to detect when Harry's computer was turned on and off. Hacking into the actual system, as it turned out, was not a viable option— the FBI software was impenetrable, therefore unbreachable.

Brent's quest to thwart Harry's work proved challenging, but Agent M continued to pressure him to ensure the FBI probe would be halted. "I am counting on you to get it handled speedily," the last message said. He pondered how to bring up to Kyle the purpose of his operation, and eventually decided to let him in on it.

"I need to put the brakes on an investigation this man is working on" he told the young man. "Their software is, no doubt, very secure, but maybe we can do something to cause a system failure, or anything to put a stop to what they are doing. What do you think?"

"I can come up with something if the price is right," Kyle told him and cocked his head to the right.

"You can count on it," Brent replied anxiously. "Let me know when you have a plan."

A few days later in mid-morning it seemed he got his lucky break. He happened to be listening that morning, when he heard Harry invite two co-workers to go out for lunch with him. He could barely contain his excitement, and called Kyle to instruct him to be ready. He sat on a bench outside the FBI building and waited until he saw the man walking with two women, then followed them to the coffee shop.

"Okay. There's $10,000 in it for you if it works. We have to wait for when they leave the restaurant, so I'll watch the exit and you'll be ready, good to go?"

"Good to go, man, but I want $5,000 up front, and the rest when it's done."

Brent drove to a local branch of his bank to withdraw the cash, and handed it over. Then he walked to a spot across the street from the eatery, pacing back and forth as he waited. He didn't know what Kyle was planning to do, and preferred it that way. But when he witnessed the explosion that had been perfectly aimed at his target, it stunned him. He was shocked to witness the chaos that followed, watching the younger of the victim's two companions bend over him. He then disappeared behind a complex into at a bus station while waiting for his frantic heartbeat to slow. Brent was not aware that Kyle's plan had involved murder, but what was done was done.

"You completed the mission, but you went seriously overboard," he texted. "I'll have the rest of your money tomorrow morning, ten o'clock." He wanted to distance himself from his cohort as soon as the money changed hands.

When he reached his apartment, he accessed the encrypted email and sent a message to his boss: "Mission accomplished. The Fed inquiry is dead." He hoped that Agent M would not see a connection between the bombing and his assignment.

His boss replied to thank him, but sent more instructions. "We must tie up any loose ends. Find Harry's co-workers and determine if the probe will continue without him. By the way, our organization NEVER condones murder. Big stain on your employment record if you were involved." That was when Brent began to trail Esmeralda, tried to learn her daily routine, and followed her to Stardust Dance Studio.

Steve

Steve had relocated to Florida, a place he believed was the farthest he could get from Celeste. He purchased a small horse ranch and hired a ranch hand. When he was not riding, he struggled to learn how to manage the assets and accounts that were newly registered in his name. When he recognized that trying to attract Brent was a fruitless effort, he decided to work independently with no partners.

Late on a Friday afternoon a young woman came to his door. He was served a subpoena to appear at an FBI office in Miami for questioning the following Tuesday. There was a reference to a mysterious case number. Sleep evaded him on both Friday and Saturday nights, until finally, on Sunday evening he took sleeping pills and eventually dozed off.

The office that Steve was led to was looked inhospitable. He was shown to a chair where he was told to wait. He did not remember any time in his life when he had been so antsy. The hum of the air conditioning unit irritated him, and he quashed an impulse to throw something at the ticking wall clock. he was tapping his foot nervously while waiting in the cold, empty room. Since rising that morning, he had been practicing responses to questions that might be asked, but it was daunting. He had no documentation related to the source of his net worth, and no investment expertise.

Two men entered the room, introduced themselves, and sat down. They started on a friendly note, asking him for his name, birth date, address—routine questions. It's just official procedure, Steve thought, trying to relax. It didn't take long for the pointed questions to come.

"Mr. Butler, I am a Special Agent in the financial fraud unit in the FBI, and our job is to look into illegal money transactions," the taller man stated. "It looks like you recently came into a lot of money. Can you outline for us where it came from?"

"My wife and I accumulated the assets together over a long time, so they were always registered in both our names. We divorced recently, and this portion of our assets is mine."

"What is your ex-wife's name?" the man continued.

"Celeste Butler."

"Mr. Butler," the shorter agent interjected. "Please explain in some detail: how did the two of you build this financial empire, and over how many years?"

It was all illegal, he told himself when he couldn't find an answer, and decided to plead ignorance.

"She was the expert, and she handled our whole portfolio. I am new at this, so I don't have the details about where any of the holdings originated."

There were a few more questions, but the investigators clearly did not believe most of what he said. Instead, they asked him for Celeste's contact information. He provided her address, email, and telephone number.

"Mr. Butler, you are a person of interest in a money laundering case, and we will most likely need to speak with you again. You are free to leave at this time. Meanwhile, the State Department will suspend your passport until this case is solved."

Steve's legs were unsteady and his head spun when he was dismissed, but he forced himself to walk steadily when he stepped out. He stopped and leaned his back against a wall in the hallway, waiting for the dizziness to diminish. A sudden despair had overtaken his whole body, and he slowly ambled into a small taqueria next door, where he sank into a chair.

He knew it was likely that his testimony might not add anything to the case, and worried about what was coming next. In fact, the FBI had already accessed every detail about his finances. The picture that emerged was that Steve had deceptively changed the ownership of the assets, but was not competent enough to manage them. They now had Celeste's name in their sights, slated to be the next domino in the inquiry.

A Love Story

Bill and Esmeralda occasionally ate dinner at each other's apartments. They had become close friends, and enjoyed spending time together. Even with intriguing conversations that lasted hours, their relationship had still not become intimate. He was fascinated with her journey from South America, and was never tired of hearing the details. She, on the other hand, had an insatiable curiosity about his family history.

On a Friday evening, they finished eating a small dinner at his kitchen table. Bill, a skillful self-taught cook, prepared baked chicken with mushrooms, perfectly seasoned, and served it with steamed rice.

"You are such a great chef... I can't fix a meal that is even close to this!"

"Believe me," he replied bashfully, "cooking is not the most important thing in the world. It just happens to be something I enjoy doing. You have the intelligence to do very meaningful things that can make a difference."

Esmeralda smiled as she went into the small living room. She noticed the nearly bare walls and simple furnishings, and thought she should suggest some decorating. When she came back to the kitchen, Bill was washing dishes at the sink. She suddenly felt a sudden, strange wave wash over her. She spontaneously approached and wrapped her arms around him from behind, barely perceiving what she was doing. He turned around and took one look at her before taking her in his arms and kissing her.

She didn't want it to end, continued to hold him, and lay her head on his shoulder. He slowly led her to the bedroom, and they fell on the bed together. Esmeralda had never experienced great physical passion before. She had always been too shy to let anyone see her naked; but now, with Bill, it seemed perfectly natural. She sensed that, beyond any doubt, he was the love of her life.

"I love you so much," he said breathlessly after they made love the second time and she lay next to him. "I knew it right after I got to know you."

"I love you too, very much..." She stopped herself, wondering whether she was being ridiculously forward, or direct. How did she not show even a little restraint?

"It's okay," he whispered, sensing her hesitation. "I could tell from the beginning that you and I were meant for each other."

Esmeralda could hear her heart beating. She thought she was in heaven; how could it be that she had also felt the instant connection when they first met? Could it be that their meeting was by design?

Magically, the evening gradually morphed into morning. I spent the night with Bill, Esmeralda thought in disbelief when she woke up next to him. Neither of them had plans for the weekend, so on Saturday they decided to spend the day together. She stopped at home to change clothes and, then he drove them to Griffith Park.

The sky was overcast, possibly smoggy, the weekend crowd filling the park, but they were oblivious to any of it. Esmeralda's mood was so elated, that she had to stop herself from displaying her joy in public. They walked hand in hand, ate hot dogs for lunch, and then raced each other to the observatory.

She did not want the day to end, but in the evening, after they ate dinner in a Mexican restaurant, they finally kissed good night. She then drove home in her car. She stood in the shower, closed her eyes while the hot water poured over her, and tried to relive every magical, sensual detail of the past twenty-four hours.

She went to bed and tried to fall asleep, but the magic of the past two days kept her wide awake. She missed her mother, and wished she could have told her about her new love. The photo she had of her had been shot at a wedding, a happy moment when she was smiling radiantly in a red dress.

"Mamá," she whispered. "I am in love with a wonderful young man. He has a kind soul, and comes from a very good family. We both know we were meant to be together, and I hope you approve."

After her brief one-way conversation with her mother, Esmeralda finally began to calm down, went back to bed, and fell asleep.

The New Maddie

Changing herself from Celeste to Maddie was not an easy process. Her attorney sent her an email describing the difficulties.

"We are not changing your existing name to a brand new one," the message read. "You are re-assuming an old name, and it's bringing up complications."

It was an ordeal that lasted nearly two months. Meanwhile, time was running out for the Titus Ellis estate to be settled. Her legal fees were mounting with the many hours she was being billed for. She worried that she might never see the inheritance, but still be saddled with the debts.

Nightmares plagued her. In her dreams Maddie was a dainty fairy-like creature that floated on water, trying to escape from the evil witch Celeste. Many nights she woke up screaming, tried to calm down, but then came the thoughts about her web of problems. A good night's sleep had become hard to come by.

The insurance fraud investigation did not end, and, to make matters more serious, the state department of insurance got involved. During a phone conversation, the examiner in charge informed her about a photo that placed her at the insurance agency on the date of the application. They rejected her claims denying her involvement, and advised her that she was facing criminal charges.

She was told in stern terms, "We strongly suggest that you revise your response to our inquiry, in order to avoid Federal prosecution."

Celeste did not want to seek Mr. Fisher's assistance in this matter; in fact, she didn't want him to know anything about it. She depended on him in the matter of her father's estate, and knew better than shatter his opinion of her.

Two weeks later she was ecstatic when he informed her that she could begin calling herself Maddie Ellis.

"I didn't record an official change of name for you, so you will not have any proof, but you will not need any. I think it's better not to leave any kind of trail that can later be tracked. This is not a problem; it is perfectly legal to assume a new name without filing any applications. Since you have your original birth certificate, that's all you will need to get a new driver's license. Your previously assumed identity of Celeste Butler has been erased."

A week later she received a package. It was cardboard box labeled "Personal effects—Titus and David Ellis." As soon as the funds came, she decided, she would offer to settle with the state department of insurance.

Celeste had become Maddie in every sense. She took her birth certificate to the DMV, passed the driving test, and got a new driver's license. Steve's death certificate enabled her to have him removed from the title to the house. For the first time in months, she believed that her life would finally be under control. Still, she could not bring herself to open her late father's personal effects package.

She had eventually received Thomas' message that he was severing contact with her, which did not upset or disturb her. She considered the relationship to be another chapter from her past life that needed closing. The dread that lingered in her was the chance of a government audit emerging from her dealings with Brent, but there had been no such sign. Maddie listed her house for sale and started to search in the San Francisco Bay Area.

Maddie wrote to the department of insurance that she decided to stop fighting them and offered a monetary settlement. To her relief, a compromise was reached and she processed a wire transfer of $150,000. Having money helps fix almost anything, she told herself. But she thought about her last conversation with Thomas, when he asked if she had ever enjoyed her wealth. She decided it was time to go in that direction.

Her house was sold for less than she had advertised it for, but she was glad to have it out of her hands. She donated all the furniture to the American Red Cross. Other people complained about the devastating effect of the Tehachapi fire on real estate values, but the financially astute Maddie accepted this negative aftermath without a second thought. After the dishonesty and breach of trust that she had experienced, this was unimportant. She was ready to begin anew.

She fell in love with a new condominium apartment in San Francisco's Russian Hill neighborhood, with a view of the Pacific. She purchased the pricey unit for just under three million, for which she paid in full with proceeds from her estate. It was no place for a dog, she decided, so Lady Windsor stayed in Bakersfield as a gift to the buyers. In her new home she hired a decorator, bought new furniture, and finally resolved to open the package of Titus Ellis' personal effects.

An investment account was soon established in the name of Maddie Ellis with the Sanborn & Willis brokerage firm. She immediately withdrew the funds to pay her lawyer, and sent him a check with a note.

Her card read:

"Dear Mr. Fisher,

I thank you with all my heart for your hard work. I sold my house in Bakersfield, came to San Francisco, and bought a condominium in a high-rise building overlooking the ocean. I wouldn't have been able to do it without your help. I am very happy to live in this beautiful city. My next plan is to meet new people and find new friends.

Sincerely,

Maddie Ellis."

The Arrest

The FBI had not found a connection between Celeste Butler and Brent Bushnell. Her good fortune was that she successfully shielded her identity from him. He had been content to be working for a secretive firm that respected his skills and paid him well. Now Brent was unsure of what was coming. His assignment to block the Federal inquiry had not been fully completed, since other FBI players might have taken it over. But, without a word, his job with Agent M appeared to have abruptly ended. He had a hunch it was best to keep away from his mysterious employer.

Esmeralda, whom he assumed to be Harry's co-worker, had turned out to be off limits for him. He hatched a plan to follow her after work and confront her in a secluded area. Therefore, with no more communication from Agent M, he no longer considered it part of his former mission. He was in it for his own ego.

Brent's scheme came to an end when two uniformed men knocked on his door and informed him that he was under arrest for money laundering. They handcuffed him and read him his Miranda rights: "you have the right to remain silent…" He was too stunned to react or speak. It was only when he was led in to be questioned that he proclaimed they had the wrong person. After having babbled for half-an-hour, he finally remembered to ask to have a lawyer present.

The Special Agents who interrogated him had documents that followed some of his money trails. He contacted an attorney who had gotten him off some charge in the past, which helped put the questioning on hold to allow time for the two to meet and discuss the case. When the session at the FBI office resumed, Brent's lawyer claimed there was entrapment. He accused the Feds of secretly wiretapping his client, and pointed to the young FBI undercover operative who had attached a wire to his wallet.

The feds were not fazed.

"No listening devices were used with Mr. Bushnell. According to our data," one of the two answered, "the device was not a microphone, but a GPS transmitter, which was lawful, since your client was a known suspect. He was deemed dangerous enough to warrant surveillance. Mr. Bushnell had become a person of interest when he was observed watching the scene of a bombing and fleeing. We are aware that he has also been stalking a female FBI intern who was present at the scene of the explosion."

It did not take long for lawyer and client to understand that prison time was a likely outcome, and they asked for a chance to chat privately.

"My client is ready to make a deal," the attorney told the investigators a few minutes later without Brent in the room. "He can give you valuable information on other people who may be of interest to you."

"That depends on how useful his information turns out to be." The reply was not enthusiastic. The feds were not moved.

Brent came when his lawyer summoned him, and the session continued.

"Who did you work for, and who connected you to the banks or other institutions where you handled monetary transactions?"

On his attorney's advice, he conceded. He described the obscure "Agent M" who had sought him out and hired him to move money abroad. He also identified the properties he had acquired on his employer's behalf.

"How did you communicate with 'Agent M'"? he was asked.

Brent had saved a string of encrypted email messages on his phone. He typed the secure code that would grant him access to the trail of their covert conversations and waited. Nothing appeared on the screen—it was as if he had entered unrecognized characters. The confidential communication system he had been using with his employer was no longer active.

"I don't know what's happening," he frowned in frustration, "Our contact was entirely electronic. We had a coded, impenetrable email address that we used to communicate. I've never spoken with this person, so I don't know if it was a man or a woman, or where they were located. Damn... Now it looks like they decided to erase my existence." He entered the code again, with the same result. He realized he had been locked out and thrown under the bus.

His lawyer signaled him to stop talking.

"There are other individuals who may be linked to Mr. Bushnell's alleged activities," his counsel offered.

"Give us names, Mr. Bushnell," the investigator said tersely, but the lawyer stopped him.

"What does my client get in exchange for what he'll give you?"

"Again, it depends on what he gives us, and if we find it useful."

Brent, after getting a nod from his attorney, resumed.

"There is one person who might also have been working for Agent M. He emailed me recently, asking me to meet him, but I didn't show up. His name is Steve Butler."

"Look," the man said impatiently, "we know who Steve Butler is, so your client is not revealing anything new."

Brent stopped and felt the blood rush to his face. What the hell happened, he puzzled, nearly hysterically, while struggling to control his emotions. When he relaxed a bit, he tried to figure out how his mysterious boss had initially found him. He thought he might have the answer.

"My supervisor at my last job was a man named Thomas Snow. He was in charge of cyber security in the firm, and I doubt he was involved in anything illegal. But it's possible that he was the source who referred me to my new employer. He might know his or her identity."

He provided the name and location of the firm, and his interrogator jotted it down.

"We will advise you after we talk to Mr. Snow. Meanwhile, you will remain in custody. We will notify you through your counsel what charges will be filed against you."

Thomas Snow

A special FBI agent arrived at the headquarters of the brokerage firm and asked to see Thomas Snow. An executive assistant led him to a private corner office on the tenth floor, with a glass wall and a view of the distant mountains. On this clear day the landscape was breathtakingly sharp.

"Good afternoon, Mr. Snow, my name is Robert Hall. I am a Special Agent with the FBI."

Thomas felt his stomach stir and he rose from his chair. It had been a long time since his days of plundering clients' accounts. Confident that the visit had nothing to do with his past, he was poised and cordial.

"What can I do for you, Mr. Hall?"

Uninvited, Robert Hall sat down and looked around him.

"We are investigating a person by the name of Brent Bushnell. He mentioned that you had been his supervisor in the past. Do you remember him?"

Thomas quickly connected some dots, and decided to think carefully before saying too much.

"Yes, I remember Brent. He worked under me for over a year, was quite capable, but he left our firm, and said he took another position."

"Do you know where he went to work after leaving your company?"

"No, I don't. We did not stay in contact."

"He referred to the code name 'Agent M' as his employer. Do you have any idea who or what that code name stands for?"

Thomas guessed who the nameless employer was, but something told him to be careful.

"I am sorry, I'm afraid I can't help you. Again, Brent and I lost touch."

"Did you provide a job reference to Mr. Bushnell when he left? Did you mention his name to anyone who might have offered him a job?"

"No, I did not. Mr. Hall, as I said, The fellow resigned from our company and went on his way, and I never heard anything about his next place of work."

"He did mention your name, and said he thought you might have put in a good word for him to his future employer."

Thomas was visibly agitated, and he rested an arm on his desk while he leaned forward, looking directly at the man.

"I did not help Brent Bushnell find another job; as a matter of fact, he didn't even ask me for a reference letter. His departure was quite abrupt. Again, I haven't spoken to or heard from him since he resigned. If that's all, I have to get back to my work."

Special agent Robert Hall was a behavioral analyst, and he noticed the tension in the man, but thanked him and left. He could not detect if it was just the unease of having an FBI investigator in his office, or if he was holding back something.

Thomas sat at his desk as he watched the special agent make his way down the hall to the elevator. He tried to gauge the best way to caution Celeste that the Feds had Brent it their clutches and that she might be next in line. He decided to email her from the corporate server rather than his own.

"Hi," the message read. "I discovered that the FBI is investigating a young man who worked for someone with the code name of Agent M. I suggest you delete any communication you may have had with him or Agent M. When questioned, I stated that I have no details on said young man's recent employer. For everyone's protection, do not contact me in any manner. I am hereby erasing and terminating our acquaintance."

It was terse, possibly cruel, but Thomas had previously determined that his contact with Celeste Butler had to end. Sometimes, he had learned, the right choices are the hardest to make. A few seconds later he saw a notification that his email message was undeliverable. The addressee could not be found.

The Financial Crimes Unit

The Financial Crimes Unit was buzzing with activity and excitement. A covert electronic surveillance was established between Brent Bushnell and Steve Butler. Albeit it thus far consisted of only two messages, it was a promising lead in the attempt to wrap up Harry's money laundering probe. Among Brent Bushnell's phone contacts, several suspicious names were identified, and a field agent was tasked with contacting each one, impersonating Brent.

Most of the names on the list were gradually eliminated, but then they came across someone named Kyle. They discovered a text from this person that asked Brent if he needed help with anything else. The message had come in after Brent's arrest, so he hadn't yet had the chance to delete it.

The FBI decided to stage a sting operation.

"Hey, I do have a favor to ask you. When can we meet?" the message was initiated from Brent's phone by the task force, and Kyle's reply appeared instantly.

"No problem. Same place tonight?"

"I think it's safer to pick a different spot. How about seven at Peet's Coffee in the Kaufman Plaza?"

"Whatever you say. See you there," the reply came immediately.

At seven that evening a male and female FBI field agents sat separately in the coffee shop, waiting for Kyle. As the minutes ticked past seven, it seemed that their target might have smelled danger and the operation was off. But then they noticed a lanky man standing outside and peering inside.

The female operative casually stepped outside and started chatting with him.

"Nice evening, huh?" she asked.

"Yeah," he said blandly. "I guess my friend's a no-show."

"Oh, that's too bad," the woman said with empathy. "By the way, my name is Megan."

"Kyle," he said and held out his hand. "Nice to meet you."

"I'm by myself too. Want to go in for some coffee?"

They went inside and ordered drinks. She chose a tall table in the corner.

"I am a hair and makeup stylist," she said, smiling. "What kind of work do you do?"

"I work for an electrician, but I'm pretty much a jack of all trades." Kyle's phone beeped with a voice text from Brent.

"Hey, sorry I couldn't make it," the message said. "Something came up, but I want you to handle another special job for me. I'll call you tomorrow."

"I couldn't help hearing," the undercover Megan said. "What special jobs do you do? I may be able to use your expertise sometime.

He began boasting about the electronic hacking and spying he was able to do using smart phone technology. She listened, hoping her partner was hearing every word through his earpiece.

"I even put a wire in the FBI office a while ago. Man, we could hear everything they were saying in there."

"Megan" waited a few more minutes before she got up from the table.

"Hey, it was super nice to meet you. Call me some time," she said and jotted down a number on a napkin before leaving.

Her male partner bumped into Kyle and planted a tracker in his pocket. While they were inside, another agent attached a GPS device to the side of his motorcycle seat. Facial recognition confirmed his name was Kyle Gordon Parker, and that there were prior arrests on his criminal record.

Esmeralda heard that Brent was under arrest, which gave her immense relief. Knowing that he had been squashed and defeated, she could stop looking over her shoulder. As soon as she left for her lunch break she called Lexi to give her the news.

"That is the best news I've heard in a long time!" her friend shouted over the phone.

"You played an important part in getting him. You were fantastic!" Esmeralda said.

"By the way, I am applying for an internship with the FBI," Lexi said. "I think I was made for this kind of job."

"I agree! I think you are right. Wouldn't it be incredible if we became co-workers?"

Kyle

It was not difficult to connect Kyle to the explosion. The forensic technicians had determined that the bomb had been activated remotely, most likely from a mobile device. Now that they had the lanky fellow in their sights, it took only two days to establish that he had been the perpetrator. Under questioning, he promptly pointed a finger at Brent and identified him as the person who had hired him for the job.

Brent, under additional questioning, tried to convince his interrogators that he had acted under orders from someone else, whom he was unable to identify.

"I think he's telling the truth that he was engaging in money laundering on behalf of another individual," The lead investigator told his team. "He is definitely not smart enough to have done it solo. I want to bring in Steve Butler and have another crack at him. Any other thoughts?"

Everybody nodded in agreement. Steve was ordered to appear at the Los Angeles office. The minute that he sat down, he again asserted that Celeste Butler was the mastermind of the operation. However, by that time any trail of her had ceased to exist. Even her email address came back as invalid. There was a trail indicating that his assets had been transferred to him from somewhere, but the source was a black hole. His fortune came from an entity that couldn't be tracked.

"Every one of our suspects is trying to implicate somebody else," another investigator said. "My gut feeling is that there was a ring leader who managed to erase his or her tracks. The good news is that we have the people who did the dirty work. We can begin preparing the money laundering charges, so we hand Brent and Kyle over to the terrorism unit."

John Pope discussed the case against the alleged bombers with his team. The two were taken to separate interview rooms and were asked similar questions. Pope himself went to grill Brent.

"So, Brent Bushnell," he began. "You seem to be a regular guy with a beautiful home and a good life. What was your connection to the explosion at the café?"

"I didn't have any connection to the explosion. I had nothing to do with it," he stated indignantly. He sat with a stiff back and his face was blank. An arrogant SOB, Pope thought to himself. He placed a grainy photograph on the table, facing the suspect.

"Take a look at this picture of you in the exact neighborhood where this incident happened. What were you doing there?"

Brent's expression changed slightly. He was getting edgy and he shifted in his chair.

"I was interested in the girl with the dark hair, so I stopped to see if I could meet her. I was just a bystander, and was completely shocked when I saw what happened. I figured it was the wrong time to chase her, so I took off."

"I wonder why you didn't rush over to help," Pope asked.

"I panicked, and didn't have time to react. I was scared that somebody might think I had something to do with it."

"Why would anybody think you had anything to do with it? You were, as you say, just a bystander."

"Like I said," Brent shrugged, shaking his head slightly, "I wasn't thinking right."

"I'll be right back," the interrogator said and left. It was a ruse; he waited five minutes before returning.

"Do you know Kyle Parker?" he sat back down and looked directly across the table.

"No," he said, his forehead wrinkling, seemingly deep in thought.

"The problem is that Kyle Parker says he knows you. In fact, he is talking to another one of our guys as we speak. He's telling us that you are the mastermind in this crime. You could be charged with murder for hire."

The color left his face. "I want to talk to my lawyer before I answer any more questions," he said, and his posture stiffened again.

Brent was allowed to call the attorney who had helped him with his previous FBI inquiry, when he was initially arrested. There was no answer, so he left an urgent message.

Kyle was being grilled in another office. Two agents came in, a man and the woman who had called herself Megan the hair stylist. He gaped at her and his hands began shaking.

"Hello Kyle," the man said. "My partner here, whom you met recently, tells me that you are quite the genius with cell phone tricks. In fact, we understand that you even bugged an FBI office. That's impressive, and if it turns out to be true, you will be charged with domestic espionage."

Kyle's face whitened. His eyes scanned the entire room, and made no eye contact with either of the two.

"Would you like some water?" the woman asked after a brief silence.

"Yes, bitch," he replied, "whatever your name is, you go get me some water."

She glanced at her partner, who just raised his eyebrows, then went out the door.

"Are you going to be all right?" he asked his suspect, who was obviously trying to compose himself. There was no reply.

She returned with a water bottle and put it on the table; the young man opened and drained it.

"Okay. We want to ask you about the day of the explosion. Where were you at one PM on the day in question?"

"I refuse to talk without a lawyer present," he blurted, turning his gaze to the wall.

The interrogations of the two bombing suspects was halted, and the two were taken separately into custody.

Helena

As usual, Bill and Esmeralda were in the cafeteria when a message beeped on his phone. It was from his mother, telling him that Grandma Helena had fallen and was taken to the hospital.

"What is it?" Esmeralda asked.

"Grandma Helena is in the hospital. I guess she took a bad fall. I keep telling my parents that they can't let her live alone. She's too frail, and can't get around well. I think we'll have to get a caretaker for her."

"I don't think she would like that," she answered. "But as I heard people say, you've got to do what you've got to do. She may have no choice. I think we should visit her in the hospital after work."

Esmeralda was worried about the old lady, more so than she let on. Early in the evening, after work, they left for the hospital.

"I have a class at 7:00, Esmeralda said. "I don't want to skip it, but I may have to, depending on traffic and how your Grandma is doing."

On the way to the hospital, she heard a call from a private number on her phone, which gave her pause. She impulsively answered.

"Esme?" she recognized Judy's voice.

"Hi Judy," she replied, glad that she picked up the call.

"I have some good news... Are you ready?"

"I am always ready for good news. What is it?" Bill looked at her for a moment from behind the wheel.

"Brent and his accomplice are in FBI custody. They are being charged for Harry's and the other victims' murders, so they will be gone, off the streets for a long time."

She was speechless for a few seconds.

"Judy, your timing couldn't be better. Thank you so much for telling me now, and not waiting until tomorrow."

"Of course, Esme. I know how much this means to you."

She told Bill the news, and saw that he was glad to hear it, but clearly, his mind was occupied with his grandmother.

"We now have some good news for Grandma Helena," she said and rubbed his thigh.

"Let's hold off on telling her right away," he said. "We have to see how she's doing. Her mental state may be a little off, so we should be careful."

"Okay, but isn't this the best news? Having creepy Brent and his fellow bombing suspect put away, charged with murdering Harry?" Her whole face smiled.

"Wow, you have a powerful way of putting it," Bill chuckled. "Obviously I think it's great that they were caught. What I'd like to find out is if they specifically went after uncle Harry, or what the hell they were plotting."

Annie was in Grandma Helena's room when they arrived. Grandma Helena was lying in bed with her eyes closed.

"Hi guys," Annie said to them. "I arrived with her, but I need to go now, so I it's good that you came. Can you stay with her for a while?"

"Sure, Mom," Bill said. "You go ahead and do what you need. We'll be here and keep watch on her." Annie rushed out.

"She's asleep," a nurse told them, "and it's better that you don't wake her up. She was pretty rattled when she arrived, so the rest is good for her."

"What happened to her?" he asked.

"She fell and broke a couple of bones in her leg. It's good that her hip is not broken."

"How was her state of mind?" Esmeralda chimed in.

"She was agitated and unhappy that she was taken to the hospital. It seems she likes her independence. It's very hard for some older people to accept that they need help."

"She is still mentally sharp, and much younger than her physical age," Esmeralda said, somewhat defiantly. "Sometimes, age is just a number."

They sat in her room, whispering, watching the clock, waiting for Helena to wake up. It was getting late; Esmeralda realized she would miss her class.

"I'll get us something to eat from the vending machines," Bill stood up. At that moment they heard a sound from the bed and rushed over. Grandma Helena opened her eyes and looked at them.

"Hi Grandma," her grandson said and took her hand. "How do you feel?"

"I feel fine, Billy," she said impatiently. "Am I still in the hospital?"

"Yes, you are. You have some broken bones, so they have to fix you up," he said. "But you look good. Esme, doesn't she look great?"

"Esmeralda, I didn't know you were here. Thank you for coming."

"Of course I came. Remember what you told me? We are both made of the same cloth, right? So I am here to help you stay strong."

Grandma Helena smiled weakly and took the young woman's hand. She looked at her and then at her grandson.

"You two look like you are in love," she said. "Am I right?"

"You may be right," Bill replied awkwardly, stealing a glance at Esmeralda. "We are trying to figure it out ourselves."

"Don't spend too much time figuring it out. If you love each other, then accept it and take the next steps. I know you are young, but life goes by quickly. You should grab every moment of happiness that comes." As if she had been holding her breath, Grandma Helena exhaled heavily and closed her eyes.

A long beep came from the monitor next to her, and then it was silent. Esmeralda ran out to call the nurse. Within a moment, three nurses and a physician surrounded the bed and tried to revive Helena. One placed an oxygen mask on her face while another pumped her chest. Nothing happened.

"She is gone," one of the nurses said after a few minutes. "I am so sorry."

"Time of death is 6:40 PM," the doctor stated, glanced at the young couple, and walked out.

Bill stepped out of the room to call his father, and then sat quietly with Esmeralda. He was crying quietly, and she grasped his hand, determined to control her own feelings so she could be the strong one.

The Sins of Omission

The greatest peace and serenity that Maddie felt came from knowing that her prior life had been obliterated. Occasionally, at night, she still had visions about sudden capture or arrest, but in her waking hours she willed herself to put it out of her mind.

She placed the package of her father and brother's personal items on her kitchen table. She had at last started speculating on what the box might contain. It felt strange, like breaking into a stranger's domain, and she hesitantly sliced it open with a utility knife. It was early in the morning, with no plans for the day.

She took out each item and lay it down carefully. There were two photo albums, a collection of old pennies, a U.S. army visor cap, a clear plastic bag filled with random souvenirs, a short newspaper clip protected in a plastic cover, and a thick manila envelope. She jokingly put a sticker on each album, labeled the thinner one "Ellis One," and the other "Ellis Two." Barely noticeable, there was a small, worn brown leather pouch with a drawstring that was pulled shut. After the entire contents were arranged on the table, she tossed the empty box aside.

The newspaper clipping described the accident that ended her father's life. It was the sequence of events she already knew: he had driven his pickup truck, crashed into an oil tanker, and died in a blaze that engulfed his vehicle. There was a reference that it was difficult to positively identify the passenger, and that he was assumed to have been his son David. She read it without emotion and set it aside.

When she began to leaf through volume "Ellis One," she thought her heart would stop. There she was, a little girl of three or four, with David making a funny face behind her. She wondered if there was an image of her birth mother, but there were none, not even her parents' wedding photo. She saw a picture of her grandfather Jack, who had died before she was born, next to her Grandmother Deborah, whom she vaguely remembered from some birthday party. The rest of the volume included pictures of her father with David on a canoe and several with an assortment of adoring women.

In spite of the memories captured in Titus' pictures, Maddie still found it hard to conjure up any feelings. She pictured her father's right eyebrow that went upward every time he had yelled at her, and now it no longer seemed comical, but sad. She still felt nothing. It was as if she was viewing a stranger's photos, so she set the album aside and flipped open "Ellis Two."

She stopped and stared at another photo of her grandfather, a young man in full uniform, standing proudly with his platoon. Next to it was a small dog-eared black and white portrait of her grandmother in her youth. A note under the image said, *"Thinking about my Deborah kept me safe and brought me home."* There was a page with award certificates, naming Deborah Ellis as teacher of the year.

The second volume included reprints of newspaper stories about the war, and a picture of General Dwight Eisenhower visiting a concentration camp. A caption below elaborated: *"This was Ohrdruf concentration camp, where our whole platoon came to liberate the prisoners."*

Maddie opened the manila envelope, which held Titus' and David's birth certificates, as well as a single marriage certificate. She was saddened to see a Decree of Divorce between Titus and Sally Ellis. Included among the contents was also a collection of about a dozen old photos. They had definitely come from an earlier generation, and she puzzled over whose they were. Then, between two photographs was an unopened envelope, with the name Titus in front. The letter inside was written in perfect penmanship. Had her father not been aware of it? He had certainly not read it.

"Dear Titus,

We, your parents, are writing to you what we should have told you many years ago, when you were a child. We provided you with all the food, clothing, and education that you needed. Our life was always ordinary and quiet, with the basics, without music, culture, or special traditions. An ordinary tree at Christmas with simple presents without fluff. We never questioned it, because after the tragedies of the war it seemed that having a simple life was a privilege.

When we met and fell in love, your mother didn't tell your father about her true heritage. Her parents were Jews who immigrated from Russia around the time of the Bolshevik revolution. Her father, your maternal grandfather, was named Mikahil Kazan. His father, Leon Kazan, had been a cantor in the great synagogue in the city of Minsk. Their daughter, your mother Deborah, was named after his mother Devora. Your mother never believed in religion, since she had been raised and indoctrinated by her own socialist mother.

After her parents divorced, your grandmother stopped observing any of the Jewish traditions, and convinced Deborah to forget about her heritage. We both now deeply regret that our home was so lacking in any meaningful holidays, traditions, or values. In this important part of life we failed. We now realize that we denied you a connection to your roots, and for that we hope you will forgive us. I, your father, have always loved your mother unconditionally, but wish I would have known about her ancestry before coming so close to the end of my life.

Your loving parents,
Jack and Deborah Ellis. "

Maddie rose from the table and absentmindedly paced around the kitchen when a sudden surge of nausea forced her to race to the bathroom to vomit. When she came out, she slowly sat down by the floor-to-ceiling window, staring at the gray-blue ocean. How was she going to assimilate this flood of family history? Until now, she had never felt that she was anyone's real daughter or granddaughter. Roots had been completely absent from her life. All at once, a new, odd, and unfamiliar sense of self was emerging.

She held the army cap in both hands, the one she recognized from the photograph, and gradually, a wave of emotion overtook her. A flood of tears came, with deep sorrow about everything: the thoughts of missed relationships, untold stories, and her grandfather Jack's sacrifice. What am I, compared to him, she lamented. All the things that I thought were so important are worthless. Jack had true love, he had a mission, and he was selfless. Everything I've done has always been only for myself...

I am a descendant of extraordinary people, she concluded, with Titus, her father, an anomaly, an unfortunate offspring. Still, as much as she disliked her father's memory, she had become conscious of the benefits she had gained from him: his own parents, Jack and Deborah, and his substantial estate. Sadly, her life journey had robbed her of knowing her grandparents, even her own mother. She, like Titus, had a hollow childhood, with no clear direction or moral compass. She made a cup of tea and sat for a while, waiting for her head to clear.

The souvenirs bag did not interest her, and next, she picked up the brown leather pouch. The string that was pulled to close it was brittle with age, and she pulled it cautiously to keep it from cracking. Inside she saw two small notes, yellowed with age. She unfolded one and tried to read one of them.

"Wir sind *zwei Familien, Berger und Berger,*
aus Weimar. Unsere Tochter ist Helena Berger"
"Bitte nehmen Sie diese Tasche zu: American
Jewish Joint Distribution Committee in America."

Maddie surmised that the language was German, but could not understand any of it except the English name at the bottom. She suspected that the original content of the bag was missing, and wondered what it might have been. She carefully opened the pouch, removed the notes, then absentmindedly lay it on the table and pressed it flat. It felt as if a small pebble or a piece of gravel might have broken loose from the inside edge of the pouch. She reached in and picked up the tiny object between her thumb and forefinger. To her amazement, it was not a pebble or a chunk of hardened soil, but a sparkling stone. Was it a real diamond, or a piece that had broken off some costume jewelry?

Impulsively, she decided to stop at a jewelry store to find out. Getting some fresh air, she considered, was also a welcome idea.

She placed the stone in a tiny ring case, put on a jacket, rode the elevator downstairs and went outside to the street. With the small case in her handbag, she walked a few blocks to a boutique shopping center, and entered the posh jewelry shop she had seen before.

"I just inherited this stone," Maddie told the elegant woman at the counter. "The thing is, I am not sure if it's a real diamond. Do you mind taking a quick look?"

The woman picked up the stone with a tweezer-like tool and placed it on a black surface. She then took a few minutes, examined it with a monocle, then looked at Maddie.

"It is most definitely a genuine diamond, and a very high-quality one," she said. "For a fee, we can appraise it for you so you will learn the carat size, the other attributes, as well as its accurate value. Congratulations on your inheritance."

The jeweler placed the diamond back in the ring case. "Thank you so much," Maddie told her after returning it safely to her handbag. "I have to think about what to do with it."

"My name is Francine, and I'll be glad to help you when you are ready," the woman told her with a warm smile.

Maddie left the shop and strolled slowly back home. She was completely baffled about all she had discovered. Did her father intentionally keep this single precious stone as part of his estate for a reason? Did he even realize it was there, or was it overlooked and left in the old pouch accidentally? The notes, written in a foreign language, were also a mystery.

Another Goodbye

"I didn't get to tell Grandma Helena that Harry's murderers were caught," Esmeralda wailed. "It would have given her some peace. There were so many open holes in her life, and this one was finally closing. But she never found out."

"Oh, Esme," Bill comforted her again. "Think about it; she lived a long, good life, even with all the holes and the tragedies. She was determined and relentless, and always knew how to move forward. She was happy to see us in the hospital just before..." He stopped.

They were on their way to the cemetery the day after Grandma Helena had left the world.

Esmeralda wore a black skirt and tights. It was a much smaller funeral than Harry's, since it was mainly attended by immediate family members and a few other relatives. She counted about twenty-five people.

One of the few speakers said, "They say that when a person passes away, it often means that he or she was finished with what they were meant to do here on earth. Helena was a survivor, a real source of strength. She was an orphan who escaped death, with the courage to change her destiny, have a successful career, and build a new life. She did it all. She was truly an inspiration."

"Her social services agency helped unfortunate people get on their feet," a woman added, "Helena mainly helped victimized women and children escape their abusers, and worked with Holocaust survivors. She received many awards over the years."

"She was the last survivor of her generation in our family," another person said.

"The world is always going forward," one of Bill's cousins observed. "The new replaces the old, and we have no choice but move with it. That's what Grandma Helena told me once."

Again, Esmeralda looked on while the mourners covered the coffin with dirt, but this time Albert handed her the shovel. She steeled herself not to break down, dug into the mound of soil to fill it, and then emptied it into the open grave.

Everyone was invited to Bill's parents' home where food was waiting on the dining room table, and the mood was more relaxed. Esmeralda recognized that the woman had lived until age 96, a long and full life.

"I was fortunate to have met this lady. I was very inspired by her," she told Bill.

"I can imagine how she would have hated to lose her independence," he replied.

After many hugs and tears Bill and Esmeralda said goodbye and left.

"Since we both took the day off, can we go to the beach, or a park, just to get some air?" she asked.

"Good idea; we can both use a break. There's a park close by with a small stream, and it's a nice place to go for a walk. My parents took us there a lot when we were little."

"You should know," Bill added later, "that our tradition requires us to sit 'shiva', which means 'seven.' We must take seven days to mourn the dead, and welcome visitors who come to comfort us. Friends and relatives are expected to bring food, so that the family doesn't have to bother with their own needs during the seven days."

"So, are you supposed to stay at home with your parents to properly mourn?" Esmeralda questioned. "You can't come to work?"

"The main requirement falls on my dad. I plan to be with my parents tomorrow, but afterwards I'll go back to work and sit with them in the evenings."

"I think it's a wise custom," she said thoughtfully. "I imagine that taking time out to get comfort from friends helps people recover sooner."

Searching for Answers

Maddie took a can of Coke from the refrigerator and sat down to leaf through "album two," hoping to learn more about the grandparents she had never known. She looked at old black and white images of Jack and Deborah, her grandmother's classroom, Titus as a boy. There was a certificate of appreciation for Deborah Ellis, the teacher of the year.

A phone call interrupted her thoughts. She did not recognize the caller ID number, and let the call go to her voice mail. She again tried to compare her own life with that of her grandparents, trying to arrive at some answers. She was convinced that, compared to her, they had accomplished important things and helped the world become better.

Maddie was amazed at her own transformation. What had been so crucial to her over the past fifteen years now seemed to have existed in another world. There was good and bad, she reminded herself again. She had been swindled and abandoned by the few people whom she trusted. But the disappearance of her ill-gotten gains turned out to be a blessing, freeing her from the constant need to hide money.

All of a sudden good fortune was smiling, something she had never experienced. Was it real, or a fantasy to forget the past, receive a large bequest, so she can plan her next life? The next question she pondered was, even if I find an opportunity to do something important, who will be there to be proud of me?

The message light on her phone was blinking, and she pressed the button to listen.

"Hi Maddie," the big voice said. She knew the caller's name before he said it. "This is Sebastian Fisher, your lawyer. Congratulations on your beautiful new home. I hope you've had time to settle down, and I want to be the first one to welcome you to the City. I'd like to invite you to dinner sometime. If you agree, would you please call me back at this mobile number to set a date."

She put the phone down and noticed that she had been holding her breath while listening. She slowly exhaled, thinking about the call. Was she dreaming? Why would Mr. Fisher, the successful lawyer, offer to buy her dinner, after all that he had learned about her? She walked around her apartment, looked outside at the clearing fog, and replayed the message. It was definitely not a dream.

New things were happening in her life, and she decided to try to digest and embrace them, one at a time. The albums with her grandparents' letter, along with the old pouch, went into a drawer in her den.

On a spur of the moment she grabbed her handbag and opened the door, but stopped when she remembered the tiny ring case in her bag. She took it out, stashed it next to the leather satchel in the drawer, and entered the elevator. Downstairs she backed her car from the garage, and pressed the remote to lower the door. She drove back to the elegant shopping area where she had been that morning.

Maddie went into a small café, ordered a sandwich and a coffee, when a woman stopped at her table. She recognized her from the jewelry store.

"Hi," she awkwardly greeted the fashionable sales lady. "Francine, right?"

"Yes, you remember! I am on a late lunch break. May I join you?"

"Absolutely!" She was thankful for the distraction. "Have a seat. My name is Maddie."

"That was a beautiful stone you brought to our store today. I was amazed by the size and quality. If you don't mind me asking, where did it come from?"

Maddie answered, "Believe it or not, I don't know exactly where it's from. I recently received a package that was part of my father's estate. It was in a small bag, which I hope to learn more about—like who it had belonged to, etc."

"Well, I hope you figure out this mystery. It sounds like a fairy tale. Are you new to the area?"

"Yes, I moved to San Francisco only two months ago. Still familiarizing myself with the neighborhood."

"Me too," Francine said. "My company transferred me here from Chicago. I am one of the master jewelers, and they needed me to replace a gentleman who left."

They ate quietly, and Maddie asked, "which do you think is the best clothing store in this center?"

"Siana's is supposed to be excellent. They are expensive, but they have great outfits. The staff will help you make good choices."

"Well, Maddie," the woman said and took her purse. "I must go back to work. It was very nice to bump into you. I hope to see you again."

There was a new spring in Maddie's step when she left to find Siana's. All at once, there were pleasant, friendly people who wanted to get to know her. She decided to wait to call back Mr. Fisher until evening, so as not to appear too eager.

It didn't take her long to pick out several slacks, sweaters, and a black dress, along with a red silk wrap. She paid close to $4,000 that she enjoyed spending, pleased with her new wardrobe. Many pieces of her old clothing needed to be donated or otherwise discarded. She arrived at home with her shopping bags, went into the large walk-in closet, then started removing hangers and throwing blouses, skirts, and slacks on the bed.

"Hi, Mr. Fisher," she said cheerfully when he picked up the call. "Wow, thank you so much for your invitation!"

"Maddie," he stopped her. "if we're going to be friends, please call me Sebastian, okay?"

"Okay, Sebastian," she said, feeling strange using his first name.

"There is a very nice French restaurant downtown, and I have a feeling you'll like it. How is Thursday around seven?" He was not the type to waste time, it seemed.

"That sounds great."

"I will wait in front of your complex at seven."

"See you then," she said and hung up.

Maddie had never gone to a high school prom, but she suddenly felt like a teenager who had to decide on a prom dress. She raced back to her closet to choose the proper outfit for Thursday evening.

Solving the Case

Kyle had been charged with murder for being the triggerman in the bombing incident and Brent with murder for hire, among other complaints. The agents in the third-floor office were in process of completing the case file. At that point, the two culprits were referred to the Financial Crimes unit downstairs. Two Special Agents were assigned to meet separately with each of them.

Kyle's examiner questioned him about the instructions he had received from Brent for their heinous operation.

"Where is your lawyer?" he asked.

"I don't want my lawyer. Let's just get this over with."

"Okay, what did Brent tell you about the target?" he asked.

"He told me that a man named Harry needed to be stopped because of an investigation he was working on. He wanted to make it impossible for the guy to finish looking into whatever it was."

"What kind of investigation did he want to stop?"

"I have no idea," Kyle said. "He wanted me to disrupt, or sabotage the operation the guy was working on. That's all I know."

"What did he order you to do?"

"He left it to me to figure it out," Kyle started and stopped briefly before speaking again. "I was positive he wanted me to take the guy out. That's why he offered to pay me $10,000. Nobody pays that kind of money just to block an investigation."

"Did he pay you?" the investigator continued.

"You bet! I got paid half before, and the rest after the job was done. I guess Brent is a man of his word."

The two investigators who watched through the one-way glass looked at each other. "Can you believe what an idiot this guy is?" one asked. "Completely clueless about how much trouble he's in."

The interview in the other office proceeded differently; Brent's attorney was present, and tried to get his client to stop talking.

"So, Brent," the interview was on. "We understand that you hired Kyle Parker to murder a senior FBI agent. What we want to know is why."

"I never told him to kill anybody," Brent blurted before his lawyer told him to stop.

"My client did not instruct anybody to commit murder," the attorney said.

"Then what did you direct Mr. Parker to do?"

"I just told him that I need to have an FBI probe stopped, and I found out that this special agent named Harry was in charge of it. Kyle is an expert in electronic disruption, so I thought he was going to insert a virus in the guy's laptop, or something like that."

"So, here is the million-dollar question," the interrogator said, and leaned forward. "What was in the probe that made it so important for you to disrupt? In other words, why did you want to stop it?"

The lawyer jumped up from his chair. "Don't answer that!"

Brent glanced sideways at his counsel before continuing. "Like I told you guys before, I was working for somebody who went by 'Agent M,' and that person handed me the assignment to torpedo it."

"If you had to guess, why was it was so important to Agent M in this inquiry that he or she wanted it to be blocked?"

"I wasn't told, but I'm pretty sure it had to do with money they were hiding. Illegal stuff."

"You mean to tell me that your employer was involved in money laundering?"

"Sir, I'm going to tell you again, that they never gave me any details about anything. I was just a highly paid gofer."

The FBI concluded that Harry had indeed been the intended victim of the explosion, apparently targeted as a result of his work. Clearly, Brent was unable to identify, or point to the specific investigation he had been assigned to obstruct. They went back to trying to weave together the three threads that emerged: Brent Bushnell, Steve Butler, and Thomas Snow. There had to have been some connection among the three, and they decided to talk to Steve and Thomas again.

Dinner

Sebastian Fisher waited downstairs for Maddie, who finally emerged from the elevator. She wore her new black dress and high heels. Her red shawl was around her shoulders. It had taken her over an hour to perfect her makeup, and she noticed the way he looked at her.

"Good evening, Maddie," he said. "You look stunning."

"Good evening, and thank you," she answered, blushing slightly.

He went over to the cab that was waiting at the curb, opened the back door for her, then went around and sat next to her. The driver had obviously been told where to take them, so he pulled out into the street and drove a short distance. Maddie saw an ornate awning with a sign "Crème de la Crème." The cabbie opened her door, and Fisher took her arm and escorted her inside.

Maddie had never dined in a five-star venue that even remotely resembled this place.

After a polite greeting, a host seated them at a table by a window, with a cream tablecloth, a rose color candle in a venetian style candleholder, and wine glasses. She wanted to appear poised and not too overwhelmed, so she continued to smile until they sat down.

Sebastian Fisher took a minute to peruse the wine menu. Apparently, he knew wines.

"I suggest a bottle of this Chablis," he said, pointing to a name on the list. "Do you have a preference?"

"No," she replied. "It sounds excellent." Maddie at last allowed herself to savor the experience, and began to relax.

A sommelier came, and after introducing himself, poured a small amount of the wine in Sebastian's glass. He nodded his approval, and both of their glasses were filled. After a few minutes of pleasantries, their aperitifs were brought to their table.

"This is delicious," she said, as both started eating the appetizers. "Thank you for inviting me here."

"You are most welcome," he said, taking another bite. "You know, Maddie, I'd like to hear more about your life. Can you tell me something about work, family, or your hobbies?"

What should I tell him, she searched her brain nervously.

"I always worked in financial services; mainly ventures in real estate and stocks."

"I gathered from what you told me that your net worth had shrunk before the inheritance. What happened? Did you make bad investments?"

"Not always," she responded thoughtfully. "I owned a few good-size assets, but my entire portfolio was stolen from me."

"What do you mean by 'stolen'? he asked with raised eyebrows.

"I had a couple of bad partners who figured out how to steal me blind—they accessed my passwords, forged my signature, then changed the ownership. It was pure fraud, but they covered their tracks so well that I can't go after them. They disappeared." He noticed a shadow that passed over her face.

"There may be a way that I can help you track them down," Sebastian said.

"Those holdings belonged to my past life, before I came back as Maddie Ellis. I am not interested in going there. I am in a good place right now."

They chose their entrees from the elegant, high-priced menu. The waiter bowed slightly and marched from their table.

After a bit of awkward silence Maddie came alive again.

"What about you? You are a successful, attractive man, and most likely unattached. Why is that?"

"Oh, I was attached before, but that didn't work well for me. My ex-wife cleaned me out, so I relate to your story."

"We all have baggage, I suppose," she said.

"I've been practicing law for a long time. My specialty has always been estate planning and management, so that's how I got your father's case. I must say it was fortunate that this estate was finally settled and closed. Unclaimed money eventually goes to the state, which nobody wants. I actually handled a few situations where I had to search for missing heirs, and found all of them except one. Some people actually disappear without a trace."

Like Celeste Butler, she thought to herself.

The conversation changed, and they talked about home values in the area.

"I think the Bay Area has the most beautiful real estate," Maddie said. "I feel fortunate that I discovered San Francisco, and it happened only because I came to see you about my father's bequest."

They left Crème de la Creme and waited for the cab to drive them back.

"I had a wonderful time," she told him when they arrived at her residence, "and the food was excellent. Thank you for a lovely evening."

"The pleasure was all mine, Maddie. I would like to see you again. Will it be all right for me to call you?"

"Of course. I'd like that."

Sebastian Fisher came around the car and opened her door. He kissed her on her cheek before going back into the taxi. Maddie was mesmerized by Sebastian's gentlemanlike demeanor, and stood outside for a few minutes before entering the foyer of the complex. She inhaled the cool air, reminding herself that she had been reborn into a different world.

New Wrinkles

The name Celeste Butler never stopped to occupy the mind of the FBI agent who questioned Steve for the second time.

"Mr. Butler," he pressed, "According to the internet, you are deceased. You are presumed to have died in the Tehachapi fire. How can you explain it?"

"It has to be a different person with the same name they are referring to," he answered with confidence. "As you can see, I am alive and well."

"There are two other individuals by the same name as yours in the area of the wildfire. One is in his seventies, and the other is a landscape architect, both alive and well. The only person matching your name and birth date is you. Did you fake your own death?"

Steve's face paled, and he felt dizzy. He looked at the wall in front of him, breathing deeply.

"I wanted to get away from my wife, so I disappeared. If they presumed me dead, that was not my doing."

"Where is Mrs. Butler now?"

"She may still be in Bakersfield, where we lived. I don't know if the house still stands, but here's the address." He wrote it on a sheet of paper and slid it across the table.

The last thing Steve was asked to provide was his former wife's birth date, which he added at the bottom of the page. He claimed he did not remember her Social Security number.

"Celeste was a very shrewd woman, and used more than one SSN," he said.

"Do you have any pictures of your wife, or of the two of you together?"

"I had to get a new phone after my older one was destroyed in the fire, so I don't have any photos left."

Those details proved to be a potential turning point in the money laundering probe. A title search of the Butlers' home indicated that it had been purchased by Celeste and Steve Butler, then recently sold by Maddie Ellis. How the title had been transferred to Ms. Ellis was not clear, but the FBI now suspected that Celeste did indeed exist.

There were no other public records that matched her name and birthdate, either before the home was bought or after it had been sold. In short order, this new lead turned out to be cold.

There was a reason for the FBI challenge in finding any trace of Celeste Butler's existence. The way that Sebastian had processed Celeste's name change, along with Steve's action of erasing all paper trails to her prior ownership of his assets, had wiped out every fragment of Celeste Butler's financial activities.

Brent Bushnell and Kyle Parker were separately arraigned and placed in a detention center under FBI custody. The news spread rapidly throughout the departments that investigated the bombing, including the plot behind it.

Summer came with a break from her classes. Esmeralda and Bill went to Yosemite National Park for a few days of hiking and relaxing. She could hardly believe the breathtaking landscape of the park. Half Dome looked like a giant against the pale blue sky, and she was mesmerized by the waterfalls.

"This place looks like a painting. It doesn't seem real, but I know it is, because you are here with me."

He smiled and said, "And you are also here with me."

"I think I'll have enough credits to graduate next June," she continued a few minutes later. "I am trying to decide which branch of the FBI I want to apply to work for. I always thought I wanted to work in human trafficking, but I am starting to rethink it. It could be that being a money laundering investigator would suit me better."

"Actually, the two are related. Traffickers sell people, as if they were cattle, and then they have to hide the money. Next, it's invested it in offshore banks, or they use it to buy real estate and life insurance policies."

"What do they do with the buildings and life insurance?" she asked.

"After they sell them, nobody knows the money came from the criminal activity, so it looks legitimate, or clean. As soon as somebody owns an asset it's possible for them to sell it. Isn't this the kind of stuff uncle Harry was working on?"

"I think so, but I was never allowed to have any knowledge about it. Remember, I am a very lowly intern," she smiled.

"Yes," Bill put his arm around her. "a brilliant and beautiful intern."

"I don't think they found the source of the financial link to the case," she said, ignoring his compliment. "They are still looking for leads."

"Some people are very good at covering their tracks," he said. "But don't worry, they will keep on digging until they catch the person or people involved."

They rented bicycles and rode through the valley, which was filled with families with children on summer vacation. Neither of them seemed bothered by the crowds. Both were content to spend time together, away from the city.

Maddie's Quest

As soon as Maddie came back from her date with Sebastian Fisher, she remembered something. She sat down on her sofa, reminiscing about how much she had enjoyed volunteering at the food bank during her teens. I should find a volunteering opportunity, she decided. She was not overly busy, and believed that doing good deeds might help erase some of her shady past.

She was eager to uncover the source of the diamond she discovered. Getting started was a challenge, and she continually turned it over in her head. She considered talking to Sebastian Fisher about it, but dismissed the idea. What would he know about old notes in German and a loose diamond in a battered leather pouch?

With her vivid memory of the horror of the wildfire, she decided to join an organization that worked with disaster victims. She knew she would understand their plight and be able to offer help and empathy. She attended an introductory session, in which instructors displayed footage of wildfires, floods, area-wide destruction, people fleeing, crying, and injured. I've been there, she thought, so I can do it.

Sebastian called her a few days after their first dinner, and they scheduled a second date for a Saturday morning, to go across the Golden Gate Bridge to Sausalito.

"Should I dress casual?" she asked him.

"Yes, definitely. Wear comfortable clothes, and bring a sweater in case it gets cold."

She dressed in her new designer jeans, a light sweater, and an old denim jacket that still looked acceptable with her signature red scarf. She reminded herself that she needed to buy a couple of new jackets.

Sebastian looked quite different, very handsome in jeans and a blue cable-knit sweater. He was driving a small black BMW.

"Good morning," she said as she slid into the front seat. "Nice car."

"Good morning to you too. It's not a new car, but it's still in great condition. I plan to trade it in at some point, but will wait a while. As I mentioned, I've been fleeced by my ex, so I pretty much had to start over."

"Wow," she said. "How could she take you for so much?"

"She had a very clever and tricky lawyer. They were sleeping together, and she provided him with records of all our assets, bank accounts, the works. She was supposed to get half of everything, including half of the value of my law firm. Then we took a loss when we had to sell our real estate. Her slime ball attorney saw to it that she got her half of the original, much higher value, and I was left with the measly leftovers."

"I am sorry..." Maddie said thoughtfully.

"No worries, I'm better off without her. The good thing is that I kept my other house—I fought like hell not to let her have it. But I am moving on, and my law practice is going well. Anyway, what's new with you?"

"I decided to join an organization that works with disaster victims. I always liked to volunteer, and I think that my experience from the wildfire will help me."

"That sounds nice," Sebastian said. "You strike me as a very kind person, Maddie, and that's one of the reasons I want to get to know you better."

"Thank you. I'm trying to be. It sounds like we both need to bring good people and positive energy into our lives."

Twenty minutes after they reached Sausalito, Sebastian spotted a parking space, and they eagerly left the car and walked along the main street. She pointed to him the hundreds of houseboats in the water, feeling the pure joy of being there.

"Let's have lunch in this trattoria," he pointed to a quaint structure. Then we can walk around more, or go into one of the galleries."

The menu in the eatery was typical Italian fare, and after some red wine they ordered Caesar salads and pasta.

"When we were talking in the car," he said, "I think you said something about trying to be a good person. What did you mean by that?"

It put her off guard. "Don't most people try to become better?" she asked.

"Of course... I may have misunderstood you. I thought you said that you were trying to change yourself in some way. But you're right; most of us want to become better people."

Something snapped inside her; she put down her fork and looked at him.

"I think I mentioned this to you when we first talked in your office. When I turned into Celeste Butler at sixteen, I became very self-absorbed, because I found myself all alone with nobody to rely on. I had to look for work and get an education on my own. But as hard as it was for me to survive, I was very pleased to prove to myself that I could make it. I was determined to become successful. My father was very harsh, undoubtedly abusive in today's terms. I remember that he cheated on his income tax returns, and was generally not likeable. I cut off all contact with him and my brother, but I guess the lesson I managed to learn from him was not the best... I had gathered that cheating the system might be a good way to get rich."

She was unstoppable. "I was working with a guy who knew how to maneuver around finance laws and divert funds from clients. Today, I realize how awful it was to engage in those activities. I had more money than I knew what to do with, and kept working to build up my fortune nonstop."

She saw that he, too, stopped eating and listened.

"When I returned to my house after the fire, I found out that I had been wiped out, totally cheated. I mentioned to you before that the only account I luckily found was one CD under Maddie Ellis. I still believe that the instant I logged on with my birth name and SSN, that old name popped up somewhere.

"That's why it took us so long to locate you," he said.

"Who is 'us?'" she asked.

"My assistant is the one who decided to search one more time, and that's when we located you at the last minute.

"Anyway, it seems that I was given a chance for a fresh start, but I don't know that I deserve it. Losing the dirty money, then receiving this bequest has changed me. Maddie Ellis was a decent person, even when she was just a girl. Now she is back as an adult who wants to make up for Celeste's wrongdoing. I can't believe I just told you all this..."

Her eyes teared, and Sebastian took her hand.

"I am glad you told me. Rest assured that this will stay between us."

They resumed eating, and she relaxed.

"I finally opened the box that had my father's personal items in it."

"Did you find anything interesting, or heart-wrenching? Any childhood memories?"

"I found my grandfather's picture album with fascinating photos. He fought in World War II, and was one of the soldiers who liberated a concentration camp, so I'm finding out that my Grandfather Jack was a hero. I was very touched to see how much he loved my grandmother. We were never told anything about our grandparents. Can you believe I've never seen my own mother? My father kicked her out when I was just a baby, and she disappeared.

"If you want to find your mother, I think I can help you," Sebastian said, clearly very engaged in her story. "What's her name?" She noticed a flicker of emotion that she couldn't read when he looked at her.

"Her name is Sally, but I don't know if she still goes by Ellis."

"On another note, if it's all right, I would very much enjoy looking at your grandfather's World War II pictures. I am a big history buff, so seeing first-hand narratives of the war will be of great interest and meaning to me."

"I'll be happy to show you the album," she said. "How about you and I sharing a small desert and getting out of here?" she suggested.

Maddie didn't mention anything to Sebastian about the leather bag with the yellowed notes and the diamond. She began to feel drawn to him, and took his arm when they strolled along the waterfront. The ocean sparkled in the sunshine, the air was crisp, and she felt blissfully lighter after having bared her soul.

Maddie liked that he was not trying to get her into bed with him. She could not foresee if their friendship would develop into romance, but she enjoyed his company. They parted with a long hug, leaving her in turmoil when she went upstairs. She believed he was kind and intelligent, and that like her, was searching for the next chapter in his life.

Hunting for Celeste

The stalled money laundering inquiry reached the desk of the Executive Assistant Director, or EAD, at the FBI. She summoned the senior special agents who had worked on the case to her office. She was a tall woman in her fifties with short blond hair and oversized glasses. The EAD was an impressive, authoritative woman, and she did not waste any time addressing her underlings.

"I want to know what the stumbling block is. What is holding you back from bringing this case to a conclusion?"

"We're coming up with a dead end on an individual who could be the key."

"And who is the individual?" she asked.

"Our mystery woman is Celeste Butler. One of our suspects, her former husband Steve

Butler, is trying to implicate her. Here's what we have: the two bought a home together, he was declared a fatality in the Tehachapi fire, while the house was later sold by a woman named Maddie Ellis. To add to the mystery, ex-husband Steve is alive and well and talking to us. Our analyst hasn't been able to find a shred of intel on Ms. Butler.

"I'll escalate this to our cyber unit. If anybody can track her down, they are the ones."

One of the cyber specialists looked at the EAD's notes summarizing her meeting with the senior agents, and thought he had an idea.

"What if Maddie Ellis and Celeste Butler are the same person?"

His first search was the California DMV, which showed an active driver's license for Maddie in San Francisco, and an expired one for Celeste with a Los Angeles address. Although each license had a different birth dates, the lapsed one proved that Celeste had indeed existed. The woman was certainly clever, but the analyst was not ready to abandon his quest. He had a strong hunch that the two names belonged to the same person. His next step was to search for her on a missing persons website, which proved worthless. Finding records of name changes was more complicated, but that's where the analyst decided to continue his hunt.

Combing through the California Department of Vital Statistics records did not produce any answers. It was known that people could start using a new name without registering it, and it appeared likely that this was what had happened. There was no record of death of either Maddie Ellis or Celeste Butler. Whoever this woman was, she was certainly among the living.

"We've been looking at the wrong name," he told his supervisor. "We have to look into Maddie Ellis, who I think is the former Celeste Butler. I am coming up empty on Celeste."

Maddie Ellis popped up as the harmless owner of a condominium in San Francisco. There was no trail of any illegal transactions. A sizeable estate had recently been willed to her from her deceased father, which did not raise any red flags.

"This woman managed to invent a new identity and erase any history of her former one," the cyber specialist said. "Financial Crimes may be right that Ms. Butler is actually a dead end. The frustrating part is that none of the other players in the case seem smart enough to continue the money laundering activities."

"I want you to look at the husband," the EAD emailed him back. "You are right, the interview transcripts tell me that Steve Butler is not savvy enough to have made his fortune on his own. I see that he stated that the assets came from Celeste. We have to do a deep dive. There must be clues somewhere."

Ironically, Steve and the feds were now facing the same challenge of finding any trace of Celeste. The professional hacker he had hired before the Tehachapi fire had erased all of Celeste's footprints from his assets. Had the accounts been registered in any U.S. institution, there might have been a trail of ownership. Since the funds had been invested in offshore banks, there was no reliable mechanism available to locate them.

The executive assistant director, however, was not ready to accept defeat. She reassigned the group who had been working on it to other investigations, and handpicked a new team of two senior cyber specialists. Those were a man and a woman who had cracked similar schemes, and were laser-focused exclusively on Steve Butler's trail.

Discovery

About one month after Helena had been put to rest, Bill and his cousins Michael and Violet were tasked with clearing the house and packing her belongings. All four of her grandchildren were the designated heirs to the property. It was a two-bedroom, two bath home that had been maintained in immaculate condition. There was no peeling paint or cracked tiles, and the plantation shutters on the windows looked new.

A local charity was scheduled to pick up most of her furniture. Violet went through her grandmother's closet and arranged the clothing in two heaps: one to be donated, and a smaller one to be looked at later. There might be one or two unique pieces that they would want to keep.

When she checked the dresser drawers, Violet noticed a small bundle, soft to the touch, wrapped in pink tissue paper. She called out to her brother and cousin.

"Hey, guys, can you come to the bedroom for a minute? I want you to see something."

The two entered the room and saw the wrapped bundle.

"What's in there?" Bill asked.

"I don't know," Violet answered, "but whatever it is, it might have been something special to Grandma Helena. I prefer that we look at it together."

She cautiously removed the tissue paper, and all of them looked silently at a little girl's yellow dress, a blue sweater, ballet slippers, and a beaded necklace.

Violet erupted. "Oh, my God!" those things must have belonged to our missing aunt Rebecca!"

Michael chimed in, "Grandma Helena apparently couldn't part with any of these. It kept her Rebecca's memory alive for her."

"What should we do with them?" Bill asked the two.

"She was your and our father's little sister," Violet said thoughtfully. "I think we should let your dad decide."

When Albert came over later and saw the child's garments, he sat down, eyes closed. He clutched the ballet shoes to his chest.

"Where did you go, my baby sister?" he asked nobody. Then he assembled all the items and re-wrapped them in the wrinkled tissue. "I'll keep these. You kids continue with the rest."

Bill was removing miscellaneous flyers, event tickets, including some from decades earlier, that the old woman had stuffed in a drawer. He dumped all of them in a large paper bag they planned to recycle, and pulled open the next drawer. Under a collection of owner's manuals for appliances and gadgets, there was a gray manila envelope. He opened it, expecting to find more worthless papers, but was dumbfounded to discover about ten photographs. Most were black and white, and one was in brown sepia tone.

He called Michael over, and they sat down on the sofa to peruse the pictures.

"I want to review everything by myself before making decisions," Michael said defiantly.

"Hey, there are no decisions being made here," Bill replied, "so relax. We are just arranging and organizing things." He hoped his cousin would keep his ego in check.

The brown photo was a professional portrait shot in a studio. It was a picture of a family of four, unsmiling, named and dated on the back: *3 Juni 1937, Peter, Hannah, Herbert, Helena.* Father and son wore suits and ties, mother and daughter in long dresses. Helena must have been fifteen or sixteen, only a year before the Berger clan was destroyed, when she had made her escape.

There was a picture of a smiling sailor with reddish blond hair, along with a few of Helena with unknown people, whose names were noted on the back. Violet guessed they might have been fellow passengers on the St. Louis. The next picture was of young smiling Helena holding a baby, and the last one was of a five-year-old girl with brown curls in a yellow dress holding a doll. "Rebecca" was written on the back.

"Why did she hide this family portrait here?" Bill asked. I wonder if my parents ever knew about it. They should have it."

"What about the rest of the photos? Did anybody except Grandma Helena know about them?" Michael asked. Bill guessed the identity of the young sailor, but kept it to himself. His grandmother's revelation that her former lover was Albert's biological father slowly began to sink in. That meant that his grandpa Villy was not his real grandfather; but then, nobody ever had a clue. Bill put it out of his mind.

"Maybe they were her private memories. We can figure out later what to do with them."

After his cousin left the house, Bill took the gray envelope with him. He knew Esmeralda would be thrilled to see the pictures, and he wanted to see her reaction to them.

When he was sitting with her in the cafeteria the following day, Bill told Esmeralda about the poignant moment when his father saw his little sister's belongings.

"It was hard for me not to break down. It was sad to see him so heartbroken."

"This is so horrible," she said. "Today when a child is missing, there are better ways to search for them. There are cameras everywhere, there is DNA evidence, and people get alerts on their cell phones. What is so hard is that they didn't even find a body, so nobody knows what happened to her."

"She may still be alive, for all we know. She would be in her seventies today."

"Make sure to check every cabinet and drawer in Grandma Helena's house. She might have kept other items that your family may want to keep."

"We'll continue next weekend," Bill replied. "We're trying to be mindful with her things, so we don't throw away anything important. You know, this is somehow bringing my cousins and me closer, which is nice. I never had a real bond with Violet, but now she and I are finally connecting."

"I would really like to meet your cousins sometime," Esmeralda said. "But, meanwhile, I am still privately celebrating. The bombing case is closed, and Brent isn't around to stalk me." She smiled, her green eyes brightening.

"You just can't get over it, can you?" Bill laughed. "You're right to think about the positive, but I'd better get back. I have to show up for a training meeting in five minutes."

"Bill, do you have any idea how scary it is that the very same person that I danced with, and who tried to stalk me, is Harry's murderer? That's why I can't get over it; I don't know if I ever will."

"I didn't think about how personally this guy got to you. I get it; it's actually pretty frightening. But you are tough, and I know you'll eventually get over it." He rose, touched her cheek, and walked out, and she followed a few minutes later and went back to her desk.

The following evening, when they were in a coffee shop, she pored over Helena's pictures, as if trying to find answers in the faces. For reasons unknown to him, Bill found himself restless and anxious, waiting impatiently while she examined the images.

"Did you notice that she wrote down each person's name on the back of every picture? I'll bet these are fellow passengers who sailed on the St. Louis with Grandma Helena. It would be an interesting project to try to look for some of these people or their descendants."

"I've got enough projects going on in at work, so thanks, but no thanks," he said tersely. "I'd rather try to find out how my aunt Rebecca disappeared. That may bring my dad some comfort. I think that being completely in the dark is harder than finding out that she had been murdered."

"We could ask the LAPD cold case department to see if they ever looked into it again. If she was kidnapped, she may still be alive somewhere. If she was killed, they would have found some remains. Poor little girl..."

Bill changed the subject. "My parents want to invite you to Thanksgiving dinner at their house. I want you to come."

"That's very sweet of your mom and dad. I only saw your mother once, so it will be nice to get to know her better. Tell them I'll be honored. Thanksgiving is my favorite holiday, because it's a time when we take a moment to appreciate the good things in our life."

"Okay," he got up. "I'd better go home. I think I need to go to bed early."

"Yes, I agree," she said with a smile. "Estás muy cansado…"

"What does that mean?" he asked, a bit perturbed.

"It means you're very tired. Good night, see you tomorrow." She rose from their table and pecked his cheek.

She called Lexi later that evening.

"I remember you once told me that you have a friend in the police department. Does he still work there?"

"I think so," her friend answered. "We haven't talked in a long time. Why do you ask?"

"It's about a cold case; a very old cold case, but maybe your friend can find out if they had ever re-opened it. It's about somebody related to Bill."

"I can ask, I suppose... Can you give me some details?"

Esmeralda briefly told her about Rebecca's disappearance when she was five, and how deeply it affected the family.

"Bill is right that knowing what happened to her will be better than never getting the truth, even if she is dead. At least there would be an answer."

Sebastian and Maddie

Maddie called Sebastian on his mobile phone.

"Hi, how are you?" she started.

"I am well, and even better now that you called."

Wow, she thought. "You mentioned that you wanted to see my grandfather's photo album, remember? Well, how about coming over for lunch on Sunday?"

She spent several hours looking up lunch menus and recipes, but finally decided to make it simple and ordered two salads and tacos. Gourmet cooking had never been of interest to her, and she was not ready to practice new recipes for a special guest like Sebastian.

He came with two bottles of wine, and greeted her with a kiss on the cheek. She liked his masculine good looks, his stylish blue shirt and leather jacket, which he tossed over to the couch. She especially enjoyed to see the way he looked at her. It seemed as if he was trying to get a glimpse of something deeper, perhaps her soul.

"Your apartment is unbelievable," Sebastian said as he looked out the floor to ceiling window.

"Thank you," she replied. "I love living here."

They sat down for lunch, drank the red wine, and finished all the food.

"It was excellent," he said. "When can you show me the album?"

Maddie carried the box of the personal items to the dining room and set it on the table. She left out her grandparents' letter to Titus, which she thought was a bit too personal. She was not yet ready to share that bittersweet, poignant, personal confession. After they sat down, she pulled out the smaller album and slid it over to him. He took a long time looking at each page.

"I've never seen original pictures of wartime Germany. I own a few from France and England, but these in front of us are more interesting. He pointed at a group photo of grinning American soldiers. "Notice at how spirited they were, against the destroyed homes you can see in the background. This must have been taken at the end of the war, soon after much of Germany was destroyed. Such a huge waste of human life..."

The newspaper clipping of Eisenhower in the Ohrdruf concentration camp gave him pause, and she noticed he frowned briefly.

"I've seen this picture before; it's actually very famous. We all read that the American generals visited the camps and made sure that the GI's saw what had happened there. But it's something else to know that your own grandfather was among them. That would have been a tough day for anyone."

Sebastian continued to scrutinize the picture collection, and finally closed the album when he reached the last page. She looked at him, then impulsively took out the old brown pouch and handed it to him.

"What's that?" he asked.

"Please open it carefully, because it's falling apart. Take a look at what's in it."

He gently pulled open the straps, opened the bag, and peered inside.

"Can I take these papers out?"

"Yes, I want you to see if you can help me figure out what they say."

He pulled the two notes out and spread them on the table.

"It's in German," he said. "My grandparents were German, and they started to teach me the language, but when the Nazis came to power, they stopped."

"Can you understand what's written on the notes?"

He slowly read the first note: "Two families, apparently related, since both were named Berger from Weimar. That's a town in Germany. There was a daughter named Helena Berger."

He examined the second slip for a minute or two, trying to interpret the words. "I think they wanted the bag to be brought to an American organization, named here in English. But there's nothing inside."

"I have a feeling that whatever was in it was stolen. But you'll be blown away when I show you what fell out of one of the stitches when I pressed on it. It got stuck inside." She brought the small case with the diamond and opened it.

"A diamond?" Sebastian picked up the stone and raised it to study it closely. "I suspect that this pouch had more diamonds in it, which were taken, or more precisely stolen, by someone. This last one was stuck, as you said, so we may have a silent witness."

"Who would have so many diamonds, and how did they get into my father's hands?" Maddie asked.

"I've done a lot of reading about World War II. There were accounts of Jewish families who exchanged all their possessions for precious gems or gold coins. Those things were worth a lot, and small enough so they could be hidden in their clothing while traveling or escaping. The Bergers must have handed this cache to someone they trusted just before they were shipped away. They wrote a request that someone should bring it to the Jewish Joint Distribution Committee in the United States. I assume they mentioned their daughter Helena because they thought she had escaped to America. That's my theory."

Maddie was without words for a minute, astonished by the sequence of events he described, and his intuition.

"What if this supposedly trustworthy person was my Grandpa Jack?" she asked.

"He was definitely there at the right time," Sebastian replied. "But what connection did someone from a wealthy, respected family have with an ordinary American soldier?"

"He might have been in the right place at the right time when they were desperate to find anybody who was definitely returning to the U.S."

"Or, by chance, he received the pouch from the person who had directly gotten it from the Bergers, for the reason that you mentioned—he was an American GI who was going home."

Their eyes met, and they clasped hands.

"I am very captivated by you, Maddie. It's hard for me not to think about you."

"I think a lot about you too," she said. "Sometimes you look at me a in certain way, and I wonder what it means."

"I admit, the second time you came to my office, I started to feel something, but I think it was mostly empathy. I was sad to hear about your tough childhood and the fact that you didn't have any family. I knew right away that you were very bright but also quite sad."

"Wow, Mr. Fisher" she smiled while still holding his hand. "You read me pretty well, but I don't want you to feel sorry for me."

"No worries there. I see you differently now—you seem very content and are finding ways to build your new life. I don't feel sorry for you at all. You are remarkable, beautiful, and I sense that there is something very special between us."

"You are not too bad yourself, coming so close to unraveling this mystery from seventy years ago. I feel lucky that I met you, and that you asked me out. We do have something special, and I wonder where it's going."

Sebastian reached over, put his arm around her and kissed her. They kissed again, then stood up and walked over to the sofa. He slowly removed her top, then her slacks, and gently made love to her. Where will it go from here, she asked herself, immersed in pure ecstasy.

Rays coming in from the mid-afternoon sun illuminated their naked bodies, and Maddie's gaze traveled over his hairy body. She barely suppressed a sudden desire to reach down to his crotch, and sat up. It had been a long time since she had experienced sexual pleasure, and she wanted more, but stopped herself.

"Let's have some coffee," she suggested, got up, dressed, and then went to the kitchen and prepared coffee. He followed her a minute later, and kissed her on the cheek.

"You know something," he said while sipping, "it won't hurt to contact the Jewish Joint Distribution Committee. They may be able to track down a relative, hopefully Helena."

"I wonder if she is still alive," she observed. "Helena would be in her nineties now."

"I think the JDC is a good place to start. They may not be able to help, but I can try.

I really should go," he said as he rose from the table. "I need to finish some paperwork for tomorrow morning."

Maddie took the two old notes, put them in her printer/copier, and made a one-page copy. She handed him the page.

They kissed again. It was hard for her to see him leave, and she clung to him for a long moment before he walked out.

Sebastian's Next Steps

Sebastian contacted the JDC, the Joint Distribution Committee that was mentioned in the old notes in Titus Ellis' pouch.

"Good morning, this is Theresa. How can I help you?" he heard after being transferred three times. Her tone was stern.

"Good morning, ma'am," he said. "I am inquiring about a family from Germany by the name of Berger. We know that most of them perished in the camps, but we hoped that you might have information on one female survivor, Helena Berger."

He provided all the details he had. After a few minutes' wait, Theresa said she found one person with that last name, but he had come from Lithuania. She suggested to Sebastian to try another resource. Before hanging up, she spelled out the other organization's name, website, and contact information.

Sebastian concluded that he had fulfilled his promise to contact the JDC, and disregarded the other institution the woman named Theresa had mentioned. He was embroiled in accusations of professional misconduct and a looming financial disaster. He saw in Maddie a vulnerable woman who had been in similar circumstances. Helping her emerge from her problems was a relatively easy process, which he had been happy to complete. He chose to keep his own challenges to himself, and decided to keep out of the Berger search.

When he and Maddie had coffee the next evening, Sebastian told her that the JDC route led him nowhere. Helena had apparently entered the United States on her own, with no involvement by any official agency.

"If it were not for that diamond I found, and possibly a loot that was stolen, I would just put it all to rest," she said. "But if it's true that Grandpa Jack actually had it in his possession, I want to look into it some more."

"Searching for public records on this matter is pretty much a dead end, Maddie," he said. "Another option may be to post something on social media."

"You seriously are a genius!" she exclaimed. "Why don't I go on Facebook and see if I get any views, responses, or whatever they are called?"

Maddie copied and pasted the note with the Berger names and posted it, along with Sebastian's translation to English. Above the image she added a caption:

"I am searching for Holocaust survivor Helena Berger or any of her blood relatives."

Within less than an hour after posting it, reactions came. One was anti-Semitic, but the rest were from people who offered sympathy, and some who encouraged her to keep searching. She shut down the computer and went for a walk. She entered a small coffee shop, ordered a latte at the counter, and sat down. To her surprise, she saw Francine from the jewelry store sitting at another table. Maddie waved to her, and the woman immediately got up from her table and sat down across from her.

After a minute or two of pleasantries, Francine's expression turned more serious.

"I wanted to talk to you, but had no idea how to reach you."

"What about?" Maddie asked.

"I did some thinking about the diamond you brought in. You may not be aware, but diamonds, like pure-bred horses, have provenance."

"What does that mean?"

"It means that when a stone like this is examined by expert gemologists, they can find out its origin. Basically, we can discover what part of the world the diamond came from, even down to the actual mine where it was extracted. We have a certified gemologist appraiser here in our location."

Maddie became suspicious. Was Francine trying to get her hands on the precious stone, keep it for the purported inspection, intending to swap it with another one?

"This is good to know," she said. "But at this time, we are just looking through our personal records to try to determine who owned it."

"I think what I'm suggesting may be useful to you in your search."

"Thank you, Francine," she said with a smile and looked at her watch. "Wow, I really have to run. It was nice to see you again." Before getting a response, Maddie rose from her chair and left.

She called Sebastian when she came back home to tell him about the encounter.

"You were right to be cautious. There are dishonest jewelers who would do exactly what you are suspecting. Besides, you don't need to find the exact origin. It's most logical that it came from Russia. There are no diamond mines in Europe."

"I'm going to get a valid, certified appraisal, just to find out the value."

"You should look for a reputable jeweler, but even then, you should insist on being present while they appraise it. Don't let this stone out of your sight."

Maddie promised herself to look for details about her grandfather's army service. She wanted to know the dates of his service, where he had been based, or any other clues that might help her learn his life story.

"I didn't know how much I was going to miss when I ran away from home," she told Sebastian later that evening.

"From what you told me, you didn't miss much. Your grandfather was already gone, and I suspect your dad was not one to tell old family stories."

"You are right, but I'm pretty sure my grandmother Deborah outlived Jack by many years. I lost out—I only remember seeing her once at David's birthday party."

"It was your dad's duty to bring the family together. Kids don't think about those things."

Fall is a beautiful time of year in San Francisco, and Maddie went outdoors as often as she could. The sky was clear most of the time, despite the chill in the air. She joined a gym and started attending meetings at the disaster relief organization. Otherwise, she typically dressed in jeans and a sweater, and drove to parts of the city she had not seen before.

As she walked through Pier 39 in Fisherman's Wharf. There was the clanging sound of a cable car that rolled by a few streets away that brought a smile to her face. She suddenly recalled the day she had taken the diamond to the jewelry store to determine its value. Francine had not been there, and Maddie remembered she was glad to speak to someone else, an older man. He took a look at her stone, and looked at her in some kind of awe.

"Ma'am, our certified gemologist is not available now, but will be back tomorrow morning. You may leave this diamond with us and come back later to obtain the appraisal, or you could come back in the morning."

She returned the following morning, and insisted on watching the diamond expert perform the appraisal. It was highly unusual, she was told, but they agreed. She paid the $100 fee and received the certificate. The diamond was slightly over 3.5 carats, flawless, and valued at $165,000.

As the thoughts of the diamond passed through her mind, while still at Fisherman's Wharf, she noticed a woman drag her crying child to a corner behind a cluster of shops. She appeared to be angry and rough with the little boy. Maddie hurried to a spot where she could observe the two. The mother was hitting the child's head with her hand, screaming at him in a language Maddie did not recognize. The boy cowered down, trying to protect his head with his small hands, but the woman continued.

Maddie approached the two and stood for a minute, ensuring that the mother knew she was there. The beating and verbal bashing continued, while the boy continued to sob.

She yelled. "You have to stop, do you understand? If you keep beating this poor kid, I'm calling the police!" She held up her phone. The woman glared at her, muttered something in her language, and dragged the boy away. Maddie snapped a few pictures and a short video of the two, just to have proof, in case she would be called as a witness. If only there had been somebody there to stop my father from beating me when I was little, she bitterly thought as she walked away.

She tried to put the scene out of her mind and bought a bowl of clam chowder with a sourdough roll, then sat on a bench to eat. The air was cold and her hair and scarf were blowing in the breeze. It was difficult for her to put the scene out of her mind. It brought back an old pain that she thought had long disappeared, and she sadly watched the fishing boats, taking in the smells of the salty air and the fried food. With her own bitter childhood memories, she pondered if there was any way to help or rescue abused children.

During her drive home, her thoughts went to Sebastian, the man who helped her change her life. She wasn't completely certain if their relationship would last, but wanted to try giving it all she could. He seemed almost too good to be real, she considered; he was intelligent, kind hearted, sensitive, definitely handsome. Still, she was unable to penetrate that exterior, to truly get to know him. She pondered if Sebastian, like her, was a needy human being searching for connection, or if there might be a hidden, more sinister side to him.

Messaging

Lexi called Esmeralda after coming home from her class.

"Hey, call me. I have some news!"

"What is it?" Esmeralda asked when she called back.

"I got the internship. I'm going to be an FBI intern, just like you! Except, I'll be working out of a resident agency in Long Beach. That's what a satellite of the major FBI office is called. This way, you won't have to see me every day." She laughed.

"Congratulations, my friend, this is such great news! When will you start?"

"Next Monday I begin a two-week training, and then I get to have my first day on the job. How are things with you and Bill?"

"He is still in the middle of cleaning out his grandmother's house with his cousins. It's difficult when they find things that bring up sad memories. Don't forget, when she came to the U.S., Grandma Helena was fresh out of the horrors of the Holocaust, only to go through even more tragedies later, here in the U.S. I am sure she carried a deep ache in her heart, but never let it show. She was unusually brave."

"Wait a minute," Lexi asked, "didn't you just call her 'Grandma Helena'?"

"Yes, that's what her grandchildren called her. Why?"

"I just saw a post on Facebook. Somebody is trying to locate a Holocaust survivor named Helena Berger, and now I'm connecting the dots. It has something to do with an old note that was found. I'll forward you the post."

Esmeralda started shaking when she heard. She turned on her computer and waited for the link. As soon as she opened Lexi's message, she called Bill.

"I think somebody found something from Grandma Helena's family. Lexi just forwarded me a Facebook post. It's coming your way as we speak."

They tried to interpret the contents of the Facebook message for a long time. They read the vast number of responses. Some wrote that their relative had been a victim in a death camp; many expressed "good luck" wishes; two were racist comments that glorified Hitler.

Bill was animated. "I am sure this Facebook post is referring to my Grandma. I am not sure how to respond. I don't want to write a random message that will go unnoticed. I have to get their attention, to get them to read what I say. We need to keep the connection alive, so we can find out what they have. I want this person, whoever she or he is, to write back to me."

Working together over the phone, they composed a simple comment responding to the mysterious post.

"Hi, my name is Bill. I am one of Helena Berger's four grandchildren. Please let me know how to contact you directly. We've been searching for many years for information about our Grandma Helena's loved ones who perished in the Holocaust."

Esmeralda and Bill each checked daily for a reply on Facebook, but even after a whole week, nothing came.

The house had finally been emptied. After endless debates among the four heirs, it was agreed to advertise it for rent.

Digging into the Past

Lexi called her old friend who was now a Los Angeles Police detective, and asked if he would inquire about the missing girl who disappeared in 1948.

"That is a very, very old case," he told her. "I doubt if anything can be discovered after seventy years."

"This missing girl was related to a good friend of mine. Do you think you could just mention it to somebody?"

"I'll see what I can do, but no promises," he said at the end of the call.

Alfonso Valdez, a man in his early sixties, was a detective in the LAPD cold case unit who had dedicated himself to cracking the oldest unsolved crimes. Therefore, when he was approached by the younger man in the department, he gave it some thought. He pulled out the evidence box that contained items originally collected at the scene, mainly a few of the girl's articles of clothing. When he looked at the aged photograph of the missing child, he thought about his own granddaughter, and decided to re-open the case, weak as it might be.

Albert got a call from Valdez, who introduced himself and informed him that he had reopened Rebecca's missing person's case.

"Thank you so much, detective. I am very glad to hear it," he said, overcome by surprise. "I think about Rebecca every day. If I can provide you with anything that will help, please let me know."

"Are your parents, William or Helena, still living?"

"No, detective. Both are deceased," Albert replied.

"I can't guarantee anything, but I will do my best to get to the bottom of this matter. It is one unsolved puzzle that needs to be unraveled."

Albert kept the brief exchange to himself, partly because he was skeptical about the chance that the seven-decade-old mystery could be unlocked.

A few weeks later detective Valdez called him again.

"I am calling to update you on the progress of the inquiry into your sister's disappearance. We came across one indirect witness, a woman whose late father had been doing yard work near the spot where Rebecca had last been seen. It was a play area where children were running around. She remembers him describing a loud brawl involving some teenagers, when one of them yelled at the small children to 'scat'." She said it was the first and only time she had ever heard that word. According to her father, the playground emptied in a flash."

Albert asked, "Did this man notice if one of the girls was grabbed, or hurt, or anything else that they might have done to Rebecca?"

"I am still talking to the daughter, and she promised to call me if she recalls anything else. But, since you were also around at the time, I wonder if there was anything that you might remember. Was there any trouble in the neighborhood?"

In spite of himself, Albert sounded frustrated. "The first time we talked I told you the exact words I had said to the police back then, when I was almost nine. I had been at a violin lesson when my sister went missing; therefore, I wasn't home. The guilt I feel over Rebecca has haunted me all my life. I was the big brother; if I had been out there on the playground, she might still be with us. I do remember that every once in a while, gangs of teenagers were terrorizing the people on our street, and by the time the police came they had already vanished."

"What did the gangs do that terrorized the families?"

"Oh, one time they spray-painted profanities on our neighbor's front door; another time they pulled off a boy's pants and threw them in a ditch. The kid ran home half naked. They were just plain mean and disgusting."

"I have a feeling that the teenagers you describe might have been connected to the ones involved in the brawl the witness' daughter is talking about. I'll keep digging."

Albert had not stayed in contact with any childhood friends from school or his old neighborhood, and now regretted it. He rummaged through his cabinets and dresser drawers, found a scrapbook from his early school years, and leafed through it. Maybe, he thought, a name or a photograph would jog his memory. He saw a Valentine's Day card from Patty, a girl he didn't remember. There was his second- grade class picture, and he scanned the faces to see if he could recognize anyone.

He tried to recall every detail of the day that he had come home from his music lesson to find his frantic parents talking to a police officer. His younger brother Harry was standing in a corner, watching quietly. They lived in the house that his mother Helena had never moved out of. He pictured the bedroom he shared with his brother, where the two of them whispered insults to each other at night when their parents thought they were asleep. It occurred to him that he was the only one left of his entire family, which meant that he had the duty to assist, as much as possible, in the detective's investigation.

The neighborhood of Albert's childhood home, where his mother continued to live, had changed over the decades.

Several houses had been remodeled, and a strip mall was built nearby. There were fewer children in the area; people's lifestyles changed, and little ones were not often allowed to play outside unsupervised. Parents now arranged playdates and drove their children to various after-school activities. It was a different world, Albert observed.

He looked for internet articles about DNA evidence. It was unlikely, he knew, that any of Rebecca's DNA would still be viable on any item of hers that was left. Even so, he asked detective Valdez if this might be an option that could be considered.

To his surprise, Valdez didn't dismiss the idea altogether.

"We have a few pieces of her clothing and a doll. If our analysts can get anything useful off them, it's worth a shot. I'll look into it and keep you posted."

Correspondence

Maddie had not checked Facebook in a few days. The negative comments enraged her, and the positive ones led nowhere. Gradually, fewer of them were trickling in, and she had assumed that, in all likelihood, the search would turn out to be fruitless.

The enthusiasm she had felt when she first posted the Berger family note and the plea to find Helena's relatives had subsided. She became apprehensive about logging in, anxious about seeing more nasty remarks. Finally, on a quiet evening, Maddie opened her Facebook page and saw a new, unread message. She nearly jumped out of her chair, and dialed Sebastian's number.

"I think I heard from somebody related to Helena Berger. I just saw a response from someone named Bill, who claims to be her grandson."

"I'll bring over Chinese takeout tonight, and we'll figure out what to write back," he said.

Sebastian brought six cartons of food, and they looked at the message together.

"His language sounds sincere, even pleading. He wants to contact you directly, not in this public forum."

"On one hand, I have my suspicions," she observed, "but on the other, I'd hate to ignore him if he is who he says he is."

"You have to think carefully here, Maddie," Sebastian said and put down his chopsticks. "Did you stop to think about how your dad got so rich?"

"What does that have to do with the Berger descenants?" she asked, and then immediately stopped herself. "What if my own father, Titus, had somehow gotten his hands on the diamonds and sold them! Oh, good heavens!" She shook her head in disbelief.

"I don't know if this kid, Bill, knows about the pouch of diamonds, so I suggest that you don't mention it to him."

"I am almost sure," Maddie said, "that Bill's father knows full well that this treasure was handed to somebody for safekeeping. I'm guessing that Helena's parents made sure that she knew about the diamonds, so that she would try to get her hands on them when she was safe. Just imagine the dangerous times these people lived in."

"Well, you know what that means. Some of your inheritance may be have come from this cache, if it really ended up in your dad's hands."

"Maybe going public was a mistake. What should I do?"

"You can give him the notes and the empty pouch," Sebastian offered. "I think you should show him the picture of the camp with General Eisenhower, with your father's caption that he had been there."

"But what about that one diamond?"

"That's your decision. You can either leave it in the pouch and give it to him; or you can keep it for now, until you decide what to do next. After all, you didn't steal it. Meanwhile, there's no harm in replying to the young man. You could set up a separate email address for communicating with him. Ask him to send you proof—some facts about Helena or her life."

Maddie sent a response on Messenger.

"Bill, thank you for reaching out to me. However, in order to verify that you are indeed related to Helena Berger, please email me some facts or about her or her life during World War II."

She added her newly created email address, then pressed the "send" key.

She and Sebastian had grown attached to each other, and spent most evenings, and some nights together. She admired his bright mind and general knowledge of the world, but couldn't see a clear path to spending the rest of her life with him. She could not forget a brief phone conversation in which she had overheard him mention the word "bankrupt" more than once. As soon as he looked over at Maddie he hung up.

"Some issues with this one client are not going away," he said afterwards, but there was no conviction in his voice. She ignored it for the moment, but decided to probe gently into his life.

"I just realized that I haven't seen your house yet. When will you take me there?" she asked him one evening.

"My house is a messy story all in itself. We'll get to it soon."

She wondered what he meant, but again chose to drop the subject. Still, she couldn't stop wondering: probably it was cluttered, or needed repairs, or could it be he had somebody living there?"

A few days later, Sebastian brought it up. "You asked me about my house, so I think this is the time for me to come clean." He lowered his eyes. It was the first time she had seen him embarrassed. "We lived in a very posh home in Pacific Heights that my ex had inherited from her mother. When we got divorced, she kept the house, and I got our small rental home that I had to move into. Whenever I come here to your spectacular condo, I ask myself how I can impress you with my little place in the Sunset district."

"Oh, please..." Maddie hugged him. "You don't have to impress me with your house. I admire you for having great character, and for being so smart. People's fortunes change... For goodness sake, look at me!"

"You are just what I needed in my life, you know that?" he said and wrapped his arms around her. They clung to each other for a few minutes. "I think you already figured out that I love you very much."

She was unable to speak as tears gathered in the corners of her eyes. She blinked fiercely to stop them and stepped back from Sebastian.

"One day I may share with you my unseemly years of shady money games. It could possibly change your opinion about me."

"Maddie, I am not a fool. I figured that you were a young woman, perhaps still a girl, completely on your own. But you were ambitious and financially astute. I guessed that you had found roundabout ways to build some real cash, which was later stolen from you. I figured that you are relieved that you can't be connected to any illegal activities, and ready for a chance to start over. You don't have to share any of it with me, because it doesn't matter. I can see what a good person you are."

"Well, now it turns out I am rich and you are poor, right?" she laughed to lighten the mood, and he joined her.

"Well," he said between the chuckles, "I always knew how to find the rich babes. But of all of them, I finally found the best one."

Maddie had been checking the email account she had provided to the mysterious Bill. Even after five days there was no response. She assumed that her caution regarding the matter was justified, and that the chances of hearing back from him were slim. She had volunteered to prepare promotional materials for the crisis intervention organization, which demanded several hours a day. She had put the Berger mystery out of her mind and worked with a few other volunteers producing radio and TV spots.

On a Sunday morning, while checking her regular email account, she saw that there were two unread messages in the new inbox. She clicked on the first one and briefly scanned it. It immediately sent chills through her body, and she read it over so many times that she practically had it memorized.

"This is Bill. I hope this will help convince you that I am sincere. Here is a summary of facts regarding my grandmother, who was born and raised in Germany:

Helena Berger was the only surviving member of her family. She escaped alone when she was fifteen, but her parents and brother were transported to a concentration camp near their town of Weimar. Before the deportation, her parents converted all their assets to diamonds. Her uncle entrusted a local priest with the gems, and asked that they would somehow be handed to an organization by the name of the Jewish Joint Distribution Committee in the United States, in hope that they would locate Helena. All her family members died in the camps. She never heard from anyone about the diamonds, and carried on to build a great life. My beloved grandmother recently passed away at age 96. She left behind one son, my father Albert, and four grandchildren."

Then she noticed an attachment, and clicked the link to open it. It was a collection of three photographs, one of Helena as a young woman, another with her husband with three young children, and one in her later, older years.

The second message was a follow up, asking if she had received the first one.

Maddie was too stunned and shocked to appreciate that her search had borne fruit. What she was reading was a dreadfully tragic family story, beyond anything she had even imagined. Worst of all, she knew she might have unknowingly been the beneficiary of all that they had owned.

Searching for Rebecca

Los Angeles detective Valdez pored over the evidence from the original police investigation into Rebecca's missing persons case. Surprisingly, there were no credible witnesses other than people who reported some gang activity, but could not remember any specific person. With the absence of the new, more advanced forensic tools, they had relied on old fashioned methodology. An extensive search for a body, including search dogs, even policemen on horseback, had come up with nothing.

Undeterred, he pursued his quest with a data base that listed families from in the immediate area who were still residing in the original homes. He called each one, started by introducing himself over the phone and asking for help in the case. Every time he heard a hint of something helpful, he drove over to meet with the resident.

He was at the home of a married couple, both retired teachers in their late seventies, telling them about Rebecca's apparent abduction, when the man interrupted him.

"I was just a little boy then," he told the detective, "and honestly, forgot about the whole thing until you called yesterday, and then I started thinking. For some reason, hearing about your investigation jogged my memory. When the girl disappeared, it sent shock waves and everybody talked about it. I remember that many parents were scared to let their kids play outside, or even walk to school alone.

"I vaguely remember the mother of my friend next door talking to my parents. She told them about an encounter with a disheveled looking young man who used to hang around the neighborhood. He bragged about having helped a couple by the name of Waring find a little girl to adopt. He told them the girl had been abandoned by her parents, and needed to have a good home."

"Do you think this disheveled fellow might have had anything to do with the disappearance of this little girl?" Valdez asked while taking notes.

"The thing is, I'm pretty sure this conversation took place a long time after the girl had gone missing, so nobody had given it any thought. I remember my father saying that the guy had always been 'a low life', and had probably made up the story. What a shame, that nobody thought there might have been a connection."

The detective went back to police headquarters to search for couples who had been looking to adopt during that time. He knew it was unlikely to find any record of what he was looking for, since there was no report of an official adoption by a couple named Waring. He wondered how reliable the information he had collected actually was. Still, having a name, even fake or misspelled, was better than nothing, and it was a start. He continued to go through paper records from schools and hospitals from that year with no results.

There was one ninety-five-year old man who lived with his daughter and son-in-law, who had been saving clippings of newspaper articles and pasting them into scrapbooks. He seemed to be eager to help, so he invited detective Valdez to sit down to look at what he had.

After going down memory lane, they came across a short article in a neighborhood publication. It was about a girl named

Lisa Waring, who had recently been adopted. Her new parents expressed their gratitude to God for bringing them this beautiful daughter, who had been abandoned. There was a picture of Lisa smiling awkwardly. Valdez asked to borrow the book so he could make copies, and promised to return it the next day. He now knew that the Waring name had indeed existed.

He posted an inquiry on all social media, asking anyone if they knew Lisa Waring or anyone related to her. He chose to wait before updating Albert until he had more solid clues. Two days later, a response appeared on one of the websites from a nursing home employee in Mesa, Arizona. He mentioned a female resident of the right age, whose name was Lisa Waring. The detective contacted the facility and verified that this patient was indeed a resident there. Was she allowed to receive visitors, he asked.

"Lisa has never had any visitors, so it would be nice if someone came to look in on her," he was told.

Valdez' excitement grew as he flew to Mesa, where he took a cab to the institution where the woman was located. He had prepared himself for a conversation with her, hopeful that she would be able, or willing, to provide him with helpful details. His second option was to somehow obtain a DNA sample from her that he could take back with him for analysis.

The nursing home was shabby and smelly. When he was led to see the presumed Lisa Waring, he was shocked. She was a tiny, grey-haired woman, hunched over in a large recliner, covered with a thin blue blanket. The attendant who took him to her bent down to talk to her.

"Hi Lisa," he said in the condescending tone that caregivers use to address mentally impaired patients. "You have a guest. His name is Alfonso, and he wants to talk to you."

He then turned to the detective. "I've never heard her say a word, so good luck..."

"Look," Valdez said, "I am an LAPD detective working on a case about a woman of her age who disappeared years ago. If it turns out that Lisa is the person in question, I want to tell her brother that we were able to find her." He showed the attendant his badge. "I think that if I can just get one piece of her clothing, we may be able to match her DNA to evidence that we have. Can you help me out?"

The attendant looked around the room. He approached her chair again, slowly removed a small handkerchief from under her blanket, then handed it to the detective.

"She hoards scraps of cloth and keeps them with her all the time. She won't miss one."

Valdez thanked the man and put the kerchief in a plastic bag he pulled from his pocket. He remained standing in front of whom he thought had once been Rebecca. He got down on one knee and touched her lightly. She moved a little, and after getting back up, he gently helped her sit upright. There was no recognition in her eyes, just a blank stare. He walked out with a heavy heart.

Bill

Bill felt discouraged while waiting for a response from the sender of the posts about his grandmother. It had taken him several days to find the photos to attach, compose his message, and include his email address. He considered abandoning the entire matter in case it was just a prank, but it kept coming back to him. What tugged at his heartstrings was the copy of the small handwritten note that he saw in the post. It was definitely a European handwriting, which he had recognized from Grandma Helena's notes and letters.

When he finally saw a reply, it came from a woman who identified herself as Maddie.

> *"Hi, Bill,*
>
> *My name is Maddie Ellis. I believe you that you are, indeed, Helena Berger's grandson. It was sad to read that her family was murdered, but heartwarming to know that she survived and lived a long, happy life. The pictures you sent helped me feel a connection with your grandmother. We should definitely talk, so would you please call me any evening. I added my phone number below. I am located in San Francisco, Pacific time zone."*

Bill was jubilant, turned on a popular song, and danced clumsily through his apartment. He barely heard the phone ring, so he didn't have time to catch his breath before answering. It was Esmeralda.

"Hi, is everything okay?" she asked when hearing his louder breathing.

"Yeah, everything is great. You're not going to believe it, but I just heard back from the person who posted the stuff about Grandma Helena. She seems like a very nice woman, and she wants to talk to me. She sent her phone number."

"What did she write?" Esmeralda asked urgently.

"That she believes me that I am Helena's grandson, and added some nice comments. I can't wait to talk to her. I'm calling her tonight."

"Hopefully, she has more than just the one little note that she put on Facebook."

"I'll call you after I talk to her." He hung up, walked in circles around the living room, and finally decided that he needed to go for a run.

At 9:00 the same evening he dialed the number, and she answered after the second ring.

"Hello, is this Maddie Ellis?" he asked, doing his best to sound cool and convincing.

"Yes, is this Bill?" There was warmth in her voice.

"Yes, that's me. I am so glad that we finally get to speak directly. It's unbelievable that you have something that had belonged to my great-grandparents."

"Yes," Maddie replied. "It really is unbelievable."

"The first thing I want you to know," Bill said, "is that my Grandma Helena was always very important to me. She was the guiding light for all of us. We lost her a couple of months ago."

"I could tell all that from what you wrote. The silver lining is that she lived a good life. She was fortunate to build a loving family here in America."

"She was a very resilient and positive woman. There is a lot that I can tell you about her, but first, I am very curious about the note you found. Was anything else found with it?"

"Yes and no; it's a complicated story. Where do you live?"

"I'm in Los Angeles."

"If you can come to San Francisco, I have a few things to show you."

"I can be there this weekend," he said.

"If you get here before noon on Sunday, I'll have lunch ready for you," Maddie told him, and a wave of excitement overtook him. He tried to keep his voice even.

"Thank you so much. I'll let you know about Sunday."

He called Esmeralda a minute after he hung up.

"Guess what, I am going to San Francisco to meet Maddie Ellis, the lady who has the original note, plus perhaps a couple of other things from my family. She invited me to lunch, so I think I'll go this Sunday."

"That's so unbelievable; I am getting goosebumps." Bill could hear her enthusiasm over the phone. "Wouldn't it be a good idea to ask your father to go with you?"

"Well," Bill replied quickly, "he doesn't know anything about all the correspondence on Facebook, so I'll have to tell him the whole story from the beginning." He slowed down. "In reality, Dad needs to go there more than me. I'll talk to him, and if he agrees, which he will, I'll tell Ms. Ellis to expect both of us. You are so smart... Thank you for bringing it up."

Despite the late hour, Bill called his father. Albert's voice sounded sleepy, but his son ignored it. It was an important conversation, and they needed to make plans for the weekend.

Albert was bewildered by the news. He was now wide awake.

"Why did you wait all this time to tell me that somebody had something from my grandparents in Germany? Didn't you think I should also be in the picture?"

"Dad," he stumbled on his words, "It was a Facebook message without any name or contact information. Basically anonymous. I didn't expect it to lead to anything, so why tell you something that was just up in the air? Now that we have a real person to talk to, who invited me to come to her house on Sunday, I figured you have to be there too. I think we should go together."

"You'd better believe I want to go. Arrange a flight for us for Sunday morning."

Rebecca/Lisa

Detective Valdez was a bit hesitant about asking his friend, a female technician in the forensic testing lab, if any viable DNA could be found on Rebecca's seventy-year old effects. The technician, however, welcomed the challenge in trying to discover a link to a long-ago crime. She took the plastic bag that contained the handkerchief, and promised to see what, if anything, could be done.

The technician/friend emailed him a week later, and explained that the items had been sent to a specialist in Genetic DNA testing. It might take a while to get the results, she wrote, but promised to contact him as soon as she had an answer. The detective still held off on calling Albert until he had solid confirmation.

He was in shock when his friend from the lab emailed him that a genetic match was found to a male in Los Angeles, most likely a brother. Rebecca's seventy-year old articles had no usable DNA, but the kerchief did. They identified Albert as the familial match, and Valdez was confident he had the right person. He knew that sharing Rebecca's circumstances would be one of his most difficult conversations, but it was an essential part of police work.

"Good morning, Albert," he said on the phone the next morning. "I have some news for you, but it may not be the kind you hoped for."

"Did you find Rebecca's body?"

"No, it's not about a body. When can you come by the police station so I can give you some details?"

"I'll be there in half an hour."

When he walked into the station and asked for Alfonso Valdez, he realized he was trembling. The detective came out and shook his hand.

"I located your missing sister."

"What?" Albert's mouth remained open.

"Please have a seat," he pointed to a chair for Albert to sit.

"Unfortunately," Valdez began, "your sister had been abducted, as we had suspected, and allegedly handed over to a couple who was looking to adopt a child. She was raised as Lisa Waring, and there are no medical or vital statistics records indicating that she had any children of her own. I discovered that she is currently a resident in a nursing home in Mesa, Arizona. I wanted to check on this, so I flew there myself to see her." Valdez paused for a moment. "I was very sad to see her condition. Unfortunately, she is suffering from advanced dementia. I couldn't communicate with her at all.

"I was able to retrieve a handkerchief from her, and that's how our DNA lab confirmed that she is, indeed, your blood sister."

"Do you have a picture of her?" Albert asked with a frown.

"No, unfortunately it didn't occur to me to snap a photo, but she is a shell of a person. I'll give you the address of the place, so you can go to see her. I have to warn you, though; it's not where you would want your sister to be. I am very sorry.

"The only thing that bothers me," Valdez continued, "is that there is no reference or record anywhere of anyone named

Waring who would fit the scenario. In other words, nobody by that name was living in your area at that time. The only couple named Waring that we discovered had several children of their own."

"Detective," Albert said, "I can't thank you enough for going above and beyond all expectations to locate my missing baby sister; even traveling all the way to Arizona. The rest is for me to do. I am the only one left of this generation in my family to try to put the pieces together. Now that we've come this far, I can try to figure out what to do next."

Steve Butler

The newly created cyber team in the Financial Crimes unit started by "backtracking" Steve Butler's various accounts. There were a few that were held by offshore institutions, shares of stock in U.S corporations, and two office buildings. They were convinced that most, if not all of those holdings were somehow pilfered from previous owners. The problem they faced was that the theft was done so expertly that the entire transaction history had been obliterated.

There was one thread they found that held some promise. It was a digital imprint they identified on two accounts, that led them to a bank in Nicaragua. That particular institution had recently been declared unlawful by the U.S government for corruption and money laundering. It has since been shut down, but some funds from that defunct bank had flowed into American banks.

"Information that we obtain on just a single one of Butler's accounts," one of them told the assistant director, "could be the thread we need to pull to unravel the whole package."

"Keep digging," she insisted. "It could turn out to be a gold mine..."

They received authorization to breach Steve's online activity, and waited. For several weeks no relevant correspondence was detected. His internet searches were innocuous, consisting of travel searches and dating sites.

One of those dating websites caught their interest, mainly because the wording used did not seem enticing, or attractive, for people looking for love. They resembled code language.

"We need a trained specialist from the Beta group to try to break this code. I've never seen it before," one of the cyber analysts said in frustration. "

"Let's get a Beta specialist to see what he or she can come up with," the other one said. "At least we're getting warmer."

A seasoned cryptanalyst was called in to decipher. She frowned when she first saw the online conversation.

"This is something new," she told them, "but I'll definitely give it a shot. I don't give up easily. Allow me a couple of days."

It took longer than that for her to decode the verbiage, but she spotted something else. The correspondence was between Steve and an unknown individual involving a purchase he was making in Panama. The next step was finding the identity of the other party and the source of the funding. The cryptologist became a part of the team, specifically assigned to interpret the communications. All the FBI departments received updates that the particular dating site was a front for a money laundering operation.

Steve, it turned out, was trying to buy a house in Panama and move there to live with his Brazilian girlfriend. They knew it was crucial to stop him before he leaves the country.

It took another month to follow the trail that led to blocking the sale of the Panama property, and then finding the link to the money funneling organization.

Steve Butler was finally arrested, and he agreed to reveal the details of all his holdings in exchange for a shorter incarceration. His continued attempts to point fingers at someone whom he claimed had been his wife were in vain. They no longer considered the elusive Celeste an immediate person of interest, although she remained on their radar. Steve's assets were seized, and he was handed a two-year prison sentence.

The EAD announced the successful conclusion of the inquiry. The team of three, including the code breaker, was greeted with a standing ovation by the entire staff. The cash funneling enterprise was identified, and the operation was shut down, although several of the main actors involved had apparently vanished.

Esmeralda was present when the cyber analysts were congratulated, but had not been aware of the details of their work.

"None of us were let in on this operation," her senior co-worker Judy told her. "The great win for us is that these guys discovered the criminal enterprise that tried to block Harry's investigation. These are the people behind Brent Bushnell and his triggerman. In other words, we got them, so we can definitely say his mission has been accomplished."

Esmeralda still did not comprehend everything she had just heard. Her mind was on her own future with the Bureau.

"You know," she told Judy, "working here makes me feel like I am part of something very important. I've been thinking about what I want to do after graduation, and I keep coming back to cracking financial and fraud crimes. Before I got my internship here, I thought that fighting human trafficking would be my focus, but the work that we do here now appeals to me more."

"There is a lot of crossover between those types of crimes. Sometimes we get cases that involve human trafficking in addition to financial fraud and money laundering, so we get to work on any of them every once in a while," Judy said. "But you still have time to decide, and soon enough you'll figure it out. By the way, I always hear good things about you--they like you here."

Heart-Wrenching Decisions

"It's not my diamond," Maddie told Sebastian over the phone, "and I don't want it for myself. I also don't think it will be right to hide it from these people. The thing is, Bill is bringing his father, and this adds a whole new wrinkle to the situation."

"What are you planning to do?" he asked.

"I'll tell them the truth, that when I flattened the pouch, the single stone was squeezed out from the seam. I'll let them decide what to do with it."

She insisted that Sebastian be there for this meeting. Her doorbell rang at 11:30 on Sunday morning; she opened the door, and saw the two, father and son, fair-haired and somewhat freckled. She greeted them with a smile.

"Hello, Ms. Ellis," the older man said. "My name is Albert, and this is my son Bill."

"I am so glad to meet you both. Please call me Maddie. I want you to meet my friend Sebastian Fisher, who is an esteemed San Francisco attorney."

He shook both their hands warmly, and the four entered the living room. The view could not have been more spectacular, with the boats in the blue Pacific in front of them, and the Golden Gate bridge off to the side.

"This is quite an apartment," Albert said and went to the window.

Maddie busied herself for a few minutes carrying the catered food to the dining room table, then asked Sebastian to open a bottle of wine.

"After lunch I will show you what I found... I mean... the items that relate to the Berger family." She stumbled on her words.

"Thank you for trying so hard to find us," Bill said. "It's very surreal for us to think that anything from our unfortunate relatives still exists."

Sebastian wisely changed the conversation and asked the younger man about his work. He was impressed when told that he was employed at the FBI.

"As for me, I retired three years ago," Albert joined the conversation. "I was an electrical engineer for thirty-five years. These days, my wife and I are trying to relax, maybe do some traveling."

"By the way, your meal is fantastic," Bill said.

"Thank you, I am glad you like it. I ordered it from a restaurant," she smiled. "Cooking is not my greatest talent."

At last they finished, and Sebastian helped Maddie clear the table. She then brought the box containing her father's personal effects to the dining room.

"I received this package as part of the estate I inherited from my father. I've had no contact with him for years; everything I found here was a surprise to me." She opened it, took out her grandfather's photo album, and let them leaf through it. Both guests stopped when they saw the concentration camp newspaper picture.

"Wow," Bill said. "Your grandfather served in World War II, and actually took part in liberating this camp."

"This particular camp was close to Weimar, the town where your great grandparents lived. That's why, when

Sebastian and I saw this next thing I'm about to show you, we knew this

must have been the camp where your relatives had been taken."

She then placed the brown satchel on the table and said, "and here is this next thing."

The two looked at the small leather bag, then at each other.

"Albert, go ahead and open it," Maddie said. "Just be careful with the straps so they don't crack anymore."

He slowly untied the two cords and pried the bag open. He pulled out two yellowed notes, and read the contents aloud. One included the names of the Berger families, Helena, and the town of Weimar. The second was a plea for somebody to deliver the bag to the Jewish Joint Distribution Committee in the United States. He stopped, absentmindedly bringing his hand to his chest.

"So, what was in this bag that had to be brought to America?" Bill quietly asked after a moment.

"Please look inside one more time," Sebastian told him. "You'll see."

Albert scanned the interior of the bag and shook it. The single diamond spilled out onto the table. He stared at it for a minute, then picked it up. It sparkled brightly, reflecting the light that came in from the window.

Maddie then showed them the certificate of appraisal, and everyone stared at it.

"This diamond is worth $165,000?" Bill asked, his voice rising a bit.

"This is the mysterious pouch of diamonds that my great uncle had given the German priest for safekeeping," Albert looked up and shook his head slowly. "Who knows what happened to the rest of them."

"My theory is that this pouch made its way through many hands," Sebastian offered, "and apparently, somebody removed the stones. We think the only reason this one stone was left was that it got stuck in the inside edge of the bag. It's possible that this particular one was the largest of all of them. Let's say there were twenty to thirty diamonds; it's unlikely, even impossible that all of them were as big and as valuable."

"Maddie," Albert asked, "do you think your grandfather, Jack Ellis, knew about this bag and its contents?"

"Sadly," Maddie said, "I never got to meet my grandfather Jack. He died before I was born. All I have is this album. But look: he was at the camp which was close to your grandparents' home town. From Bill's email about a priest, we assume this man of God was given the satchel with the diamonds and the notes for safekeeping. It seems plausible that he later handed the bag to an American GI who happened to be my Grandpa Jack. He presumably pleaded with him to bring it back to the U.S. and take it to the JDC. But how did Titus get it? I found it in the box with all his stuff."

"That doesn't matter now. The most important thing is that your grandfather's actions brought our family heirloom to us. It seemed to have been an incidental act, but fate, or perhaps God, made sure it fulfilled its purpose. I'll say that the Berger and Ellis families have somehow been connected by history," Albert said.

She was silent for a moment, deep in thought. "This anecdote," she finally said, "aroused my curiosity about my Grandpa Jack's army service during the war. I went through the war records online, and tracked down the dates and location where he had been stationed. I was very moved to see how much he missed my grandma Deborah while he was deployed."

"His hope to come home and see her again almost certainly helped him survive the war. Love is a very powerful motive to stay alive."

"Sorry, Dad, we should get ready to get back to the airport soon," Bill interjected.

"We still have a few minutes," Albert said.

"Before you go," Maddie stood up, "I want you to take this satchel and what's inside it, as well as the appraisal. It belongs to you."

"I can't imagine what we would do with this diamond," Albert said quietly.

"You know how much it's worth, so you can either sell it, or use it for a meaningful cause. It's your decision."

"If you'll indulge me, "Albert said with a slight smile, "I want to tell you a story about our family. My parents, Helena and William, whom everybody called Villy, had three children: I, the eldest, Harry, and Rebecca. My sister vanished into thin air at age five, but nobody ever found out what her fate was. They searched exhaustively, but never came up with a dead body or any leads. It broke my father's heart; my mother said it shortened his life.

"Then, a few months ago, my brother Harry was murdered in a bombing in downtown L.A. His killing was targeted, because he was investigating a money laundering operation at the FBI. The sad thing is that my mother passed away with no answers about Rebecca or Harry.

"Back to Harry, the FBI finally caught his killers and arrested them, and also cracked the money laundering case. The other part, umm... and, I'm sorry, Bill--I didn't get a chance to tell you about it yet--is my sister Rebecca. A very dedicated police detective tracked her down to a nursing home in Arizona. She is mentally gone, and doesn't recognize anybody, and she apparently had never married or had a child. I hope to find some facts about what happened to her, or see if I can find a trace of the individuals who raised her.

"I wish my mother would have lived long enough to learn that her daughter is still alive. Although...." he stopped for a moment. "On second thought, under the circumstances, it's probably better that she never knew. People always talk about having closure, but I don't think this would have been good closure."

"Dad, I can't believe it!" Bill stared at his father. "Why didn't you tell me, Michael, and everybody else the minute you found out about Rebecca?"

"I just heard about her two days ago, and was going to tell all of you. I plan to fly out to Mesa to see her, so we can figure out how to move her to another facility, close to us."

Maddie and Sebastian sat quietly, listening without saying a word. A heaviness descended on the dining room table, and nobody spoke. Sebastian came to the rescue.

"Hey, guys, there is a cruise ship sailing under the Golden Gate bridge! Come, look! Have you ever seen anything so magnificent?"

Maddie, Albert and Bill rushed to the window to see the spectacle.

Bill said, "There is something that Grandma Helena once told me: the world moves forward, so we have no choice but move with it. We shouldn't dwell on the past more than we have to. I'm sure she would be very pleased that we actually have some remnant from the family she lost. If she is looking down at us now, she surely wants us to do something positive with it."

Albert looked at his son in surprise, clearly moved by his words.

"We should discuss it, and try to find a worthy cause to donate the proceeds from the diamond," he said. "We'd better go, son."

"Please let me know what you decide to do," Maddie said, and handed them the satchel and appraisal in a small bag. "I promise to make a generous contribution of my own." She wept when the two men embraced her at the door, and Sebastian, too, hugged them warmly. They waited and watched the guests make their way to the elevator.

A Closure of Sorts

It was a few minutes before Esmeralda grasped that the case that was just closed had to do with Harry's investigation. His work was done at last, she thought to herself, so the time came to spread the word. She picked up the phone and called Elizabeth, Harry's widow.

"Hi Elizabeth," she said cheerfully, "This is Esme Santoro. How are you?"

"How nice to hear from you, Esme," the woman said. "I am doing all right, I suppose. Still picking up the pieces."

"I want to share some exciting news. You know that Harry was looking into a money laundering operation. He came very close to solving it, and this is what got him killed."

"Yes, we all figured that out, although it doesn't make it any easier."

"Well, the investigation he worked on was just completed. The culprits were stopped and arrested. Everybody in our department congratulated the team for completing Harry's mission."

"I thought they already had the murder suspects in custody," Elizabeth said, her voice even.

"Yes, but they were just the hitmen, and we eventually got to the bottom of the plot. I am not sure they found all the individuals involved, but the ones we caught are being brought to justice. It would have meant a lot to your late husband."

"Well, I guess that's good. Thank you for calling," Elizabeth ended the call.

Esmeralda was uncertain how much this mattered to Harry's widow, but she was pleased that she had something positive to tell her.

She called Bill, but got his voice mail and hung up.

Lexi, the next person she dialed, answered her phone after the first ring.

"Guess what, something good just happened. An elite team from our group finally broke up the money laundering scheme that Harry was trying to get to. I just wish he was here with us to savor the moment."

"That is great to hear. But... I have news too..." Lexi blushed. "I think I finally met somebody. He is an intern like me, and I kept having butterflies in my stomach every time I saw him. Finally, we figured out that we like each other, and we hit it off. It's another office romance, just like yours, huh?"

"Butterflies, huh?" Esmeralda laughed. "I am so happy for you! It's about time you had a good guy in your life. Can I meet him sometime?"

Esmeralda waited until Sunday to go to the cemetery. She bought a bunch of white carnations and went to visit Harry's grave. When she lay the flowers on the flat part of the tombstone, she noticed a few small stones on the headstone. She looked around, picked up a pebble, and added it to the rest. Then she sat down on the grass, taking in the peaceful scene. Waiting for some inspiration, she closed her eyes. She had prepared some things to say to him when visiting his grave, hoping to be able to speak from her heart. It had to be better than the mundane message she had just told Elizabeth and Lexi.

A sudden breeze rustled her hair, and she sensed a mysterious warmth travel from her head down to her feet. It was an odd, but pleasant feeling, as if she were floating, hovering over the grave. The words came to her slowly, and she waited until the sensation subsided while she looked at the gravestone, hugging her knees. For a few moments she watched an elderly woman standing by a tomb two rows away, and finally started speaking quietly.

"Harry, I know you are no longer with us on earth, but I still sense your presence. It's hard for me to see somebody else sitting at what used to be your desk. You most likely see everything from where you are, but I want to tell you how much you meant to me as a mentor and a friend. I am relieved that justice prevailed; the people who were responsible for your murder are in prison.

"At your funeral somebody said that when a person passes away it means that their purpose on this earth has been completed. But you were taken from us by violence, it was not yet your time, because your work was not finished. I sensed the clear clue that you sent me when I dreamed about crickets, and that's what turned us in the right direction in solving your murder. What gave all of us at the FBI a cause for celebration is that a few days ago, we finished the task that you were working on. The money laundering outfit was finally discovered and shut down. I told Elizabeth about it, but for some reason it didn't seem to bring her much comfort. She misses you so much."

Esmeralda felt a huge lump settle in her throat as she struggled to transition to her more deeply personal message. She tried, to no avail, to stop the tears that gathered in her eyes, and almost choked on them as she continued.

"You once asked me if I had a boyfriend... Well, looking down at us, you surely know that your nephew Bill and I are now a couple, and I hope you approve. Fortunately, I got to spend some time with your mother Helena before she passed away. Her courage and strength inspired me more than anything I've ever experienced, and it transformed me. I realize that, beyond being just co-workers, your spirit and mine have become intertwined. Through the powerful bond that I share with Bill and Grandma Helena, perhaps, it seems, I am becoming a part of your family.

"I hope you rest in peace, knowing that many of us down here miss you and will always remember you."

She hurried away, sniffling while replaying in her mind what she had said. I am whole now, she whispered to herself. I finished what I needed to do. Hopefully, she thought, Harry appreciated her words, ones that she would never have spoken had he been alive.

Going to Arizona

Albert and Bill flew back to Los Angeles after they left Maddie's apartment. Both father and son were overcome by what they had in their hands, very moved by the experience. They spoke about the compassion that was expressed by their hostess.

"I don't have a good read on Sebastian," Albert said. "He is certainly smooth, intelligent, and handsome, but something seems off about him."

"Wow, Dad," Bill replied. "I was actually quite impressed by him."

"You are young," his father said. "It's easy to be dazzled by his type. The thing is, you have to look deeper. Anyway, back to our business: before we do anything with this diamond, I want to visit Rebecca and move her to a closer location. She may not remember any of us, but I understand that nobody has inquired about her or visited her in Mesa. No matter what, she is ours, and we have to take care of her."

"Don't you want somebody to go with you?"

"No, this is something that I need to do for myself. I prefer to do it alone."

"I think Mom should go too. You've always been each other's rock."

"Good point," Albert conceded. "In fact, your mother isn't going to hear of me go by myself anyway, and I know she will help me figure things out. Your mom is a very smart woman."

Annie, Bill's mother, had started visiting nearby care facilities immediately after her husband told her about Rebecca. Then she and Albert came up with a short list of the best ones. They boarded the one-and-a-half-hour flight to Mesa and rented a car at the airport.

"Can we squeeze in a day to do some hiking? The cool weather is perfect," she said. "It will help clear our heads."

"I don't think hiking is something I can even think about now..." Albert answered, a bit surprised about Annie, but knew it was her way to try to brighten his mood. "I want to deal with Rebecca. Don't forget, her official name is Lisa Waring, so that's how we must address her."

They arrived at the shabby nursing home, and exchanged glances with the same thought: they had to move her out of there as soon as possible. A woman at the front desk was cordial enough, and asked them to wait. Annie noticed and pointed to the peeling wallpaper, and the stench was inescapable. It was about ten minutes before a male attendant arrived and led them to Lisa. She was sitting in her oversized chair in what looked like a community hall among other patients.

"Lisa has never had visitors," he said. "But a couple of weeks ago a cop from L.A came to see her, and today the two of you. I wish she could talk to you, but she hasn't spoken a word as long as I've been here."

Albert had to control his disbelief when he saw the scrawny, bent over woman in the armchair. She was clutching a blanket. It was impossible for him to conceive that this person had once been his pretty, lively little sister.

They approached her, pulled over two chairs, and sat across from her. Her eyes were vacant, but Annie said she could see deep sadness. Albert held a childhood picture of Rebecca and himself in front of the silent woman. He started to talk to her.

"Hi Lisa... I am your brother Albert; remember me? We used to call you Rebecca when you were little." He broke down and turned his head away and Annie took over. She was holding an Oreo cookie, that had apparently been Rebecca's favorite when she was a child.

"Lisa, my dear... How are you? Would you like an Oreo?" she held the cookie in front of the woman's face.

"I just noticed," she tugged at his arm, "that something changed ever so slightly in her face when she saw the cookie. Perhaps, with time, she'll gradually remember something."

She lightly patted Lisa's shoulder and arm, while still holding up the treat in front of her. There was no reaction, and a few minutes later they left the community room to talk to the administrator.

"We want to move her to a nursing home near us in Los Angeles," Albert told him. "What is the process?"

While Annie stayed to get the details on the needed steps, her husband went back to sit with Lisa, and showed her the photo again.

"Remember this picture? It's from your fifth birthday." He repeated, "you were called Rebecca back then, and I was your big brother Albert." He then took out pictures of their parents from that time. "This is Mommy, and this is Daddy, remember?"

"I don't think they feed her enough here," Annie came back and said, "and she is definitely not getting regular showers. She smells awful. Young man," she called out to the attendant, "when was the last time Lisa had a shower?"

"They are bathed twice a week, so the last time was..." he stopped.

"I want her washed right now," she demanded. "She smells awful!"

"I'm sorry," he replied defensively. "It's close to dinner time here, so there's no bathing until tomorrow."

"If she doesn't get a bath or a shower immediately, I'll go do it myself!" she shouted, and a few heads turned.

It took about fifteen minutes until a female orderly came with a wheelchair, lifted the tiny woman and placed her in it. She then wheeled her away while the two waited.

Lisa was wheeled back half an hour later. Her gown had been changed and her wet hair was combed. The foul odor was gone.

"Thank you," said Annie. "When will you give her dinner?"

"We'll feed her soon," the orderly said, stepping away.

"Ma'am," Albert called out to her. "If you can bring her meal here, I want to feed her myself."

Lisa slowly ate a few bites of mashed potatoes and two pieces of fish, and then she was taken away to go to sleep. Albert and Annie left and drove to a nearby sandwich place.

He didn't order any food, just sat quietly, looking away from the table and his wife, staring at nothing.

"I wonder what was easier," he finally spoke, "being in the dark about Rebecca, or seeing her like this. By the way, you were pretty powerful in there, yelling at them to tend to her."

"Well, it had to be done, right? On another subject, do you remember any songs you sang together when you were little?" Annie asked him.

He thought for a moment. "I remember, 'I've been working on the Railroad.' When we got to the part 'Dinah won't you blow' Rebecca always yelled it at the top of her voice. The only other song that comes to mind right now is 'Itsy Bitsy Spider.' Why do you ask?"

"I thought that if she hears those songs, it may wake up some buried memories. They say that music sticks in people's minds more than stories. Did your parents teach you any German children's songs?"

"That language was completely outlawed in our home," Albert said emphatically. "There was no speaking or singing in German."

"Any Yiddish tunes?" Annie kept asking.

"Neither my father or my mother spoke or sang in Yiddish. My father had studied French and Italian, so he could carry on conversations in those languages, but that's it. We were an all- American, English speaking family."

"Your mother spoke perfect English, even with her slight German accent, which I know she didn't like," Annie said.

They returned to the nursing home the following morning to sit with Lisa again. At Annie's urging, Albert started to sing "Itsy Bitsy Spider," while they searched her face for any sign of recognition. He looked at his wife, who said, "try the other song, please."

"I've been working on the railroad, all the live long day..." he sang, and stopped. Lisa made a sound, so he smiled and continued singing, but she remained silent.

"Something inside her is dormant," Annie said. "Could be that with therapy there might be some improvement. Anyway, let's get her moved to L.A."

They both kissed her on their way out, then drove to the airport to fly back home.

Finding a Worthy Cause

Albert invited Bill, Harry's children, Michael, Violet and Todd, and their mother Elizabeth for dinner after the visit to Arizona. After they finished the meal, Annie and Elizabeth cleared the dining room table. Albert looked around him at the young people before he started speaking.

"Bill and I were very fortunate, through a Facebook connection, and got our hands on something that came from my grandparents, Peter and Hannah, back in Europe." He showed them the contents of the brown satchel, carefully placing the diamond on a dark cloth he laid on the table.

They stared at the stone, then at the yellowed notes, and then at each other. Albert didn't give them an opportunity to say anything before continuing.

"Miraculously, out of all the diamonds that my great uncle gave the priest to safeguard, this one remained. That's because whoever swiped them was too careless to check that nothing was left, and thank God for that. Maybe this stone has a special meaning, a significance. I thought of perhaps having a diamond broker sell it, which will enable us to make a worthy donation.

"As you already know, at long last, we found my poor sister, your aunt Rebecca. I haven't been able to get a decent night's sleep since we saw her. She's a shell of a person with her mind gone."

He stopped for a moment and took a deep breath before moving on. Bill put his hand on his father's shoulder. This wasn't easy, even for the eloquent, well-spoken Albert.

"The theory is that somebody snatched her when she was about five, and brought her to a family who was looking to adopt a child. She grew up as Lisa Waring. There are no public adoption records, so we assume it was done secretly, most likely illegally. We haven't been able to track down anybody who knows anything about her life, but we have the last name of her adoptive parents. Meanwhile, before we go into investigating her past, we arranged to transfer her to a nice nursing facility close by.

"So, with all this new drama that's playing out, I'll stop talking, so I can hear from you. All of you are legitimate heirs to your great grandparents' possessions. What are your thoughts about gifting the proceeds from this diamond? Would you prefer to have it divided among the four of you? As your parents, Elizabeth, Annie and I figure that we have all we need, so the decision must be yours. I'll let you talk, debate, or argue about it. After you discuss it, if all of you are not in agreement, we'll forget the idea and split the money four ways."

Albert joined Annie and Elizabeth in the kitchen while the four cousins remained at the table.

"I think each one of us should get a turn to speak up," Bill took the lead. "Michael, what do you think?"

Bill was afraid his cousin would disagree, since he usually liked to be in charge. There was a collective sigh of relief when Michael, after glancing at Violet, said, "We're not going to get rich from the cash that will come from selling this stone. We know how much it's worth, which is not exactly millions and the diamond broker will take his share. After splitting it among us-- Yeah, we'll get something, but then it will get swallowed up with other money, and it won't mean anything. I agree that we should find a way to memorialize our heritage."

"Look," Violet started and her voice quivered. "This may be a message for us to use this money to create a legacy. How unimaginable is it that Aunt Rebecca came back into our lives at the same time that the old notes and the diamond showed up? All the sorry missing pieces of our family are coming together, so I definitely don't want to take any of it and spend it. I'm voting with uncle Albert and my brother Michael."

The other three looked at Violet thoughtfully.

"What about you, Todd?" Bill asked his youngest cousin. "We are all single, but you have a whole clan with five kids. We know it's not the same for you."

"Actually, we just found out that my father-in-law had a brother who had no children, so when he died, he left us a good sum of money and some real estate. What a great relief for us... It seems we'll be in good shape without this gift. But regardless, I am inspired by what Violet said about a legacy, and I think we have a duty to honor it. It's about taking the high road. But, Bill, you've been running this show, so what do you say?"

"Well," Bill said, a bit embarrassed, "I have an advantage here because I had more time to think about this. Dad and I went to San Francisco together to visit Maddie Ellis, the person who posted the message on Facebook. She gave us the pouch with the notes and the diamond. In fact, she even suggested that we might consider using it for a higher cause. Our great grandparents and great uncle were generous, intelligent people, who were shipped away and exterminated. There's no doubt that we have to memorialize them. We'll all manage without the extra cash."

The entire discussion lasted less than ten minutes, and Michael stepped out to call Albert back. Elizabeth and Annie joined them.

"It looks like we have a unanimous decision," the announcement came. "We all agree that, if we can sell this stone, we should figure out where to donate the proceeds in memory of the Berger family."

Annie and Elizabeth looked at each other.

"I must say that I am impressed," Albert said with a smile, the first that anyone had seen in a long time. "You are all young, but you have a greater nobility and more heart than many older people. I promise you that your father, Harry, is watching," he addressed his late brother's children, "and he is proud."

The four cousins went to the den to chat.

A Sad Truth

Esmeralda and Lexi walked to a movie theater, where a popular new film had just opened.

Laughter engulfed the two when they recounted the adventures with Brent, and Esmeralda amplified Lexi's quick rise from an outsider to an FBI intern.

"It took me over a year to get to where you've gotten in only three months," she said. "How fair is that? I admit, though, that it took courage for you to take the assignment to go to Brent's house to bug his computer. It could have gone badly for you."

"I think I despised him so much, that it almost blinded me," Lexi answered. "It wasn't just for the Bureau that I did it. It was personal to me, because I knew what a crook he was. I was determined to stop him from continuing to do his dirty business and get away with it. Who knows how many people he cheated in his life."

Esmeralda said, "Bill's father just located his younger sister who had been missing for seventy years, since she was just a little kid. What we heard was that she had been abducted by some stranger and given to another family to raise. It sounds so strange... She grew up under a different name, but they have no way of finding out the circumstances or anything else, because she has acute dementia. They had assumed that she'd been killed, so there was hope and comfort in knowing she's still alive, but it's still painful."

"Do they have any details about the people who adopted her, or raised her?" Lexi asked.

"The only known detail is a family name."

"My boyfriend mentioned a P.I. agency he had worked with in the past. They have a great reputation, and may be able to dig more deeply into it. If the family is interested, I can ask him to find out for you."

"Can they look all the way back to seventy years ago?" Esmeralda asked.

"From what I was told, they worked on a similar situation and got the answers. All I can do is ask, so it's up to Bill's dad."

The movie was starting and the conversation ended.

Esmeralda told Bill about the private investigation firm. Bill mentioned it to his father the same evening. "They may be able to unearth the mystery of Rebecca's past, Dad. What do you think?" he asked.

"Let me think about it," he told his son. "I'll let you know."

Lisa, or Rebecca, was admitted to an upscale nursing home where she had a semi-private room. The facility was painted in bright colors, had large windows, and the quality of the food was significantly better. There were music performances for the residents, and the staff included more trained nurses and caretakers.

"We'll have to make some changes in our budget to be able to pay for Rebecca's stay here," Annie mentioned one evening. "She is in a high-priced facility."

"We'll find a way to make it work," Albert said. "I'll have to pull some money from my retirement account. Look, it's the only kindness Rebecca has ever seen in her life, even if she is unable to recognize it."

They visited her daily. Over a few weeks they showed her, time after time, pictures of herself with her two brothers, of her parents, and of herself with childhood friends. Lisa/Rebecca remained unchanged, silent and hunched over. A resident therapist came over to talk to them one afternoon.

"I understand how hard it is to see a loved one who can't communicate, especially when you have things you want to tell them. Sadly, dementia is a deterioration of brain cells, and it's usually irreversible. I overheard you call her 'Rebecca.' May I ask why?"

"It's a complicated story. My sister's birth name was Rebecca, but she was taken in by people who chose to change it to Lisa. It's a long story."

The therapist stared at him, evidently avoiding unnecessary questions. He then smiled briefly and went to sit with another patient.

"Do you think it makes any sense for us to pay a private investigator to find out what happened to Rebecca?" Albert asked Annie. "What good will it do at this point?"

"I think your sister should be remembered for who she was when she was lovingly named at birth. When the time comes that she passes on, she should have a traditional burial and a headstone bearing her real name."

"So, do you believe that we should hire the P.I?"

"If you're asking me, yes, this is what I would do, but you're the one who should make the decision."

"It could get expensive."

"Like the kids told you, it's only money. If it's important enough, you do it."

"As long as we can make it work out financially, I agree. We'll have to crunch some numbers later."

Through Esmeralda, Bill forwarded a message to Lexi, asking how to contact the sleuths.

The private investigator, named Victor, contacted Albert by email, and they set a

meeting at a nearby Starbucks. Victor listened patiently to the older man, and wrote down the meager particulars that were known about Rebecca.

The investigative agency had, over the years, amassed inside data about old crimes. Their trove of information included school records, church membership lists, scoutmasters from the local Boy Scouts chapters, and more. Some of it dated back many decades. They agreed to take on the Rebecca, aka Lisa case. The price tag was $100 per hour.

"Waring... The name rings a bell," Victor told Bill over the phone two days after they met. "I'm pretty sure we've run across it before. I'll get back to you guys soon."

"I hope that by 'soon,' he means 'quickly'," Albert told his son. "I prefer that this doesn't add up to thousands of dollars." But they were encouraged and hopeful.

Esmeralda had a premonition. She remembered a human trafficking case from a few years earlier. She had, quite accidentally, had become an important player in solving it, because the culprit had been her estranged brother. She recalled seeing young women with crying children climbing into vans after having been freed by FBI agents, and the images had haunted her over the years.

"What if Rebecca was a victim of child trafficking?" she asked Bill one evening. "She was a beautiful and friendly girl, who was, I'm afraid, noticed by some awful people. It's possible she was too trusting, which made it easy for someone to lure her away. I am just trying to think..."

"We'll see what this guy, Victor, finds out. They seem to have access to quite a bit of historical data about people from that time."

"I read some Bureau material about human trafficking, and it's astonishing," Esmeralda continued. "Trafficking has been practiced for centuries, but had not been considered an official crime by law enforcement until twenty or so years ago. They didn't investigate these incidents back in Rebecca's time."

Bill tried to put this conversation out of his mind. He suspected that Esmeralda's hunch might be correct. What had been baffling to him were the people who had taken her in and allegedly raised her under a new name. Why couldn't the police detective find any trace of that family?

The answers came within two weeks, much sooner so than anyone had anticipated. Victor called Albert and told him he had more information. He asked to meet again.

"Bill," his father said over the phone, "Victor, the P.I., said he wants us to meet again. He found something, and, truthfully, I am a little afraid to find out what."

"Look, Dad; we already figured that whatever happened to Rebecca couldn't have been good. I think we are more or less ready to hear about it, so we can put it all behind us. I'll come with you."

He was very uneasy when he and his father arrived at the coffee shop to wait for Victor. Esmeralda's words had been echoing in his head, but he put on a cheerful face. They chatted for a few minutes until the private investigator arrived.

"I'll cut to the chase, guys," Victor began. "I must warn you that this will be hard to hear. The good news, if we can call it that, is that we were able to trace the chain of events. Rebecca was most likely snatched and allegedly handed over to a family named Waring.

"The initial step was checking school enrollment records, yet none of the schools in the area had Lisa Waring on their list. We did, however, come across Rebecca's name as a kindergarten pupil. Next, we searched for anyone by the name of Waring, which might have fit the scenario: age, marital status, whether they had kids, etc. We found none."

Albert had already heard that from Detective Valdez. He sighed, and let Victor continue.

"A newspaper article from that time described a big house where young girls of all ages had been living. Occasionally, one of them would walk over to the corner store and buy herself a treat before hurrying back. When two neighbors noticed that men were coming and going to and from the house, they suspected foul play. The police were called, but believed what the adults in the house had told them, that all the girls were runaways."

"That was all? The cops didn't want to get into it, or what?" Albert asked, his eyes narrowing.

"When they entered the home, the officers observed some of the young women and girls, who appeared quiet and subdued. They questioned a few, but the victims had obviously been coached and warned. The message the police had gotten was that a wealthy benefactor had been financially supporting the home, and sending inspectors regularly. The ugly truth about the real situation had never been discovered.

"The Waring name was a sham, or a front for this prostitution ring. It seems that the youngest of the victims, like your sister, were home-schooled for a year or two, with the basic 'three Rs'—reading, writing, and basic math. After that they were subjected to the sexual fantasies of the male clients. None of the children had any birth or school records, so they simply got lost in the system."

"Was that what happened to my sister?" Albert exploded, his face red with fury. "This little girl was molested like a piece of meat?" A few customers around them hushed and averted their eyes. "Is this information reliable?"

"Sir, you hired me to investigate, so my partner and I did a lot of digging. It appears that Rebecca, or Lisa, ran away from that so-called group home at age ten or so, to live with one of the men. She moved with him from Los Angeles to Arizona. We didn't find anything indicating that she had ever married or given birth. Over the next ten years, she escaped a few more times from other places. She was arrested more than once for disorderly behavior. Fast forward twenty years, Lisa came to the attention of a social worker, who referred her to a psychiatrist.

"She was diagnosed with schizophrenia, and committed to a mental hospital, where she spent much of her adult life. Seven years ago, she was moved to the nursing home where you found her. She had become eligible for Medicare."

Albert wept quietly, his elbows on the table, holding his head in his hands. Bill put his arm around his father's shoulder and lay his head on it. Neither of them said a word.

Finally, the older man composed himself and addressed Victor.

"I apologize for my outburst. It's hard to believe that your private agency, rather than law enforcement, was able put together this sequence of events. In my heart, I was afraid that human trafficking might have been involved, but prayed I was wrong. A life wasted! What a damn shame!" He was letting his emotions overtake him again.

"I am truly sorry to bring this news to you, but at least now you know the facts about what happened. I'll mail you a statement. You two take care."

Albert awkwardly waved his hand in a thank you gesture as Victor left.

"Look, Dad... At least she's alive."

"Yes, but what kind of life did she have? Was it worth living?"

They walked out into the street. An unexpected rainstorm was in the making, and the first drops started falling. They ran to the car and drove away, miserable and silent.

"I'm wondering how much of this filth we should share with the family," Albert finally said.

"We don't have to give them the line-by-line scenario, but they should all be aware that Rebecca was a victim of sex traffickers. It's easy to think that things like that only happen to other people, but we are the living proof that it's not true. You're right, it is filthy and obscene, but we should all be aware that it exists."

"It's a good thing that your Grandma never found out. No matter how tough my mother was, I doubt if she would have been able to live with this."

"You're right," Bill observed quietly. "Rebecca's life was pretty much wasted. Who knows what kind of future she could have had if this hadn't happened to her?"

A Reckoning

Sebastian told Maddie about a large case he had completed for a builder in the city, and how pleased he was with the outcome and the sizeable compensation.

"Let's celebrate," he told her over the phone. "How about dinner tomorrow at Crème de la Crème?"

"That's where you took me on our first date, and it was heaven. I have no objections."

She quietly wondered if he was in a position to pay hundreds of dollars for a posh meal.

A crowd had gathered in the area in front of the restaurant, and the two stopped to have a look. They saw a man lying on the ground with one paramedic rendering first aid, as two others brought a stretcher from an ambulance. Two police cruisers arrived.

"What happened?" they heard somebody ask.

"This man was run over by a hit and run driver," a woman replied. "I hope he makes it. It's a San Francisco disease, drivers who hit pedestrians and don't stop."

"Are there any pictures of the car, or the license plate?" Maddie asked. "This is awful."

A reporter and cameraman stood in front of her and videotaped her statement.

"You will be on the eleven o'clock news, ma'am," the reporter said. "Can I get your name?"

"My name is Maddie Ellis," she said, and then turned to enter Crème de la Crème with Sebastian.

"I guess you made an impression," he told her when they sat down. "They want to put you on the news."

"It's not a big deal," she replied casually. "They always like to show passersby who witness a crime. It adds to the drama."

Dinner was not quite as charming as the first they had at Crème de la Crème. Sebastian seemed unusually distracted. They walked around the city for a while after dinner, and then he drove to her home.

"Is everything all right?" she asked on the way.

"Sorry, Maddie. My mind has been elsewhere," he said before dropping her off. "The thing is, I just took on a new case for a client in San Diego, so I'll be out of town for a few days."

"Wow," she said, "you are on a roll!"

"I guess you can say that," he answered casually.

"Well, I'll miss you," she replied, but detected a sudden coolness, possibly some distancing, in his tone.

Three days later, when Maddie was leaving her complex, she noticed a man standing directly across the street. She ignored him and continued to the coffee shop where she planned to meet two people from her volunteer organization. The man was loitering nearby when she returned. She was curious and uneasy, but walked back home without turning her head.

He followed her back to her building. She stopped, turned around and looked at him.

"Why are you following me?" she asked him gruffly.

"I recognized you from the news," he said. "Aren't you Celeste Butler?" He was a short man with a cropped beard and hard brown eyes, wearing a black baseball cap.

She thought she was about to faint, and reached her hand to the wall next to her to steady herself. The blood drained from her face.

"You are obviously mistaken," Maddie said after gaining some composure. "My name is Maddie. They actually had my name in the news story."

"I can see you are startled, so I'm going to leave, but I'll be back."

Maddie waited for him to disappear, then rode the elevator back to her upstairs apartment. She collapsed into a chair in her dining room and burst into tears.

Her mind was in turmoil with endless thoughts that swirled around, as if all vying for her attention. Why are her demons coming back? How did they find her former name? Who was this man who was watching her? Did somebody send him? Can her prior activities be traced? Should she call Sebastian?

She chose to hold off so she could calm down before calling him. She reminded herself how capable she had always been at handling challenges. She wrote down the questions that were in her head on a pad of paper. She found the recording of the news piece about the accident, and watched the brief clip of herself with her red scarf wrapped around her neck, commenting about the rogue car. Below her picture was the name "Maddie Ellis." Damn. Why did she have to open her mouth?

She then searched the internet for Celeste Butler, but found nothing. Absentmindedly, she went on to check for entries about Steve Butler. She gawked at what appeared on her screen. One older link listed him as a fatality in the Tehachapi fire, but according to the more recent ones he was alive and breathing. Her allegedly deceased husband had been living in Florida, and was recently arrested on charges of money laundering.

It took only seconds for her to gather that the man she had loved and mourned was the one who had pilfered her assets.

She remembered the orange sneakers and charred body in the Bakersfield morgue. How could it be that she had identified the wrong body?

It was likely, she knew, that Steve tried to find a way to implicate her in his newly found schemes, and that was how her name had come up. It baffled her that he would have been capable of accomplishing it. She then pondered if, since her spouse was alive, she was still legally married to him. Could that be the case, although his death by fire had been officially recorded?

The next search she started was for the current Maddie Ellis. She was listed as the owner of a condominium in San Francisco, and a member of a rescue organization. It certainly did not make her look suspicious, nor did it show any connection to the nonexistent Celeste.

So why was she being followed? Was somebody trying to extract money from her, or was it possibly the long arm of the law? She guessed it was the former. Either way, she knew she was in trouble, but all she could do was wait and think. Sebastian had not called her from San Diego.

Maddie decided to keep a low profile and avoided venturing outside. She told the chairwoman of the volunteer group that she needed a couple of weeks to take care of important personal business. She noticed the man with the baseball cap sitting on a bench in the street opposite her residence.

I definitely cheated and took money from accounts belonging to real people, she kept berating herself. What had gotten into me that I thought it was a perfectly harmless practice? Her records were gone, but she still remembered a few of the unscrupulous money managers she had dealt with. She began to make a list of institutions who might come after her for financial restitution, then looked them up online, just to see if they were still in existence. She was fully aware that any of the involved individuals would, under pressure, easily throw her to the wolves.

Using her own phone might be risky, she thought in angst, in case someone had installed a listening bug in the device. She remembered the isolation and helplessness she had experienced before she left Bakersfield. The familiar feeling was creeping back. Her heavenly new life now seemed to have been a deceptive illusion. More than anything else, she needed somebody to trust and with whom to confide.

"Hi Sebastian," she texted him, "you haven't called. Is everything all right?"

A half hour later his response came: "Sorry, I've been very involved in this case. Everything is fine." Cold, she thought. Very cold, and who knows why.

Maddie's thoughts again took her to Thomas Snow, her former partner-in-crime who had long since become a solid citizen. He was the only person she knew who was above-board, but it was doubtful if he was still an ally.

With a shrinking amount of food in her kitchen, she finally ventured outside through a side entrance of her condominium complex. She walked at a brisk pace and avoided glancing sideways. In an electronics shop she bought a cheap phone that was not connected to any plan provider. She then went back, pulled out her car and drove to a nearby supermarket.

The guy with the baseball cap was not there when she returned, which gave her some relief. She came up with a strategy, but allowed herself time to refine it. At last she decided it was worth a try, and used the new phone to dial Thomas' phone number.

"Thomas Snow, how can I help you?" He sounded cheerful enough, Maddie thought. She altered her voice to make it sound higher.

"Hi, Mr. Snow, my name is Maddie Ellis, and I am a potential investor. Can I schedule an appointment with you?"

"What type of investments are you interested in, Ms. Ellis?"

"I like the stock market, but I want to work with an expert who can make good recommendations."

"May I ask who referred you to me?"

"It was my cousin's friend. Unfortunately, I forgot his name, but if you need it, I'll get it for you."

Maddie was afraid that he might recognize her voice and hang up. But Thomas, apparently eager for a new client, scheduled a meeting for the following day. She booked a round trip airline ticket for Los Angeles for the next morning.

A few minutes later, when she glanced out through her window, she saw her stalker, but this time he was not alone. There were two more men with him, and all were casually scanning her location.

The Value of a Diamond

Albert was tossing junk mail into a recycling bin, and stopped when he noticed a letter from an unfamiliar bank. It was addressed to the estate of Helena Berger, and he took a long look at it before deciding to open it. It reminded him that his mother hadn't taken his father's surname when they married, and remained a Berger.

The document in the envelope astonished him. It was a statement for an account that belonged to Helena Berger for the benefit of her daughter Rebecca. The balance was slightly over $380,000, which was unfathomable to him. The attached transaction report indicated that the deposits Helena had consistently made, augmented by the accumulated interest, albeit low, had built a significant nest egg. Children of Rebecca's age had not been assigned Social Security numbers at birth. Therefore, the account was registered solely in his mother, Helena's ownership.

He remembered the appraised value of the single diamond given to him by Maddie, and had just engaged a jewelry broker to sell it. He calculated that, between that and Helena's newly discovered account, there would be over half a million dollars available to help a charitable institution.

Albert asked Harry's family and Bill to come over once more the following Sunday afternoon to discuss the bequest. It had been a few weeks since the San Francisco visit with Maddie

Ellis, so he decided to send her an email "just to say hello." A week had passed since he sent it, but to his surprise there was no reply.

Annie brought out a chocolate cake and offered drinks to the cousins, and Albert spent a few minutes chatting with them. He wanted them to relax, thereby avoiding any tension or unpleasant arguments. The younger people were cheerful, clearly delighted to see each other and catch up.

"Okay, kids..." he started. Bill held his breath, waiting for the speech to start. Why couldn't his dad refrain from formal oratory?

Albert started. "Remember, we agreed that we should support a worthy cause with the proceeds of our prized diamond. This is an important, historic time for all of us. What we have here is precious not only for its financial value. It came directly from the hands of my grandparents and your great-grandparents, and wasn't meant to be used for adornment, but for survival. That's why I agree with you that it's important that we gift it to an institution that supports survivors.

"But, there's more: I just received in the mail a statement belonging to your grandma Helena. She had apparently been setting money aside for decades for the benefit of Rebecca. Can you believe it? The incredible part is that it has grown to a total of more than $380,000. It took me some time to realize that this account can't go to charity. It seems fair to me that we use these funds for the purpose that my mother intended—to pay for Rebecca's care. I must tell you that the cost of her nursing home stay is not cheap."

Annie, his wife, chimed in. "We can't forget that Rebecca is a descendant of the Bergers like all of you. She is entitled to share in the inheritance, and this is the only way to use it for her benefit."

Everyone nodded in agreement; it was great relief for all that there was a source of money to cover the high monthly nursing home fees.

Violet was the first to speak up.

"Going back to our charitable contribution, I've been searching for organizations that would fit. There are two things I suggest we should consider: the first one is that Grandma Helena's social work involved helping survivors. The other is that aunt Rebecca was a victim of human trafficking. I think that our choice has to be based on those two facts."

"Violet," her brother Michael said, "you've always been the smartest of all of us, and you expressed our situation perfectly. Good job, sis..."

Violet blushed and smiled, but said nothing.

"Dad," Bill spoke, "With this amount of money, we have to be careful. I've also been searching, and came across The Organization for Abused and Missing Children. I think we should check them out."

Elizabeth nodded her head. "I agree that this type of entity would be the most appropriate. We want the money to go to a worthwhile cause."

"Once we come to a decision on where we make the donation, we should tell Maddie Ellis. She said she would add a generous contribution. Remember, Dad?"

"Well, I sent her an email about a week ago just to say hi, and haven't heard back. She may, or may not, actually come through."

Todd's wife and children came over, and the rest of the afternoon was spent playing games. Bill called Esmeralda and privately recounted the family conversations. Everyone stayed for dinner, which Annie had been preparing while the discussions went on.

No Escape

Maddie cancelled her ticket promptly after she saw the trio outside her apartment. She threw open a suitcase on her bed, and devised an escape plan. She packed as many clothing items and toiletries as she could fit in the bag. Then she took her passport along with other important documents and placed them in a briefcase, along with her mobile phone and charger. She dressed in black and pulled her hair back under a hat.

As soon as darkness fell, she left her unit, pulled her rolling suitcase down the stairs to the first floor, then went to the side door, cautiously stepping outside. She didn't notice anyone suspicious, but decided not to take her car. Using the burner phone, she called a rideshare company for the trip to the Caltrain station.

It only took fifteen minutes for the driver to drop her off, and Maddie grabbed her suitcase, briefcase and handbag. Her panic had not subsided when she entered the station and scanned the train schedules. She had pre-planned her trip to Nevada, and soon she spotted the first train she needed to take. Just as she took her first step towards the platform, two men approached her.

"Maddie Ellis, aka Celeste Butler, I am FBI agent Sean Aguilera. You are under arrest. Please come with us."

She was too stunned to utter a word, and stared at the man.

"What am I being arrested for?" she finally asked, and hated herself for her shaky voice.

"Fraud and money laundering."

The second man grabbed her big luggage, but she held on tightly to the briefcase that had her phone as she was placed in the back seat of a black SUV. Maddie was dizzy with terror, worried that she might faint, but she somehow persevered. Nobody spoke while they drove her away, and she wanted to call Sebastian. She silently took her phone from her briefcase.

"Can I make a phone call?" she asked.

"Go ahead," the man behind the wheel said coldly.

She dialed Sebastian's number and waited for him to answer. Desperate, she left a message: "I am in big trouble. Please call me. Please!" Resigned to the fact that she had run out of options, she forced herself to cool down and clear her head.

Just before the car stopped and she was escorted into a building, Maddie saw a text from him.

"Dear Maddie, I am very sorry about everything. I've been under a Federal investigation for tax fraud, and my office was raided. They turned everything upside down, and found a small note with the name Celeste Butler, which for some reason gave them leverage. I guess they had been searching for you for months, but couldn't find you under that name. I had to tell them who you were in order to avoid prosecution and possibly imprisonment. It seems that I can't be your knight in shining armor, but I did not lie about my feelings for you. You brought a lot of joy to my life, and I am grateful to you for that."

Maddie was put in a holding cell by herself, and knew an unpleasant interview was inevitably coming. She had enough of her own history to confess, but also remembered the other players who might be of interest to her interrogators. Perhaps she would try to follow Sebastian's example—trade information for a lighter sentence, or possibly even freedom.

It turned out that it was none other than Sebastian, the man whom she thought loved her, who betrayed her. She pondered why the FBI was investigating him, and realized that he had not been forthcoming with her about himself. While she had exposed her entire life story to Sebastian, he kept his skeletons hidden. Apparently, she concluded, it would be wise for her to keep him at a distance. Completely exhausted, she lay down on the cot in the cell. When she woke up hours later, she was not sure if it was morning. She remembered her vivid dream about Steve, and it astonished her. She had actually felt him kissing her and fondling every point in her body, and, even after waking, still felt the pulsating orgasm. Did it make me scream in my sleep, she wondered? How about that, she slowly considered... Hey, Steve, we are both behind bars now... That thought jolted her into reality.

Her Legacy

Even with all the contacts and details that Maddie provided, the gravity of her financial fraud weighed heavily. She held out as long as she could. Finally, after she had divulged every bit of information they asked for, she learned her fate.

"Ms. Ellis, I must tell you that you got yourself a favorable deal," she was told privately by a friendly FBI agent, "without the help of a lawyer. You are a smart and savvy woman. The standard penalty for committing the kind of serious financial crimes you are charged with is a life sentence. As agreed, in exchange for the intel you provided, we are recommending a lighter sentence of five years in Federal prison."

Her bench trial was brief, since she had already agreed to the plea deal. Maddie was aloof and didn't react. She nodded her head, and a female deputy led her out of the courtroom. I am paying the price for my father's deeds, she told herself. Not only did he treat me miserably, he stole the Bergers' diamonds, sold them, and kept the money. She had become, she realized, the unwitting beneficiary of his malice and dishonesty.

Maddie started to ask herself what and whom she would go back to after she had served her time. For the second time in her life, and now more seriously, Maddie considered suicide. She decided to give it more thought before doing anything, but contemplating various means of self-destruction gradually became an obsession. Sleep eluded her as strange and sinister visions swirled in her subconscious mind.

Maddie began to serve her time in the Federal Correctional Institution in Dublin, across the bay from San Francisco. About two weeks after her arrival, she asked to meet with her attorney, and Sebastian was called to visit her. She was taken to a room where she could have private conversations with visitors. They sat at a table across from each other.

He was visibly uneasy, keeping eye contact with her to a minimum. She didn't care; she had quashed her feelings for him, and went straight to business.

"Thank you for making the trip here. I appreciate it."

"Of course," he replied. "I owe you that much."

She asked, "can you help me prepare some paperwork?"

"What kind of paperwork?" he asked.

"I want to deed my condominium to Albert and his family. It's not rightfully my own property, so I want it to go to them. Can you get it done?"

"Of course," he said, and finally looked at her. "But... Are you sure this is what you want to do?"

Maddie had started having persistent headaches that were not going away. She wondered if they were migraines, and planned to ask the prison nurse for medication.

"As you can imagine, I have all the time in the world to think. So, yes, this is what I want to do."

"All right," he replied. "I'll get it done for you."

"As soon as possible, please. Okay?"

"I'll get to it right away. I'll be back with the documents you'll need to sign."

"There is something else that I want to talk to you about," she said with more softness in her voice and paused while he stood up and sat down again, waiting for her to proceed. Maddie started to speak, and stopped. Sebastian stared as she seemed to struggle to form words.

She finally began talking. "I've been having trouble speaking here and there. Sometimes The words just don't come out. Maybe it's all the stress, who knows?

"Anyway... I need somebody in whom I can trust to follow my wishes in the event of my death. As you know, I don't have many such people in my life. This will sound strange, but hear me out, please. As you know, I used part of my father's estate to buy my condo, but invested the rest of the proceeds in a brokerage account. It's a lot of money. I never took the time to prepare a will, but it's important to me to make my wishes clear. My intentions are to leave everything I own to the Helena Berger's descendants, and to specifically name Albert as the recipient. I know it would be impossible to give him power of attorney, because he would be considered an interested party."

"Where are you going with this, Maddie?' Sebastian asked her.

"To be blunt, I have a hard time trusting you with anything, because I know you sacrificed me for your own benefit. On the other hand, I remember how well you handled the transfer of my father's estate to me, and your general legal expertise. Can I possibly count on you to fulfill my wishes in the event of my death?"

Sebastian looked at her for a long moment and lowered his eyes. "I don't blame you for losing trust in me. I was under too much pressure, and I caved. But, Maddie, I swear to you that I will faithfully do whatever it is you want. I owe you everything."

"Then," she slowly asked, "if I grant you power of attorney, can you make sure that the money will go to where I designate it?"

"Maddie, I don't understand what you are thinking," he looked at her quizzically.

"I have a lot of loose ends that I need to have tied together, that's all," she replied.

"Look, Maddie, five years will go by faster than you think, and then you'll be free. They may even release you earlier. You are not going to die tomorrow, and you'll need some resources when you get out. Think before you do something that you may regret."

Maddie looked at him for a long moment. In some way she despised him, but she could not think of anyone else she could turn to.

"I can always revoke your power of attorney" she said, "but for now, what kind of authority do I have to give you in order to handle my finances?"

"You will need to grant me durable power of attorney. If you are sure about this, I'll prepare the paperwork, and then it will be official. You will have to provide me the numbers and locations of all your accounts. We will need to have your signatures notarized, so I'll bring a notary with me, and we can get it done."

"Good. How soon do you think it will take for you to have everything ready?"

"Give me a week," he said.

Sebastian was let out, and Maddie went back to her cell, feeling that a great weight had been lifted from her. She swallowed two Tylenol tablets the guard had brought her, and lay down, waiting for the headache to abate. The pills were not helping, but she kept taking them. Somehow, she didn't care about what was wrong with her, and focused on having her last wishes in order. She hadn't given much thought to the fact that handing Sebastian durable power of attorney would give him total control over all her assets.

A month later, Albert received a thick envelope by certified mail that came from Sebastian Fisher's office. He was baffled to see a handwritten letter along with official documents.

"Dear Albert,

I must tell you a long, sad story. Do you remember that you told me that our families were connected by history? You were so right about that. You heard some of this before, but I have now pieced all of it together. My grandfather, Jack Ellis, was among the soldiers who liberated Ohrdruf concentration camp near Weimar, Germany. It was there that he was handed the leather pouch with your grandparents' two small notes and diamonds. The priest who had given it to him implored him to bring it to America, turn it over to the JDC, so that they would find Helena Berger and get it to her.

When Jack returned from the war, he married my grandmother and had apparently forgotten about the Bergers' pouch. Shortly Before his death, he discovered the small bag and entrusted it to his son, my father, Titus Ellis. He must have asked Titus to fulfill his promise to take it to the JDC.

Titus was not a kind or ethical person. He had your family's treasure, and must have chosen to keep it for himself. He managed to sell the stones (except the single one that was stuck in the bag), and keep the cash. I had had no contact with my father for many years. After he died, I learned that I was his only heir to an estate of millions of dollars. I had no idea where this fortune had come from, but, truthfully, I was glad to start a new life and buy my new apartment. I recently discovered that my paternal grandparents, Titus' mother's father and mother, were Jewish immigrants from Russia.

After I met you and Bill, I realized that much of my inheritance was not rightfully mine. As luck would have it, I am currently serving a five-year sentence in Federal prison for crimes that I don't wish to mention. While here with time to reflect, I decided to transfer ownership of my condominium to you. It would be immoral of me to keep it. Putting it in your hands helps me absolve myself of some of the guilt I carry for what I have done over the years.

You will find the deed of trust and a key to the unit enclosed with this letter. I trust that you and your family will know what to do with it, and I wish all of you the very best that life can offer. In the event of my death or incapacity, I've granted Sebastian Fisher durable power of attorney, so he has control over my other assets. He knows my wishes that every cent is to go to your family for the purpose of donating it to the charitable organization that you choose. You see, I am fulfilling my promise to make a substantial contribution to whichever worthwhile cause you decide to support. It gives me great joy and comfort to be able to do so.

Affectionately,
Maddie Ellis"

Albert re-read the letter a few times, and remained at the kitchen table, his eyes blank. He had never imagined that the gracious Maddie Ellis might have had a criminal past. He considered himself a good judge of character, and she had impressed him as a genuine, above-board woman. The fact that she was partly Jewish unexpectedly kindled in him a sense of kinship with her. He weighed in his mind whether to ask Sebastian where Maddie was being held, and perhaps pay her a visit.

Annie and Bill were equally perplexed when Albert showed them the letter and the deed of trust.

"I can't imagine what Ms. Ellis might have done that would land her in Federal prison," Bill said.

Albert replied, "Unfortunately, we don't always know about people's past. Think about it; we only met her once. Her letter, though, gives a glimpse into her life, which tells me she didn't have it easy."

"Maybe she got involved with the wrong people, Dad. That kind of thing has gotten a lot of people into trouble. I've seen it at my job."

"You may be right on. But for now, I suggest that we drive to San Francisco to take a look at this condo unit. We'll have to figure out what we should do with it, and we'll need to have a car to get around."

Sweet Philanthropy

Albert and Bill spent a weekend in San Francisco. Uncomfortable with staying in Maddie's condominium, they spent the night in a nearby hotel. After meeting with Sebastian in his office, they made some decisions.

They arranged to have Maddie's personal belongings taken to a storage facility near the residence. The apartment still contained all of her possessions, which complicated matters for them. They decided to donate the furniture and clothing to the disaster relief organization she had worked with. Then they selected a real estate agent, a woman with an impressive track record, and listed the unit for sale.

Multiple offers came immediately, and within two days Albert decided which offer to accept. The chosen buyer paid in cash, and the Berger heirs were faced with the question of what to do with three million dollars. After income taxes, there would be two thirds of it left.

"Dad," Bill asked, a bit uncomfortably, "don't you agree it would be fair for some of the money to go to Grandma Helena's grandchildren?"

"You're thinking about yourself and your three cousins, right?"

"Yes, I am," he lowered his eyes.

"You have a point, so let me ask the ladies what they think."

After Annie and her sister-in-law Elizabeth made some calculations, they agreed to divide one million among the four grandchildren. It would be in addition to Helena's house, which the kids had already received from their grandmother's estate, Annie reminded her husband.

When Michael, Todd, Violet and Bill were informed of the gift, all were astounded.

Todd spoke up, "I already told all of you the great news that we received an inheritance from my father-in-law's brother. So, it seems that we will be in good shape. Still, I'm grateful to get this quarter of a million. We have to save for our children's college education."

"To be perfectly honest," Violet said, "it's great to get this windfall, but... I thought we decided we weren't going to keep any of it."

"Violet, all in all, the total we received is a substantial amount," her mother, Elizabeth, said. "A large part of it came from your ancestors through Maddie Ellis, but we don't know the exact amount. Ms. Ellis expressed her wish that her portion be used for a donation. In good conscience, we, your parents, thought it through, trying to figure it out. At the end of the day, you are still the Berger descendants, so it's fair that you should receive some of the inheritance. Don't worry, there is plenty left for a charitable gift."

Bill, Michael, Todd and Violet got up and embraced their parents. Albert, Annie, and Elizabeth were smiling, visibly pleased with how the estate distribution was proceeding.

Albert had contacted the director of the Organization for Abused and Missing Women and Children. The man scheduled a meeting with the entire family in their Los Angeles office, so everyone was asked to arrange to take the day off work.

All of them wore dressy attire—the men in suits and the three women in black dresses and high heels. They were met by a charming woman who led the way to an executive office. The director greeted all of them, and after shaking everyone's hand, invited them to sit down in chairs that had been set up in advance.

"We are very grateful that you selected us as the beneficiary of your gift," he said.

There was a brief silence, they all glanced at each other, and Bill began to speak, his voice shaky at first.

"My father is much more articulate than I am, but I was elected to speak on behalf of our family today," he started. "We want to tell you what brought us to our choice. You'll have to bear with me; I jotted down some notes."

"I apologize...Please give me a second," Albert interrupted when his phone chirped with a text message. It was from Sebastian Fisher.

"Albert," the message read, "I have very sad news. Maddie was just diagnosed with the worst kind of brain cancer. It already spread to other parts of her brain. She is mostly incoherent, and the doctor is not giving her much time. By the way, at the prison she is listed under the name Celeste Butler. I'll keep you informed."

"Please, go ahead, young man," the director said when Albert nodded, and all eyes were on Bill, who had a sheet of paper in his hands. He began.

"The funds that we are donating came from my great grandparents, who were my father's grandparents." He pointed at Albert. "Before they were shipped to a concentration camp, they arranged to hide a cache of diamonds from the Nazis. These stones wound their way to the United States, and were later sold. Although most of the proceeds have disappeared, we fortunately received a small portion, for which we were very grateful.

"My grandmother, Helena Berger, after escaping Nazi Germany, made a new life for herself in America. She became a social worker who spent all her time helping all kinds of survivors—people who were threatened, or in danger, or just needed help. Grandma Helena built a new life and had three children. One day, her youngest child, my father's sister Rebecca, was abducted. She was only five years old. We recently discovered that she had been snatched by human traffickers, and had a very tragic life. Today she is living in a nursing home, suffering from dementia.

"Each one of us," Bill, with more confidence, turned to face his family before continuing, "is a part of this tragedy, and we want to turn our pain into something positive that will keep our ancestors' memory alive. Inspired by our Grandma Helena, we decided that these proceeds should go to an organization that helps abused and missing women and children. Our intention is to make a philanthropic gift by founding a small foundation that will give grants to those victims."

The director, who had been listening intently, interjected. "We have a number of programs that provide such people opportunities to rehabilitate themselves, and if you so choose, your foundation would help fund these initiatives."

"Can we assume that there are more details and fine print, so that at this moment we are only setting up the basics?" Annie asked.

"Yes, that's definitely correct. Will you want to establish this foundation in your family name to memorialize it?" the man looked at the small assemblage.

Albert began to speak, but stopped for a moment, seemingly overcome by emotion. "This foundation must honor two names: Berger and Ellis."

"Dear, I think you should explain the connection," Annie said.

"Okay, so here's a brief explanation... Jack Ellis, an American soldier who fought in World War II, brought back with him our ancestors' bequest, put it away, and forgot about it. Over the years, after his death, the proceeds from our inheritance unfortunately became intermingled with the Ellis family's assets.

"Years later, Jack's granddaughter, Maddie Ellis, received the estate of her father, Jack's son Titus. It included something that had the Berger name on it. She therefore sought us out, then contacted us and handed us what was left of my grandparents' hidden cache. Maddie later became convinced that nearly everything she owned had dishonestly come from our inheritance. As a result, she transferred to us her entire wealth, with the express wish of donating it to this memorial fund."

Albert was visibly upset when he stopped, having heard about Maddie's condition.

The entire group exchanged questioning looks. While this was an emotional day for all of them, none of them understood Albert's sudden gloom.

The director listened, and asked no questions. He responded, "You have a very moving narrative to share with the world. With your help in providing the material, we will publish an authentic description of your ancestors' and Jack Ellis' journeys. On behalf of those who will benefit from your generosity, I want to express my sincere gratitude for your well-thought course of action."

"I think your dad would be pleased," Elizabeth whispered to Violet with teary eyes. "I feel his presence. I know he is watching us." Violet took her mother's hand.

"There will be some official documents," the director went on, "that will require notarized signatures, which will allow us to arrange for the funds to be transferred to us. As soon as all of this is finalized, we will contact you to determine the specific department or program that you wish to fund."

All seven walked outside into the bright sunshine and hugged each other.

"Why don't you treat all of us to lunch," Annie looked at her husband. "We have to lighten our mood and celebrate. It's a beautiful day."

"There is an Italian restaurant around the corner. Let's go," Albert declared and stopped. His voice was uncharacteristically weak. He looked up to the sky and spoke quietly, "Harry, you would be proud of how our children chose to spend their inheritance. We did raise good kids."

He avoided mentioning Maddie, or the Ellis name, during the meal. After dinner he took his son aside and showed him Sebastian's message. Bill read it twice, shaking his head in sorrow. He wished he could talk to his father about Maddie and how unfortunate, even tragic, her life had turned out.

The Ellis Ghost

Sebastian sat at his desk, wearing old jeans and a t-shirt and sipped from a can of Coke. With no appointments scheduled, he planned to go through an assortment of messages and papers. He was reading some email correspondence and was about to jot something down on a legal pad before his office phone rang.

"A woman just walked in and asked to see you," the receptionist said. "She will only identify herself by her first name, Lillian."

"Give me a moment, please," he told the receptionist. Walk-in prospective clients were unusual, but not unheard of. He finished writing down a note on a yellow pad before buzzing the front office back.

"Send her in," he said.

A pretty Asian woman, approximately thirty, walked in. She wore a short skirt over black leggings and a black long-sleeve T shirt decorated with gold swirls. Sebastian looked her over, trying to assess what she was about.

"Hello, Mr. Fisher," she started in heavily accented English. "My name is Lillian. I wonder if I can have a minute of your time."

"Lillian, would you please introduce yourself by your full name?"

"All right... My name is Lillian Chang-Ellis," she said evenly.

Chinese, he gathered from the name. But where did the Ellis part come from? It was uncomfortably familiar. Was she somehow related to Maddie's family?

"Good morning, Ms. Chang-Ellis. Please have a seat. How can I help you?"

"Actually, I go by Lillian Ellis," she started and sat down. "I understand you are the lawyer who handled my late husband's estate. His name was Titus Ellis. I am here to talk to you about that."

"Ms. Ellis..."

"You can call me Lillian," she interrupted.

"I am confused. First of all, Titus passed away about three years ago. Secondly, his marital status was single at the time he died. What exactly are you here for?"

"Titus and I were not legally married, so I was his common-law wife. We had a child together, and that's why I'm here." Her tone grew more aggressive.

"Why did you wait all this time? As I said, it's been three years since he was killed."

"It's a long story. When we split up, I went to Hong Kong to visit my parents. I found out I was pregnant, and my baby was born there. I just came back a couple of months ago and found out that Titus died. His house was sold, even his car dealership. My son is now almost four years old, and I am having trouble finding work."

Sebastian listened quietly, half knowing what was coming. He waited for Lillian to continue. She stared at him for a few seconds, the look in her eyes becoming combative, which troubled him, but he kept quiet.

"Well," she continued in a louder voice, "I know that he was well off, and left some money behind. Back then he told me that he had a will done, and I'm pretty sure I would have been included."

"If you were not officially married, why do you think you should have been included in Titus' will?" Sebastian asked, looking directly at her.

"Like I said, I gave birth to his baby."

"Look, Lillian... you can't barge into an attorney's office and make groundless demands. Without getting any documentation from you, I am unable to give you any details, except that the estate was distributed and liquidated a long time ago. The official records were filed with the County of Los Angeles. They are public, and you are welcome to look through them."

"You mean to tell me it's all gone?" Lillian rose from her chair, and Sebastian held himself back from ducking behind his desk to avoid flying objects being hurled toward him.

Instead, he stood up and glared back at her.

"I'm afraid you are correct, Lillian, and I think our conversation is finished."

"Who else was in his will?" she demanded, now practically yelling.

"As I said, our conversation is over. I am asking you to leave now."

"I am leaving..." Her l's sounded like r's. "But I am not going away. My son deserves to have financial support from his father."

She grabbed one of Sebastian's business cards from his desk and slammed the door on her way out.

He remained standing at his desk, shaken and troubled by the exchange. Lillian appeared to have been one of Titus' numerous girlfriends. It was clearly too late for anyone to come after his estate. Still, even at the time he died, would she have had a claim to any of it? Who was she, and was there really a child? It occurred to him that she might be involved with a criminal gang, the kind that specialized in extortion.

Sebastian turned off his desktop computer and took a few minutes to arrange the papers on his desk. He grabbed his briefcase and exited his private office.

"I won't be taking any calls today," he told his assistant. "Please ask the receptionist to transfer all calls to you, and I'll check my messages later. I'm taking the rest of the day to finish some personal business." It was time for him to visit the Sanborn & Willis brokerage branch in order to liquidate Maddie's account. He desperately needed the cash, and between him and God, whose existence he had always doubted, nobody would ever know.

The Breaking Point

The next day, an overnight letter was delivered to the law office of Sebastian Fisher. His assistant handed him the envelope.

"There is no return address, but it looks official, so I think you should open it," he told his boss and placed the packet in front of him. The assistant stepped out, and Sebastian slit the top with his letter opener. He saw a photocopy of a Chinese document, presumably a birth certificate, with a note:

> *"Mr. Fisher,*
> *"I enclosed a copy of my child, Darren's birth certificate. "I am demanding my share of my late husband's estate. I should probably receive all of it, since his son died with him and, to the best of my knowledge there were no other heirs. I am putting you on notice that you will find yourself in a very unfortunate situation if my wish will not be satisfied.*
> *I am connected with a network of nasty individuals who can easily come after you. You will hear back from me very soon.*
> *Lillian Chang-Ellis."*

Sebastian placed the note and the Chinese document back in the envelope and put it in a briefcase, then grabbed the case and walked out of his office.

"Are you coming back, Mr. Fisher?" the receptionist asked him on his way out. He replied without turning his head, "not today," then closed the door behind him, emerging into the humming streets of downtown San Francisco.

Bittersweet

Two weeks after the meeting with the organization's director, Albert and Annie drove north to Dublin, across the bay from San Francisco. They had called the prison to confirm that they were coming to visit an inmate known as Celeste Butler, whom they knew to be Maddie Ellis.

They were asked to wait in a small room. Ten minutes later the door opened, and a nurse rolled in Maddie in a wheelchair. She was sitting up, supported by a pillow, her head wrapped in a scarf. She smiled weakly when she saw Albert, who did his best to mask his overwhelming anguish.

"Hi Maddie," he said with a forced smile and went over to her. Annie followed behind, waiting for her husband to introduce her.

"I am so sad to see you under these circumstances. This is Annie, my wife. Annie, dear, this is Maddie Ellis, the lovely lady Bill and I told you about."

Annie approached the wheelchair and took Maddie's hand. "I am very honored to meet you, and sorry to see you so ill." Maddie pressed her hand weakly, but said nothing. "I want you to know," Annie continued, "that your generosity means the world to our family."

Albert brought a chair closer to her, and his eyes teared as he sat down. "You gave us everything you own. I can't imagine you have so many sins to repent for."

"I am repaying a debt that my grandfather, and then my father, owed you. Each of them, in turn, had something that belonged to you. But beyond that, I want to be part of the effort that you are making to honor the memory of Holocaust survivors, especially your ancestors. Obviously, I will not need anything when this is over."

Albert saw Annie turn her head away. "We are also honoring your grandfather, Jack Ellis," he said. "I have the letter that states that your gift is being presented to the Organization for Abused and Exploited Women and Children. They are setting up the Berger-Ellis Memorial Fund, named after both families."

Albert took out a copy of the letter he received from the director of the organization that received their gift. He placed it in Maddie's lap, and she picked it up and read it slowly.

She looked at the two of them with sad, tired eyes. Annie, who managed to overcome her emotions, was silent.

"You know, I didn't always make the right decisions," Maddie finally said. "My life has been complicated, and I wanted to fix the mistakes that I had made. Of course, we can't undo the past, but, fortunately, I've now been able to make some difference. Thank you for helping me honor my grandfather and your grandparents. I am happy to know that their names will always be linked together."

"So, what are the doctors saying, Maddie?" Albert asked.

"It's not good. My headaches have been unbearable, so they are giving me strong medications that wipe me out. For some reason, I also find it hard to speak sometimes, which is another symptom of my illness. I don't have much time left, I'm afraid. It happened so fast... Just like that, from one day to the next, I found out that I am terminally ill with an inoperable brain tumor." There was awkward silence, but she continued. "Thank you for coming all the way from Los Angeles. I am so grateful that I got to see you, and for the news about the memorial fund."

Annie rose and hugged Maddie, and they left.

Two weeks after the prison visit, Albert received a call from Sebastian.

"Good morning," he answered. "It's good of you to call. How is Maddie?"

Sebastian's voice was heavy with tears. "She died yesterday. I can't believe it happened so fast. Since she's been incarcerated, I haven't seen her much. What they told me is that she started getting severe headaches. After she fainted a few times, the prison doctor sent her to Stanford Hospital for tests. They discovered the growth too late, so there was nothing they could do for her."

"I am very, very sorry to hear it," Albert said as grief overcame him. "She had impressed me as a very special person, and appeared healthy."

"You are right. She was special and much more than that. Sadly, I have to confess: I betrayed Maddie, not because I wanted to, but because I was threatened. It's very complicated, but bottom line, she was incarcerated because of me. I owe her, I really do, but she is gone. All I can do now is arrange her funeral, and I'm afraid it will be very small. I hope you can come."

"I certainly will. Just tell me when and where. I'll ask Bill to come too."

There were about a dozen people at the gravesite service, mostly those who knew her through her volunteer work. Sebastian stepped forward to say a few words.

"Life was not always good to Maddie, but still, she was the kindest human being I've known. All she wanted was to perform good deeds, whether on a personal level or through her work with the survivors' organization. She truly wanted to make the world a better place."

"I haven't known Maddie for very long." Albert spoke up, "I'm sure you all heard that actions speak louder than words. From her actions, which spoke volumes, I can tell you she was kind, generous and intelligent. May she be remembered in all our hearts."

She was entombed, the handful of acquaintances shook hands with Sebastian, and he remained with Albert and Bill.

"Maddie somehow suspected that her life was going to end soon," Sebastian told the two when they were alone. "She must have had had a strong premonition, and that's why she was in a rush to deed the San Francisco condo to you. Something told her there was a pressing need for her to put her affairs in order."

"Remember what I said when we had lunch at Maddie's house?" Bill asked the bereaved man to try to comfort him. "My Grandma Helena always told us that life is for the living, and that we have to keep moving on." He could see that his words didn't sink in. He and his father invited Sebastian for coffee, but he declined. After they shook hands, he waved to them and walked away.

"I feel sorry for Sebastian, Dad," Bill said on their way back. "He was crying his heart out."

"Don't," his father told him. "He is a hypocrite, and was crying crocodile tears. He is charming and knowledgeable, but very lacking in the soul department."

"He and Maddie seemed like a nice couple."

"Yes," Albert said sadly, "they appeared that way, but when Sebastian said he had betrayed Maddie to save his own skin, it showed how little depth there was in their relationship."

It was while they waited at the airport for their flight back to Los Angeles, when Albert noticed a small card that Sebastian must have shoved into his hand when they were saying goodbye. He showed the card to Bill after reading it:

"Albert, I want you to know that I left my law practice. I will be taking a long trip out the area, perhaps out of the country. It has been a true pleasure to have met you, and I hope our paths will cross again. Best wishes to all of you,
Sebastian Fisher

Albert was notified that all the official steps had been finalized for creating the Berger-Ellis Memorial Fund. The family had been anxious to mark the occasion of their charitable endowment with a celebration. He, however, said he wanted to hold off a short while longer. In his heart, Albert was privately honoring a traditional Jewish thirty-day mourning period for Maddie. Because he felt connected to her, and the fact that, at least in part, she had a Jewish soul, he thought it would be appropriate to pay her this small measure of respect. There was nobody else who would properly mourn her.

"Dad, Maddie mentioned that some more money should be coming from her," Bill asked his father, "and that Sebastian has power of attorney and will have the details, remember?"

"I think we can forget about anything coming from Sebastian. Between Maddie's wishes and his own, it's pretty clear to me which he will choose to satisfy. I think he turned out to be another part of Maddie's miserable past."

"You were right about him since the first time you met," his son said.

Then, at last, it was time to celebrate. Bill invited Esmeralda, Lexi, and her boyfriend to the special gathering. Violet, Michael, and Todd's wife and children arrived. Detective

Valdez was invited, and although he came late, Albert was delighted to introduce him to everyone. The guest of honor was the assistant director of the Organization for Abused and Exploited Women and Children.

It was a festive party, for which the living room was decorated with old and new family pictures surrounded by flowers, and catered food was served. They had briefly considered bringing Rebecca from the nursing home, but later abandoned the idea.

The assistant director announced the newly established charitable fund dedicated for funding special grants to the organization's victims. The gift donated by the family was to be invested and overseen by an independent auditing firm. The recipients' identities, she added, would be verified and confirmed by the organization, but kept confidential. She then displayed a newly designed plaque intended to be posted in the main lobby, which read: "The Berger-Ellis Memorial Fund." After a brief silence, applause erupted.

Bill, at his father's request, recorded the announcement.

"I wish Maddie were here," Albert said. "We are honoring the memory of her grandfather, Jack Ellis, who carried our ancestors' small satchel home to America. She would have been very happy to come to our party."

Esmeralda contemplated that it had been over a year since Harry's murder, as she sat in a corner, looking mournful. She was overcome by the memory of the struggles, battles and victories that happened along the way. Why do the lives of many good people have to be sacrificed to help the world become only a tiny bit better, she asked herself.

"Listen, Esme," Elizabeth came over to talk to her quietly, "just look at the world and keep on enhancing it, one step, one day at a time. Unfortunately, it's usually the tragedies that push us to be strong so we can take action. My nephew Bill, your boyfriend, told me a lot about the kind of person you are. I am sure you understand."

"Yes, I agree with everything you said. I've been thinking about the victims in those tragedies: my mother back in El Salvador, Harry, and Rebecca, to name just a few. But I can see how their inspiration is guiding us. It seems that they sacrificed their lives in order to push us to take action. I finally made my decision about my future job with the FBI. I'm going to apply for a position in the human trafficking department at the Bureau."

Most of the guests were leaving when Esmeralda and Bill finally got a chance to try some of the food. Eventually, Lexi, her boyfriend, and Esmeralda were the last ones to go. Albert, Annie, Elizabeth and the four cousins sat down and relaxed in the living room while Todd's children played outside.

"Today was a very good day," Violet said.

"Yes, it was," Bill agreed. "Our endeavor is finished successfully."

Albert called Elizabeth and Annie to him, and they stood together. He scanned the younger generation and said, "Bill, Michael, Violet, Todd; your mothers and I realize how special all of you are. In our hearts you'll always shine just like all those diamonds."

CPSIA information can be obtained
at www.ICGtesting.com
Printed in the USA
FSHW010621261020
75177FS